THE
HACKER

ALSO BY NANCY HERKNESS

The Consultants series

The Money Man

Second Glances series

Second to None: A Novella
Second Time Around
Second Act

Wager of Hearts series

The CEO Buys In
The All-Star Antes Up
The VIP Doubles Down
The Irishman's Christmas Gamble: A Novella

Whisper Horse novels

Take Me Home
Country Roads
The Place I Belong
A Down-Home Country Christmas: A Novella

Stand-Alone novels

A Bridge to Love
Shower of Stars
Music of the Night

THE
HACKER

—NANCY—
HERKNESS

 Montlake

Published by Montlake, Seattle

www.apub.com

Amazon, the Amazon logo, and Montlake are trademarks of Amazon.com, Inc., or its affiliates.

ISBN-13: 9781542018333
ISBN-10: 1542018331

Cover design by Eileen Carey

Printed in the United States of America

To Patti Anderson, dear friend and expert personal trainer,
who kept me healthy in more ways than just the physical.

Chapter 1

"Five more reps," Dawn Galioto commanded her friend Alice Thurber, who was lying on her back on a weight bench.

"I think I hate you," Alice gasped out as she struggled to lift two ten-pound dumbbells into the air above her chest.

"You want to look good for your wedding, don't you?" Dawn gave Alice her best encouraging but no-nonsense smile. Six years of being a personal trainer had allowed her to perfect it.

"Low blow. Only for Derek would I let you torture me like this," Alice said, shoving the dumbbells upward with renewed determination.

"He's pretty good motivation, I gotta say," Dawn agreed with a nod that made her straight, dark-brown ponytail swing over her shoulder as she knelt to spot her friend. Alice's fiancé looked like a movie star.

"You know," Alice said, "I can always have my dress made with long sleeves."

Dawn smirked. "That would be cheating."

Alice pushed out the final few reps, and Dawn relieved her of the dumbbells. "My arms feel like rubber bands," Alice said, sitting up and shaking out her abused limbs.

"Yeah, but flex them, and then check out how amazing your back looks in the mirror."

Alice flicked her long braid to the side and craned her neck to see her reflection in the mirror. "Oh my God, I have actual muscles!"

"Because I am very good at my job." Dawn slotted the weights back onto their stand and tugged down the electric-blue tank top all the trainers at the Work It Out gym wore over their black leggings. "Now head for the mat. It's time to stretch."

"And it's going to hurt so good," Alice said with a grin as she quoted Dawn's favorite saying.

"Admit it. Stretching feels great." In fact, Dawn wished she could have someone stretch her the way she did her clients. But having anyone looming over her while she lay on the floor freaked her out. It yanked her back to a bad time.

"Depends on the day." Alice grabbed her phone. "Just let me show you the headpiece for the veil I'm considering and see what you think." After she tapped at her phone, she looked up. "You haven't forgotten about coming to my house next Sunday to help me with the wedding dress design?"

Dawn sighed inwardly. She spent all her time in workout clothes or jeans. What did she know about designing a wedding gown? But she was a maid of honor so she had to support her friend. "I'll be there with bells on." Luckily, the other maid of honor, their friend Natalie, had serious fashion sense.

Despite her worry about advising Alice, a warm, fuzzy feeling spread through Dawn's chest. She was still amazed that Alice wanted her to have such an important role in her wedding. She wasn't used to having close friends anymore. Her kind of baggage was more likely to scare them away. "Okay, I'll take a look at the veil thingie."

Alice stared at her phone in exasperation. "What is *wrong* with the gym's internet service these days? It's about as speedy as a teenage snail on its way to school."

"I didn't know snails went to school." Dawn grabbed a paper towel to wipe down the weight bench.

"You know what I mean." Alice checked her phone and blew out an exasperated breath. "Are they ever going to fix the problem here? No one's been able to stream TV on the treadmills for the last two weeks, at least."

"Yeah, the customers are pretty grumpy about it." Dawn shrugged. "Vicky's brought in a bunch of different tech geeks to try to get it back to normal but none of them can find the problem. My personal suspicion is that they're all relatives of hers and she's giving them the work as a favor." Vicky was the wife of the gym's owner, Ramón Vazquez, the man whom Dawn owed her present career to.

"You know who could fix it? Leland Rockwell. In about five seconds with one hand tied behind his back."

A little jolt of awareness zinged through Dawn. She had met Leland Rockwell a couple of times at parties Alice and Derek had thrown in their spectacular Manhattan penthouse apartment.

Leland was the computer genius at KRG Consulting, the firm Derek, Leland, and their third partner, Tully Gibson, had founded. Dawn had never said much to him because he was scary smart, and she felt intimidated since she was a college dropout. Although she loved listening to his honey-smooth Georgia drawl when he talked to other people. It seemed to wash through her like a warm sea and softened the intimidation factor somewhat.

She'd also noticed his lean, sculpted body with the surprisingly wide shoulders because that was her job . . . or so she told herself. His face had the elegant bone structure of old money, and there was a courtliness to his manners that screamed private school. He tried to disguise that by wearing the computer nerd's uniform of T-shirt and jeans, even at the parties. Behind his tortoiseshell glasses, his vivid blue eyes gleamed with that formidable intelligence that Alice was referring to.

And Dawn always knew exactly where he was in the room at those parties.

"Finally!" Alice jerked Dawn out of her daydream by holding up her phone with photos of an embroidered lace veil attached to a crown of pearls and white silk flowers.

"It's beautiful," Dawn said sincerely. "It looks like it could be on the cover of one of those Regency romance novels you love so much. But not outdated or anything."

Alice beamed and took the phone back before she hugged Dawn. "Thank you! That's what I hoped you would say. I'm so excited!"

After a split second of hesitation, Dawn returned the hug. "You're going to look amazing no matter what you wear." She stepped back. "Now it's time to stretch."

Alice obediently lay down on the foam mat, and Dawn gently pushed her friend's bent knee across her body. Alice made a little groaning sound before she asked, "Who's the new trainer over at the ellipticals?"

Dawn glanced up at the muscle-bound blond man in his late twenties. He was berating a sweaty, middle-aged client with a paunch to leave it all on the gym floor. "That's Chad, the former high school quarterback and new favorite of all the ex-jocks and wannabe ex-jocks. He's got that whole 'no pain, no gain' vibe going."

"You're not a fan," Alice said.

In fact, Dawn had turned down several invitations to go out for drinks with the new trainer. The man couldn't take no for an answer, so now she actively avoided him. "I prefer to find other ways to motivate my clients to work harder."

"Like reminding them they will be wearing a wedding dress in six months."

"You pushed out those last five reps like a champion, didn't you?" Dawn moved to Alice's other side. "Why are you even looking at other guys with a fiancé like yours?"

"I'm not looking at them *that* way. I'm interested in the people you work with because you're my friend."

Dawn grunted, but the happy warmth returned to her chest. Alice was good about showing her that friendship went both ways. Dawn struggled to remember that sometimes.

"Which reminds me . . . I wasn't kidding about Leland."

Dawn pressed her friend's shoulder to the floor. "I'm pretty sure the gym's tech budget isn't up to paying KRG Consulting's fees."

"He'll do it for free," Alice said. "Don't you remember that's how I first contacted Derek? He started their Small Business Initiative, KRG's program that offers complimentary assistance to businesspeople like me and Ramón who don't have the extra resources to solve problems. I was trying to figure out what was wrong with the accounting software my clients were using."

"I'd forgotten the part about it being free." Dawn hated to ask for help from anyone, but this wasn't for herself. It was for Ramón. He had pulled her back from the brink. "Yeah, maybe ask Leland if he has someone who could look into it." Because she couldn't imagine the gym's issue needed the kind of genius Leland was.

"As soon as you're done tormenting me," Alice said with a grin.

⌐

Two hours later, Dawn stood at her kitchen counter, eating organic Greek yogurt, when an email from KRG Consulting popped up on her phone. "That was fast," she muttered, putting down her spoon to swipe into the message.

"Shit!" she said when she glanced at the signature.

It was from Leland Rockwell himself. She glanced at the display on her microwave: 9:35 p.m. Alice had said something about the man being a workaholic, but Dawn's problem wasn't exactly a high priority for KRG.

Dear Ms. Galioto,

I understand the gym where you are employed is suffering from issues with Wi-Fi performance. I would be happy to help. Perhaps it would be easiest to put me in touch with the person responsible for the computer systems. I will, of course, keep you in the loop as to my progress on the project.

Regards,
Leland Rockwell

Should she answer him tonight? She supposed it wouldn't hurt since he could always read it in the morning if he'd sent it right as he was leaving.

She plunked down on a wooden barstool and frowned at her phone. What kind of response should she make to the founding partner of an international consulting firm? Brief, so she wouldn't betray the fact that she wasn't accustomed to business correspondence at such a high level.

Dear Mr. Rockwell,

I will speak with Mr. Ramón Vazquez, the owner of Work It Out, tomorrow and let him know of your kind offer. Thank you very much for your assistance.

Sincerely,
Dawn Galioto

She read it over half a dozen times, debating whether her wording was too stiff, too obsequious, not appreciative enough, or too vague. Finally she hit "send." When his return email dinged into her phone, she took a deep breath before she swiped it open.

Dear Ms. Galioto,

I look forward to hearing from you.

Regards,
Leland

P.S. Perhaps we could dispense with our surnames?
They seem somewhat unwieldy since we've met before.

She bit out a laugh, then wondered if he was making fun of her. No, *teasing* her. That was a better interpretation. She could give it right back to him.

Hey, Leland! You're right.
Dawn

It took mere seconds before his response pinged in.

Dawn, I'm always right.

That made her laugh again before she stuck her phone in her sweatshirt pocket and finished her yogurt.

⁓

Leland was disappointed when Dawn didn't rise to the bait of his provocative remark about being right. He leaned back in his chair in the room his partners had dubbed Mission Control due to its array of computer screens. This was where he spent most of his work time, rolling his chair among various stations as he juggled multiple projects. Hell, it was where he spent most of his time, period.

When Derek had called to say that his fiancée's friend needed help through their Small Business Initiative, Leland had felt an odd rush of interest. Dawn was Alice's personal trainer. Her self-defense instruction had played a significant part in saving Derek's and Alice's lives when a psychopathic hacker had held them at gunpoint six months ago. That meant Leland was grateful to her.

He'd met her a few times at the social events surrounding his partner's engagement, the only parties he felt obligated to attend. He admired her straight, dark hair, body honed as taut as a bowstring, and lips like tempting pillows. The contrast between soft lips and hard muscles had stirred something low in his belly.

However, she tended to say three words to him and then move along. He'd laid on the full southern gentleman treatment, his Georgia drawl as thick as honey. She would give him a long look from those huge, dark eyes of hers and make an excuse to leave. He couldn't figure out what he'd done to offend her.

Tonight, he'd decided that charm might be the wrong approach. She was a warrior in teaching women self-defense, so maybe she would like a fight. Or at least some mild provocation.

Too bad she hadn't taken up the challenge. He expected that straightening out the Wi-Fi problem would require about sixty seconds of his time, so the project wouldn't offer any further contact with her.

Just as well. He had a dozen other jobs to do that contributed to the firm's bottom line, unlike Derek's pet pro bono project. He knew in his gut that he was overloading himself because he didn't want to face the sudden profound absence in his life. But that was what work was for.

Chapter 2

Dawn stuck her head in the door of the office that Ramón shared with his wife, Vicky. "Got a minute?" she asked, relieved that only her boss was occupying the room. She wasn't sure how Vicky would react to Dawn trespassing on her computer territory.

"For you? Always!" Ramón's smile transformed his rough boxer's face into a benign uncle's. He waved to a turquoise chair in front of the blond-wood desk his massive body dwarfed. Vicky had done the decorating. "Everything okay?"

"Better than okay." Dawn dropped into the chair. "I've got some expert help for the Wi-Fi problem and it's free."

"There's no such thing as free in this world. But no one's mentioned a Wi-Fi problem to me."

"Because you're big and scary." Dawn grinned.

In fact, her boss was beloved in the gym, where everyone considered him a gentle giant. The wannabe boxers had long ago given up challenging him to a bout in the ring. He adamantly refused, claiming he didn't want to be thrown in jail for manslaughter. Even more, he'd sworn off violence of any kind once he'd ended his boxing career, saying he'd seen enough hurt to last the rest of his life. She admired him for that.

But she owed him even more. He was the one who had encouraged her to become certified as a personal trainer. She'd been teaching her self-defense classes at the gym—the only bright spot in her life at the time—when he'd told her she'd make a great trainer and offered to pay for the courses she needed. She sometimes felt as though he had saved her life—or, at the very least, her sanity.

Dawn raised her eyebrows as he continued to look at her in bafflement. "Seriously? Vicky didn't say anything?" she asked.

He shook his head. "Although I remember some guys messing around with the computers a couple of times last week. I don't pay much attention to the tech stuff."

"Well, for the last ten days, the customers have been giving all of us trainers an earful about how they can't stream TV or movies on the treadmills and ellipticals. It seems no one can break a sweat without entertainment anymore."

"I wondered why it was so quiet in the equipment room recently, but I didn't pinpoint the reason." Her boss tugged at his short ponytail, which meant he was worried. "So people are really annoyed?"

"Yeah. I even switch off the Wi-Fi on my phone when I'm at the gym because it's so incredibly slow. I thought you knew about the issue."

"Vick usually takes care of stuff like that."

"From what I can tell, she's tried, but I guess the people she's brought in couldn't fix it." Dawn sat back in her chair. "Luckily, I have a solution."

"The free one?" Ramón looked skeptical.

"Yup. My friend Alice—who's a member here too—is engaged to a very fancy consultant from New York City. His firm, KRG Consulting, runs a free program to help small business owners with problems. Alice hooked me up with their computer expert. All you have to do is agree and he'll jump right on it."

"It sounds too good to be true." When Ramón shifted in his chair, it creaked so loudly that Dawn feared it might collapse under him.

"I'd agree with you except that I saw what they did for Alice's book-keeping issue." Of course, Alice had nearly gotten herself killed when she and Derek uncovered the fraud that had created the problem. "They put every resource she needed into the project, even rented a private jet. At no cost to her."

"I'd have to run it by Vicky." Ramón still sounded dubious.

"I know. She's the tech queen." Although how Vicky could even type without ruining her jewel-encrusted manicure, Dawn couldn't figure out. She stood up. "Let me know if you want to use KRG's services."

As she walked away from the management office, she frowned. It surprised her that Ramón wasn't aware of the Wi-Fi problem. Why the hell hadn't Vicky told him after all this time?

It also complicated things for her because she had expected Ramón to hail KRG's assistance as a lifesaver. Now she was in the awkward position of having asked for help for someone who might not accept it. Hopefully, Leland was too busy to care whether a gym in Cofferwood, New Jersey, wanted his assistance or not.

No such luck, though. After she finished with her first client, Dawn checked her email messages. She grimaced when she saw one from Leland.

Ready when you are.

She considered ignoring it until she'd heard Ramón's decision. Leland would figure that she was working and hadn't read it yet. She started to slide her phone back into her sweatshirt pocket and then stopped. Leland was a computer expert. He might be able to tell that she'd read his email.

She growled in frustration, pulled out her phone, and read it again. On second glance, it seemed a little provocative. She was only supposed to put him in touch with her boss. His words made it sound like they would be working on the problem together.

No, she had to be imagining things. After a minute's thought, she typed out a careful response.

My boss is excited about the opportunity, but his wife
is the IT person so he doesn't want to step on her toes.
He's going to get back to me after he speaks with her.

Thanks,
Dawn

That was only a slight lie. A polite one.

She started to stow her phone but decided to wait a minute.
Without the Wi-Fi connection to screw things up, her regular phone
service still worked fine. Sure enough, an email came back from
Leland.

Ah, the joys of a family-run business. Not only office
politics but domestic dynamics to contend with. This
may be more than I can handle.

She snort-laughed. Mr. Southern Charm could probably talk a state
trooper out of giving him a ticket after being clocked at a hundred miles
per hour on the New Jersey Turnpike. Even worse, she was enjoying his
email messages way too much.

I have a client. Catch you later.

She shoved her phone in her pocket and strode past the grunting,
sweating gym rats to the lounge, where her next client, Leslie, was chatting with the blond ex-jock, Chad.

"Dawn, baby," he said, flashing his whitened smile. "If I didn't
respect you so much, I'd steal away this lovely lady and train her
myself."

Leslie, a frazzled mom with three small kids and a husband who
traveled for business three weeks out of every month, trilled a giggle.

Dawn didn't begrudge her the pleasure of flirting with a guy whom some considered good-looking. So she just narrowed her eyes at Chad in a warning before turning to Leslie with a wink. "Don't let that dazzling smile fool you. He's way meaner than I am."

"Did you just call me dazzling?" Chad pressed his hand to his chest in mock astonishment.

"Don't let it go to your head," Dawn said. "Leslie, let's get you warmed up and ready to work."

Leslie rose from the couch and touched Chad on his bulging biceps, her fingers lingering slightly. "Thanks for keeping me company."

"My pleasure." Chad looked deep into Leslie's eyes. "I hope our paths will cross again."

Dawn controlled the urge to gag and shepherded her client away from her cliché-spouting fellow trainer.

*

Dawn was eating a kale-and-quinoa salad in the employee break room when Vicky sashayed through the door and up to the small white plastic table where Dawn sat.

"Ramón told me about your offer," the owner's wife said, jutting out one hip and resting her ring-laden hand on it. "That's real nice of you, but my guys say the Wi-Fi will be fixed by the end of today. So no need for your consultant friends to get involved." With her free hand, she toyed with her dark-blonde curls.

Although Dawn didn't like Vicky, she admired her. The woman had big hair and snapped her gum like a diehard Jersey girl, but she ran the administrative side of the gym like a corporate CEO. Bills got paid on time, payroll was never late, there were always clean sweat towels, and the equipment was updated regularly. That's why Dawn had been surprised when the Wi-Fi problem had persisted.

Dawn put down her fork. "That's good news. Thanks for letting me know." But disappointment tweaked at her chest. No more email exchanges with Leland.

Vicky nodded. "I've got the tech stuff covered. No need to worry about it."

Dawn forbore to point out that the issue had continued for a couple of weeks. "Got it."

"By the way, you're doing great on billing training hours," Vicky said. "You're headed for a quarterly bonus at this rate. Good job."

The comment might have been patronizing from someone else, but Vicky cared intensely about how many training hours could be billed to clients.

"Thanks," Dawn said again. "I always like getting bonuses." She just socked them away in a conservative mutual fund because she had all she needed in the way of material things like furniture and workout clothes. She also had an apartment five minutes from the gym, a job she cared about, and a few trusted friends. She was as safe and secure as she could make herself without becoming a recluse.

"You've got a good touch with the customers," Vicky said. "Tough but encouraging. It keeps them coming back."

A surprising glow of satisfaction warmed Dawn. She put a lot of thought, study, and effort into her work. It was nice to have the hard-to-please Vicky notice. "It's a pleasure working here."

Vicky gave her a thumbs-up, the rhinestones decorating her leopard-spotted manicure glinting in the fluorescent light. She turned toward the door but stopped to say over her shoulder, "And you don't create drama. I appreciate that."

Dawn laughed. Her fellow trainers, both male and female, sometimes acted like feuding cats. "I try to stay away from the hissing and clawing."

"Thank God!" Vicky swayed out of the break room on her four-inch silver stilettos. She wore them with a tight-fitting turquoise tracksuit that somehow worked for her.

Now Dawn had to call off the big gun at KRG. She pulled out her phone but couldn't start typing. Was it embarrassment at having solicited his services when they weren't wanted? Or was she trying to prolong their brief email relationship? Either one was not useful.

She forced her fingers to tap the screen.

> The boss's wife just informed me that the Wi-Fi problem
> will be resolved by the end of the day. I'm sorry I raised a
> false alarm. It was nice of you to be ready to jump right
> in. I appreciate it.
>
> Dawn

That seemed to strike the right note of friendly professionalism. She hit "send" and picked up her fork again, jabbing a mouthful of grains and greens.

Before she could finish chewing, an email from Leland popped up in her in-box. The man must type at ninety miles an hour.

> Shall we make sure the problem gets fixed before we
> call it quits? Many an IT expert has made promises they
> can't keep, myself excluded, of course. Let me know if
> the Wi-Fi indeed recovers by the end of the day . . . or
> not.
>
> Leland the skeptic

"Ain't it the truth?" Dawn muttered as a smile tugged at the corners of her mouth. One more email exchange at least.

Skepticism is usually my job, but I'll keep you posted.

D.

She left her fork in the bowl while she waited.

I knew I recognized a kindred spirit.

L.

A kindred spirit. That was a laugh. He was rich and famous for his tech genius on an international level; she worked as a personal trainer in a Jersey gym. He had the elegance of a southern aristocrat; she was pure peasant Italian.

But his words twirled like a happy pinwheel in her mind for the rest of the day, giving her a tiny lift every time she remembered them.

At about six thirty, a cheer sounded from the room where the ellipticals and treadmills were lined up. Dawn was in the midst of demonstrating how to do a burpee using a BOSU ball.

"What's that all about?" her client asked, staring in the direction of the racket.

"We can find out or you can start on your burpees."

He draped a sweat towel around his neck and grinned at her. "What do you think?"

She leaped to her feet with a mock glare. "Fine, but you'll have to do five extra to make up for the break."

They walked into the big space swirling with the motion of customers of all shapes and sizes, dressed in outfits that ranged from knock-your-eyes-out neon to gray sweats. Now the only sounds were the hum of treadmills rolling and the metallic clunk of weights being lowered.

"What was the celebration about?" Dawn asked a trainer who was restocking the towel shelves.

"The Wi-Fi's normal again. Everyone's streaming on the machines." He gestured to the pulsating glow of the built-in screens.

Her disappointment was more than a twinge this time. It was a downright sinking feeling. All because of that damned "kindred spirits" comment.

"Yeah!" Her client pumped his fist. "I run a lot longer when I'm distracted by the news. Sometimes it makes me so mad that I go even harder to blow off steam."

Dawn knew all about sweating off emotions. That's what had drawn her to the gym in the first place.

"Okay, back to burpees," she said, waving toward the training room.

"At least I got to catch my breath."

"You'll need it."

As soon as she was done with the session, she headed for the break room, where it was usually quiet at this time of the evening. The staff was busy since many people trained after work. She wanted to be able to focus on her last communication with Leland. Plunking down on a white bean-shaped chair in the corner, she pulled out her phone.

There is great joy at the gym tonight. The Wi-Fi has returned to full speed. Who knew that people were so dependent on distraction from their sweating? They literally cheered.

Again, thanks for taking the time to email with me about this matter. I'm sure you could have fixed it in a lot less time than it took Vicky's boneheads to finally come through.

Dawn

She was sure he would answer her immediately. She might be flattered by that if she didn't suspect that he was always at his computer. Although he must be working on other projects, so it was *kind* of flattering. Of course, her messages took him mere seconds to respond to. He didn't need to weigh each word and phrase like she did.

> I am less joyful than your patrons. Out of curiosity, I took a quick, cursory look at the general data inflow/ outflow at the gym earlier today. The amount of traffic passing through it was extraordinary. It's no wonder that the streaming had no bandwidth to utilize. Now I am thoroughly intrigued but have no authority to intervene. Perhaps the problem will recur, in which case I am eager to be at your service.

Dawn rocked back in the puffy chair. He'd already looked into the problem . . . and found something weird. She didn't know what caused "traffic" on a Wi-Fi router other than streaming videos and gaming. There was no use pursuing that now since it must have stopped.

The words that she came back to were: "I am eager to be at your service." Was that just his southern courtesy or did he mean it?

It didn't matter because Vicky had gotten the Wi-Fi fixed.

> Thanks for taking a look at the issue. The traffic is weird but I guess it's gone now. I appreciate your time. I'll let you know if there's any more trouble.

And that was the end of that. She waited a minute but Leland must have agreed with her because he didn't respond. What more was there to say anyway?

Leland rested his elbows on the arms of his chair and steepled his fingers as he reread Dawn's email. Nothing to indicate she wanted anything further from him. He stared at the ceiling for a long moment before he hit the delete key. He had the idle thought that a delete key in his brain would be useful too. He'd like to erase the disappointment he felt at not having a reason to communicate further with her. Their exchanges had given him a surprising amount of entertainment.

An internal message from Derek popped up on his screen.

Leland, can you come to my office in ten?

Leland glanced at the programs running on his screens and sent back: "Yes." He took off his glasses and rubbed his eyes as he hoped like hell this wasn't another well-meant but misguided intervention from his partner. Both Derek and Tully had the idea that he was working himself too hard because he was trying to somehow forget his mother's death three months before. They didn't understand that he was honoring her. She was the one who had taught him his work ethic. Every project he completed was a tribute to her.

Ten minutes later, he braced himself mentally and sauntered into Derek's corner office with the wraparound windows that showcased the towers of Manhattan, now blazing with myriad shades of artificial lights. Leland had a similar office that he almost never used, preferring his computer cave. Tully's office faced the Hudson River because he liked to watch the boat traffic.

Tully was already seated on the leather sofa with his sock-covered feet propped up on the coffee table, his cowboy boots resting neatly side by side on the carpet. Derek sat in a chrome-and-leather chair opposite him, looking like a casting director's image of the perfect consultant in his custom-tailored navy suit, albeit without a necktie.

It was a bad sign that both of them were there, especially in the evening. They seemed to feel it was okay to deal with personal stuff after normal work hours.

"You're here late," Leland said to Derek as he eased into a chair beside Tully. Since his partner had fallen in love with Dawn's friend Alice, Derek spent more time out of the office, although he often worked from home.

"I have a personal request," Derek said.

Leland steepled his fingers again as he waited with a faint sense of dread.

"You're the only person I know who can do that and pull it off," Tully said, imitating Leland's gesture. "When I do it, I look like an asshole."

"I could say that you always look like an asshole but it would be unkind," Leland said.

Derek gave them a tight smile. "Could we focus here?"

"My posture indicates that I am focused," Leland said.

"Right." Derek cleared his throat. "Now that Alice and I are engaged, we are planning a wedding."

"That generally follows an engagement." Leland restrained himself from doing a fist pump of relief. This meeting wasn't about him.

"Unless you elope." Tully sounded hopeful. "I'll drive the getaway vehicle."

"We're not eloping," Derek said.

"Do you have a date yet?" Tully asked.

"As soon as possible," Derek said. "Which means in about six months."

"Your Alice is very organized," Leland said. "Most New York metro–area weddings take at least a year to plan. Unless you're considering a destination wedding?"

"We're not . . ." Derek glared at his friends and partners. "Trying to talk about this with you two is like herding cats."

Leland was enjoying himself now. It was rare to see his unflappable partner off-balance.

"Forget all the details," Derek said. "I've been thinking about my best man. I know it's supposed to be just one man, but this job calls for two. You've both been there for me through all the ups and downs of our roller coaster ride with starting KRG. You helped me make my proposal to Alice an event straight out of her dreams."

"Leland even wore a wig. He gets extra credit for that," Tully interjected.

Derek's fiancée loved Regency romances, so Derek had rented a mansion in New Jersey and asked his friends to dress up as a coach driver—that was Tully, since he somehow knew how to drive a team of horses—and a nobleman's butler. Hence the wig, which had itched like the devil.

"You're the kind of friends a man is lucky to have one of, let alone two." Derek swallowed visibly. "It's a little unorthodox, but I would be honored if you would both agree to be my best men."

"Hell, yes!" Tully said. "I'll drive you to the church in a coach-and-four."

Derek chuckled. "That won't be necessary." He turned to Leland.

"The honor is mine." Leland meant it. The three of them had been through hell and high water together since business school. They'd had each other's backs when they thought KRG was going to fail. They'd celebrated every success, of which there were pitifully few in the beginning. They'd beaten the odds because when one of them got discouraged, the others were there to shore him up. These men were more than brothers to him.

"Are we going to have a group hug?" Tully asked. "Because I'm in."

Derek laughed. "Maybe at the wedding. Thank you, both of you. You are indeed the *best* men."

The happiness that glowed around Derek these days would have been nauseating if he didn't so richly deserve it. Leland hadn't believed that any of them could find that kind of love. They were too driven by their own personal demons, always striving for the next level of success.

All this talk of Alice brought his thoughts back to her friend Dawn and his disappointment that the Wi-Fi problem had been resolved without his help.

Although he still wondered what had generated such a high level of traffic on a local gym's Wi-Fi. Especially since it had continued for two weeks without anyone detecting or blocking it. Even an idiot could see that it was what had caused the streaming impairment. Did that mean they weren't able to stop it, or they didn't want to? The second possibility intrigued him.

Leland started when Derek plunked a glass of neat bourbon down on the coffee table in front of him.

"A toast," Derek said. "To best men and best friends!"

Leland raised his glass and let the smooth whiskey burn down his throat while he celebrated with his partners.

But part of his brain was still back at the Work It Out gym. He hated an unsolved puzzle. Even more, he would miss the little edge of fun in his email exchanges with Dawn.

Chapter 3

"Okay, that's it for today," Dawn said to her client, a high school tennis player who came after classes to improve his flexibility. She offered him her hand to get up from the mat.

"That was a good workout, Coach," the young man said, wiping his face with his sweat towel. He draped it around his neck, grabbed his water bottle, and checked his cell phone.

Dawn sighed. Getting a kid to leave his phone in the locker room was nearly impossible, but she'd insisted that he put it on mute.

"Shi-oot!" he said with an apologetic glance at her. "I'm running out of data allowance again. I don't get it because I'm on the gym's Wi-Fi." He tapped at the phone. "Mom's gonna be pissed."

"You're the third person who's complained about that today, so I don't think it's your fault." She grinned at him. "Tell your mom I said so."

"Thanks, Coach, I will." He looked relieved as he started toward the door.

Dawn smiled as she picked up the mat to clean and rehang it. She got a kick out of being called Coach. Her smile turned to a frown as she remembered his complaint.

The customers were getting cranky about the ongoing IT issues at the gym. That was bad because people were often just looking for an excuse to cancel their membership. She didn't want to see Ramón's business get hurt because Vicky didn't know what she was doing on tech matters. Ramón was more like an older brother than a boss to Dawn.

An image of Leland's sharp, intelligent face flashed across her mind. She'd been thinking about him a lot, all because of a few emails. Those had ended a week ago and she still missed them.

So maybe this was her chance to connect with him again.

If just one more person mentioned the data usage to her, she would take it as a sign that she should offer Leland's services to Ramón one more time.

She nearly danced a jig when her very next client turned off his phone because his data usage was blowing up his limited plan.

As soon as she finished with her session, she went in search of her boss. She found Ramón and Vicky in their shared office, which suited her just fine. Ramón worried more about keeping the customers happy while Vicky's eyes were firmly on the bottom line.

"What's up?" he asked, waving Dawn in. Vicky ignored her and tapped at her keyboard, her long, flashy fingernails clicking against the plastic.

"I've gotten some customer complaints about high data usage on their cell phones when they're here." She decided not to reference the earlier Wi-Fi problems. No point in rubbing Vicky's nose in it. "It happens even when their phones are connected to our Wi-Fi. I thought you might want to know about it."

Ramón glanced at his wife. "*Querida*, we're having internet problems again."

"Yeah, I heard about that," Vicky said, still focused on her computer. "It's not a big deal. Most people have unlimited data plans anyway."

"Vick," Ramón said. "If people are complaining, we need to fix it."

That's why it was good to have Ramón present for the conversation.

Vicky stopped typing and gave Dawn an irritated look before she smiled at Ramón. "Ray, sweetie, don't worry. I'll take care of it."

"Good." Ramón nodded to Dawn. "Thanks for letting us know."

Dawn walked back to the staff room unsatisfied. Vicky seemed dismissive but Ramón was now involved. That might get his wife to address the issue. Or she might drag her feet like she'd done with the Wi-Fi problem. It left Dawn with a dilemma, though. She'd asked Leland for his assistance previously, and then Ramón had turned it down. She didn't want to be in that awkward position again.

After her last client, Dawn walked home and showered before dropping onto the sectional in her living room and flipping open her laptop. Could she justify contacting Leland or not?

She wrote and deleted four versions before she decided to send the fifth one.

Dear Leland,

We've got a new problem at the gym. The Wi-Fi is working fine but now people are complaining that their cell phone data usage is high, even though they are connected to the gym's Wi-Fi. Any theories about that?

Regards,
Dawn

She had no idea if he would still be working at nine o'clock on a Tuesday, so she pointed the remote at the television in search of a light, fluffy rom-com. Her taste in programming surprised her friends, but she couldn't deal with violence or shocks when she wanted to relax. No sooner had she gotten the menu up than an email appeared in her in-box.

An involuntary smile curled her lips, and she wiggled her butt to settle into the cushions so she could enjoy Leland's message.

> Aha! The nefarious data gobbler strikes again! I have
> theories but they will require proof. I think I need to
> join your gym.
>
> L.

A shiver of excitement ran through her. Leland Rockwell wanted to join her local Jersey gym. But she hadn't asked for his help, just his theory. Maybe he had misunderstood. She didn't want to be embarrassed by turning down his high-level assistance for the second time.

> My boss's wife is supposed to be working on the prob-
> lem. I was just curious as to what you thought might
> be causing it.

She hated to hit "send" but she pressed the key.

> I'll work undercover because I'm intrigued by the
> strange goings-on in Cofferwood. Does the gym have
> a pool, by any chance?

Excitement turned to intense anticipation. She would see him in person, not just email the man behind the computer screens.

> Actually, it has a half Olympic-size pool because it used
> to be a college gym. Are you a swimmer?

That would explain how nicely he filled out his nerdy T-shirts.

> I swim when I need to think. My membership applica-
> tion will be sent in by morning. Do you have any train-
> ing time slots open this week? We can talk while I sweat.

He wanted her to train him? She had to remind herself to take a breath. And that was a problem. She needed to control her expectations. This was his job, even if he was doing it for free. It had nothing to do with her personally. She was helping out her boss by bringing in a consultant. That's what Leland was: a consultant. They came into a business, they fixed a problem, and they departed. The latter was what she should keep in mind.

Besides, she barely knew the man, hadn't thought anything—well, much—about him until they started emailing.

She switched screens to check her calendar and realized why Vicky was so happy with her productivity. It was very high because she liked to work and it allowed her to hang out in a clean, well-lit place surrounded by people she was familiar with and trusted. So her goals and Vicky's aligned in this case.

She sent him back an email with a list of the limited times she had open.

I see you are very much in demand. I'll take one open session every day, your choice of when. That will give us an opportunity to consult regularly.

Every day. Maybe that was good. It was surprising how much you learned about a person when you put them through rigorous physical exercise. People responded to the challenge in very different and revealing ways. She could get to know him well enough to find out she didn't actually like him.

After confirming that he genuinely had no preference as to what time of day they worked out, she sent him back his training schedule and added: Do you want me to train you seriously or is this just a cover?

His response was: I always do things seriously.

She sucked in a breath, suddenly insecure about creating a program for someone like Leland. After all, he could afford the best of the best.

For all she knew, he already had a personal trainer. She sat up straight and squared her shoulders. Just because she didn't work at some fancy gym in Manhattan didn't mean she should worry about her ability to supervise a rich guy's fitness routine. Bodies behaved the same no matter how much or little money a person had.

We'll talk about your goals at our first session.

When his response came back, it brought out her evil trainer's smile.

That sounds ominous. Remember that I need to be able to walk when you're done. Until tomorrow.

She typed back: You'll be able to walk, but not without groaning.

She waited a moment to see if he had anything more to say, but no new email showed up. So she logged into her fitness-planning program. She was going to put together a routine that would test what he was made of.

Better to write him off sooner than later.

At nine forty-five the next morning, Leland stepped out of a limousine around a corner three blocks away from Work It Out. Arriving at the gym in a limo felt too conspicuous, but he didn't want to give up the time that being chauffeured gave him to work on the trip from Manhattan to New Jersey. After all, he was playing hooky from the office.

As he hefted his gym bag and headed up the street, he found himself surprised by the vivid colors of the turning leaves in contrast to the still-emerald grass along the curb strip. It felt strange not to have to battle for space on the clean, well-kept sidewalks. He spent all his time among the hard, gray surfaces of Manhattan: steel, cement, and glass. He'd forgotten that other places could be softer, slower, and quieter.

He drew in a deep breath of the sunny autumn air and considered whether his partners were correct in saying that he needed to get out more. His daily forays to the lap pool on the top of their office building didn't count, since he took the elevator to a glass enclosure within a skyscraper.

Maybe he *was* using his job to keep himself from feeling the absence in his world, but it was what he needed to do right now. His mother shouldn't be dead. She deserved to live a long life enjoying all the luxuries he could give her since he had become successful. Familiar pain jabbed at his chest.

So he turned back to work, as always, wrapping his fingers around the cell phone in the pocket of his blue hoodie. He'd loaded so much monitoring software onto it that even the phone's vastly expanded memory was strained.

He lengthened his stride as he recollected that Dawn was waiting at the gym for him. He wanted to see if his memory of her silky, dark hair, slashing cheekbones, and dark, watchful eyes was accurate. Although maybe her avoidance of him at the parties had made her seem more interesting than she really was. An unusual buoyancy bubbled in his chest at the prospect of actually talking with her at last.

He crossed an intersection to see a large, redbrick building dominating the entire block. It looked exactly like what it once had been: a college gymnasium built in the late 1940s, with a double row of tall windows and a convex metal roof. The entrance had been updated with several plate-glass windows on either side of big glass-and-steel double doors. The neon sign over the entrance said WORK IT OUT in bold turquoise letters that glowed even in the daylight.

A cell phone antenna perched on the apex of the roof. It was surprising because the gym wasn't that much taller than other nearby structures. Maybe the antenna was just a signal booster.

As he approached, a flock of women in yoga pants spilled out the doors, some chatting, some staring at their phones, some looking harried. He held the door as a couple of stragglers sauntered out. One looked him up and down as though she were considering bidding on him at a livestock auction before she said, "Nice manners and good-looking too. You must be taken." She kept walking.

He felt a smile tug at the corners of his mouth as he stepped into the gym's double-height lobby. Maybe the occasional interaction with random strangers wasn't so bad after all.

His pleasure was overlaid by another wave of sadness. His mother had insisted that he hold the door for women, children, the elderly, and the infirm. When he asked with teenage sarcasm if there was anyone he *shouldn't* hold it for, she'd just given him one of her looks. From then on, whenever he held a door open for anyone, he'd looked at her and she'd smiled.

As soon as he turned toward the blond-wood reception desk, he saw Dawn, and his melancholy blew away like wisps of smoke.

Because Dawn was more than his memory of her.

Her olive skin had the sheen of satin, while her dark eyes were luminous and less wary than he remembered. Maybe because she was on her home turf at the gym. The slight smile of greeting curving her lips was professional, but the lips were soft and full, a delicious contrast to the strong cheekbones and jawline. A high ponytail rippled like a dark waterfall when she nodded to him. She pushed away from the desk with her hip and walked toward him, every movement betraying a coiled energy tamped down under tight control. He had a strong desire to make it explode.

He hoped Dawn remembered that he had signed up using one of his online aliases—Lee Wellmont—so his identity would not be easy to track down if his unauthorized meddling was discovered.

"Hey, Lel . . . Lee. Glad to see you're smiling," she said. "That means you're looking forward to a hard workout."

"Or maybe it means I'm extremely pleased to see you." He poured on the Georgia drawl.

Discomfort flickered in her dark eyes. So she didn't want to flirt at her job. Or maybe she didn't want to flirt in front of the huge man who had risen from the desk to join them, his baseball mitt of a hand thrust out.

"Welcome to our newest member," the man said. "I'm Ramón, the owner of this place, and I'm pleased to have you here."

He'd bet that Ramón had been a boxer . . . or a linebacker. The man's nose had been broken more than once and his neck was as thick as a telephone pole. His smile, though, held nothing but kindness and affability.

"The pleasure is mine," Leland said, relieved not to find Ramón's handshake crushing. "I've heard great things about both Dawn and your gym."

Ramón's smile turned into a beam. "That makes me real happy, Lee. Who'd you hear it from?"

"Dawn's friend Alice Thurber. We went to high school together."

"Alice is good people. Any friend of hers is a friend of mine," Ramón said.

Dawn cleared her throat. "Talking isn't going to build you any muscle. Let's get to work."

"I hope Alice warned you that Dawn believes in a challenge, both for herself and her clients," Ramón said, a note of pride in his voice.

"I'm counting on it," Leland said. "I spend all day in front of a computer, so I need someone to whip me into shape."

"I'll give you a quick tour before we get started," Dawn said, pivoting on her heel and heading toward the smallest of three doors that led off the lobby. He followed, enjoying the swing of her hair and the sway of her surprisingly lush butt under the black leggings she wore with a tight turquoise shirt. The shirt matched the general color scheme and had "Work It Out" embroidered on the back.

He followed her down a hallway past the men's and women's locker rooms to a door marked CONSULT ROOM. Dawn knocked and opened the door into a small space that held a desk and two bright blue chairs, gesturing for him to go in.

"This is where we talk with clients about private issues like medical problems or past-due bills. It used to be a supply closet." She gave him a wry grimace and hesitated for a moment before saying, "Maybe you shouldn't tell people you work with computers. You're supposed to be just an average Joe." She threw him a quick glance. "Not that anyone is going to believe that once they talk to you. Well, except Ramón. He assumes everyone is honest until proven otherwise."

"I didn't say I worked with computers. I said I sat in front of a computer. You just have inside knowledge."

She frowned, her strong brows drawing down in the middle until the ends seemed like uptilted wings. "You're right. I'm sorry. I guess I'm just nervous about this."

"Why?" He felt nothing but the exhilaration of finding and fixing a problem.

"Because you're pretending to be someone you're not. I might slip up and get you in trouble."

"If you call me Leland by mistake, I can always say that Alice called me that in school so you picked it up from her." He gave her his best disarming southern smile. "It's almost the truth."

"I guess almost truths are better than outright lies. You ready to sweat or do you need to do spy stuff first?"

"My spy stuff is on my phone and collecting information as we speak, so let's sweat." He was curious to find out how she conducted her training regime.

"You said to keep it real," she said, "so let's stow your bag in the locker room like everyone else's."

After he'd stashed his gym bag in a blond-wood locker, he rejoined Dawn in the hallway. "Could I take a look at the pool first?" he requested. "I might stay to swim. That will give my software plenty of time to dig in."

She nodded, the light catching in the sleek strands of her hair, making his fingers itch to see if it felt as satiny as it looked. She led him back into the lobby and through a room lined with treadmills and ellipticals, about one-quarter of which were in use. No pulse-poundingly loud music blared through the gym, so he could hear the thud of running shoes hitting the rubber tracks.

The far wall was composed of a row of floor-to-ceiling windows that overlooked the promised pool. It glowed a sparkling turquoise, clueing him in to the source of the gym's eye-popping color scheme. He had to admit that the pale wood floors and paneling provided a nice balance to the brilliant blue, evoking a white sand beach by the Caribbean Sea.

Only one woman plowed through the water in one of the lanes, her stroke slow but steady. The nearly empty pool beckoned to him. "I'm definitely doing some laps after our session."

She bared her teeth in a mock-sinister smile. "If your arms aren't rubber by then."

"Do your worst." He liked her edge.

"Okay, let's warm you up." She pointed to an empty treadmill. "We'll talk while you walk." She narrowed her eyes and scanned him up and down with purely professional interest. He caught himself wishing her gaze held a different kind of appreciation, more like the yoga woman's.

Her fingers danced over the control panel of the treadmill and it began to move at a pace he considered a saunter. "I mentioned that your initial session is ninety minutes and that the first thirty minutes are free. We'll use the free time to warm up and discuss your fitness goals. On your next visit, you can warm up yourself before your session begins if you'd like to get the maximum benefit from it."

Her tone was pleasant but, again, all work and no play. He missed the snappy teasing of her email messages.

"I'll get my tablet to input your program. And some water for you. Be right back." She took off toward a glass-fronted refrigerator so he could savor her distinctive stride, which somehow combined propulsion and seduction.

As he strolled, he redirected his thoughts to his phone, now tucked away in the locker, sucking in data from all over the gym. Would it confirm his working theory?

"Here you go." Dawn slotted a water bottle into the treadmill's console. "Hydration is important." She tapped a button on the tablet. "Let's talk goals. You don't need to lose weight, so we can cross that goal off."

"I appreciate it." His tone was dry.

One corner of her lips twitched. "You're welcome. Muscle mass looks pretty good too."

"I'm resisting the urge to flex in confirmation."

She hummed at that. "I guess I shouldn't write down 'figure out why cell data usage is so high at the gym.'"

"Probably not wise." The treadmill suddenly accelerated as it followed Dawn's programming.

"How about increasing your flexibility?" she asked.

"I like to think that I'm quite flexible already, but go right ahead." She ignored his comment and tapped at the tablet.

The treadmill quickened to running speed and tilted to a high incline. He increased his pace to accommodate it. "Did you add 'run up Mount Everest' to my goals?"

She chuckled and hit a button on the control panel, causing the track to slow and flatten. "I was just messing with you."

So the teasing was still there. A blip of pleasure twanged at his chest.

She asked him a few basic questions about his general health, raising her eyebrows when he told her he swam every day for an hour or more. "So we don't need to work on lung capacity or stamina either, it sounds like." She made a note.

The treadmill slowed and stopped. Dawn tucked the tablet under her arm and gave him a full-on grin. "Let's see what you're made of."

The next fifty-five minutes were a challenge. She pushed him to see where his strengths, weaknesses, and limitations were. By the end he was breathing hard and his glasses had fogged up enough to require wiping off.

Then the real torture began. She had him lie down on a mat before she knelt beside him. "As your reward for working so hard, I'm going to stretch you. Bend your left knee and put your foot flat on the floor. Good. Turn your head to the left."

She circled his left wrist with her fingers in a firm, warm grasp and pulled his arm out straight on the floor so it lay a mere inch from her folded legs. Releasing his wrist, she shifted one hand to his left shoulder and put the other on the outside of his bent knee. She pressed his shoulder down and his knee to the right, ever so slowly but inexorably.

He barely noticed the pleasant pull in his back muscles because he was enveloped in Dawn. A faint scent of something lemony emanated from her body. With his head turned sideways, he had a close-up view of the black fabric of her leggings stretched over her deliciously rounded hip and strong thigh. The warmth of her palms seemed to soak through his T-shirt and running pants, creating pools of sensation on his skin that migrated straight to his groin. He closed his eyes and began mentally coding the most boring program he could think of.

"Tell me when it becomes uncomfortable." Her voice was so close, almost by his ear, which made him think of lying in bed beside her. Both of them naked.

"Stop there." His command was more abrupt than he intended.

"Sorry. Did I hurt you?" She sounded contrite.

"Not at all, but as you said, I need to work on flexibility." He rolled his head back to center. A mistake. Her face with its elegant angles hovered over his, a look of concern darkening her brown eyes. If he pushed up on his elbows, he could just reach that lush mouth of hers to see if it was as soft as it appeared.

He would not allow himself more than a passing glance at her breasts, their tempting curves suspended above his chest. However, when her ponytail fell over her shoulder so that its silk nearly brushed his cheek, he considered winding it around his fingers to bring her down to him. The thought of those lush breasts pressing into his chest made him stifle a groan.

"Let's try the other direction. Stop me the moment you feel any discomfort." She stood and skirted the mat to his other side.

He almost laughed since he was already feeling plenty of discomfort. He started on the computer code again the moment she touched his wrist.

You are a professional and this is just another client, Dawn repeated to herself for the fifteenth time. She forced herself to ignore how Leland's pulse beat against her palm as she positioned his arm. She kept her eyes fixed resolutely on the mat somewhere to the side of his shoulder as she eased his knee across his body, testing for the kind of resistance that indicated pain. It had been a mistake to look down into his eyes the first time she'd touched him, because she'd seen a flare of something that had sent heat rippling through her own body.

God knows she'd trained good-looking men before. Some of them had even hit on her. She'd never felt any desire to take them up on their offers.

So why the hell was she hoping that Leland would say something inappropriate?

"Stop there," he said.

"You have excellent flexibility on this side," she said, lifting his knee back into neutral position. She took a deep breath and reminded herself again that this was just a body that needed stretching.

Then she pushed his bent knee gently toward his chest. There was no way to avoid looking into his eyes now. She needed to gauge his reaction to the stretch so she didn't overdo it. Not to mention that she would appear distracted if she gazed off into the distance when her position put her face-to-face with him. Maybe he would close his eyes the way some of her clients did.

No such luck. As she carefully shifted some of her weight onto his shin to deepen the stretch, the blue of Leland's eyes blazed up at her, sending little flickers of sensation dancing over her skin. She had the strangest desire to taste the sheen of sweat that glazed his forehead. Or to brush back the strand of his brown hair that clung to it.

And his mouth. Oh dear God, she wanted to trace the sculpted lines of it with her lips and her tongue and maybe even her teeth.

"I think that's far enough," Leland said, his voice strained.

Dawn eased off quickly. She'd been so caught up in her fantasy that she'd forgotten to check for signs of tension. "Okay, I'm going to straighten your leg upward now."

Leland nodded. Dawn wrapped one hand around his ankle and placed the other flat on the back of his thigh. As she pushed his leg toward his head, she tried to ignore the press of his tendons and bones against her fingers. This time she kept her mind on the task, helped by the fact that Leland had transferred his gaze to the ceiling, although his attention seemed inward.

He even *smelled* good. There was a faint aroma of laundry detergent emanating from his gray T-shirt that blended with his own scent of clean, healthy male, made stronger by his exertions. She wanted to bury her nose in the crook of his neck and inhale him.

She couldn't decide whether to cut the stretching short so she could regain her sanity or whether she preferred to prolong the exquisite torture of touching him and being allowed to manipulate his big, toned body in any direction she felt like.

She would have the same decision to make tomorrow . . . and the next day.

But she had a job to do and she intended to do it right. After the final stretch, she settled him back into a neutral position on his back, her pulse speeding up as she let her gaze skim down the impressive length of his body. "Okay, good work," she said, standing up to put a little more distance between herself and his magnetic pull. "I'll walk you to the locker room."

His chest rose and fell as he took a deep breath with his eyes closed. "I can't decide if I'm grateful or in pain. I'm afraid to find out by standing up."

"Coward." She reached downward, palm open. Touching him again was a bad idea if she wanted to maintain her professional composure. But she couldn't stop herself. "I'll give you a hand up."

Those intense eyes opened again and his long fingers wrapped around hers, his grip sending a sensation of warmth and strength vibrating up her arm. He bent his legs and rose to his feet with barely a tug for support. He didn't release her hand until she forced the issue by pivoting toward the exit door.

"Give me a minute to check the status of all my body parts," he said, rolling his head and shaking out his arms. "All right, I think I can move."

"It wasn't that bad, was it?" She gave him a sidelong glance when he fell into step beside her. It felt good to know that she had challenged him with her program. But he challenged her peace of mind with those intelligent eyes watching her through his nerdy glasses and the athlete's body trying to hide under a geek's clothing. It was like unwrapping a package to find a surprising gift within. A really hot gift.

"I'm used to swimming, where I am in control of my own fate. I'd forgotten how useful it is to have someone push you in new directions."

Pleasure surged through her but she brushed it aside and lowered her voice. "Are you going to check your phone before you swim?"

"I'll take a quick glance at it, but I need my office computers to dive deep." His honeyed drawl sounded close by her ear as he bent to keep their conversation private. It seemed to flow downward to pool in her belly.

"You'll email me?"

"Don't I always?" There was an undertone that heated the honey as it poured through her.

She managed a nod and lengthened her stride. She needed to get away from this madness. "Make sure to drink plenty of water," she said as they reached the hallway leading to the locker rooms.

"I figured on absorbing it through my pores while swimming."

She couldn't stop herself from glancing up. His lips curved in a teasing smile, but his eyes glinted with something hotter.

"I'm pretty sure that won't work." Her voice came out all wrong, like she'd been on the treadmill running hard.

"Another urban legend shot down." He flicked the end of her pony-tail so that it flipped over her shoulder. "I'll find you after my swim."

The playful intimacy of his gesture sent a shiver of heat spreading through her. She had to swallow hard before she croaked, "I'm tied up with a client for the next hour."

"Then it will be a long swim." He pulled open the locker-room door and left her with an accelerated heart rate.

She needed to make sure she trained her next client far away from the windows that offered a view of the pool. In her experience, work was the best antidote to the kind of insanity Leland evoked in her brain and other parts of her body.

After the final stretches with her client, she checked the email that had come in fifteen minutes before. Leland was waiting at the juice bar, staring at the glass in front of him with a dubious expression. His longish brown hair was still damp and showed more curl than usual. He was dressed in jeans and a clean dark-blue sweatshirt that somehow made the blue of his eyes behind his glasses all the more vivid.

Dawn tried to quash her reaction as she slid onto the bamboo stool next to his. "Not a fan of protein shakes?"

"It tastes like suntan lotion and trail mix combined in an appalling way."

"Must be the Caribbean Zen. Let me get you a Jamaican Karma. You'll like it better." She signaled the bartender.

Leland pushed the half-empty glass away. "That's enough healthy intake for today. Just water for me."

"Didn't swallow enough in the pool?" If she kept sparring, she wouldn't think about the texture of his skin where it stretched over his sharp jawline. Much.

He ignored her jab as the server produced a glass of water with lemon slices floating on top. "What would you like to drink?"

"I'm good. I've got all the bottles of water I want back in the gym."

Leland picked up his glass. "In that case, let's sit over in the corner, where we can speak without being overheard." He cut his eyes toward the server and the two other customers sitting at the juice bar.

He offered his hand to Dawn to help her off the stool. How could she refuse to take it? When his warm, solid palm met hers, sensation sizzled through her arm, and she let go as soon as she could without being obvious. She turned her back to him and headed for the wooden café table in the corner.

This was the one room where Vicky had taken a break from turquoise, going for a rain-forest effect with potted palm trees and the piped-in twittering of birds. It was supposed to be soothing to go with the names of the drinks on the menu. Or maybe it was the other way around.

Leland had chosen the location well. The only other occupied table held two women having what looked like an intense gossip session, but it was on the other side of the space.

Dawn took the chair that allowed her to see anyone approaching and kept Leland's back to the room.

He sat down across the small tabletop from her. His wide swimmer's shoulders dominated her view, but out of the corner of her eye, she could still see his long, powerful legs stretched out and crossed at the ankles. All his exertions seemed to make him radiate strong, male pheromones. At least her receptors were picking up the signals.

"The data usage is off the charts again, as it was when you had the Wi-Fi issue," he said, his voice low. "This time, however, someone is harnessing all the phones in the gym to handle the massive stream of traffic."

She jerked her wandering mind back into business mode. "What kind of traffic? Is it some kind of illegal activity?"

"I won't know until I get back to my office. My phone can collect the data but it doesn't have the capacity to analyze it." He put his elbows on the table and touched all his fingertips together, his gaze fixed on her above them. She'd only ever seen people do that in old movies, but somehow it worked for him. "I have a theory that someone is utilizing the phones as a deep web or dark web node."

A frisson of nervous excitement tingled through her. "The dark web sounds like something Darth Vader would use. Is it illegal?"

"Not necessarily. The deep web, which encompasses the dark web, is used by legitimate businesses who want very secure information transfer, since deep websites are all encrypted and don't show up on search engines. Some regular folks simply believe they have the right to be anonymous on the internet. Even more important, since its users cannot be tracked, citizens living under totalitarian governments use the deep web to communicate with the uncensored outside world. Which is why the *New York Times* has a deep website. I personally use the dark web to track possible data sales if a client gets hacked."

"So it's a good thing?"

"Sometimes. But it was also home to the infamous Silk Road website, which dealt—and in fact might still deal—in very illicit goods and services."

"How illicit?"

"Guns, drugs." Leland's expression of distaste was even stronger than when he had been sipping his protein drink. "Child pornography, sex-slave trading. Truly horrible things. Unfortunately, others have picked up where the Silk Road left off. Supposedly, you can even hire an assassin, but most of those websites have turned out to be scams."

"So what exactly does being a node for the deep, dark web mean?"

He smiled briefly at her feeble joke. "The deep and dark webs are based on anonymity. In the simplest terms, users obtain that anonymity by having their internet access randomly bounced through multiple servers called nodes. That makes it virtually impossible to trace activity back to the end user."

Dawn frowned. "Would someone at the gym have to know about being a node?" She just couldn't picture Ramón aiding and abetting an assassin or a child pornographer.

"I would think so. Some router has to be feeding the traffic through the phones. It's an interesting hack. I'm wondering if it's related to your earlier Wi-Fi issues." His face was lit with interest, his eyes practically glowing. His drawl had melted away as he talked. "Using the phones would probably make the users even harder to track because the IP addresses are bouncing through multiple devices. But why? What are they trying to hide?"

His gaze still seemed aimed at her, but his attention had turned to the problem. He was talking to himself. "Money laundering of some kind? Data theft?"

"The secret recipe for Jamaican Karma?"

His lips quirked in a half smile and he laid his hands palm down on the table. "Sorry. Puzzles enthrall me."

"No apology necessary. I just wondered how far away your mind had gone."

"I should get to the office to find out what's really going on."

She felt hollow at the prospect of his departure. Even potential assassins couldn't dampen the pleasure of basking in his company. "At least you got your exercise done for the day."

"So I will glow with virtue for the next twenty-four hours." He pushed his chair back.

Dawn tried to delay his departure. "Did you get a lot of thinking done in the pool?"

An odd expression crossed his face. "I did but not on the most useful of topics." He eased out of his chair with a surprised grimace. "I stiffened up. You get the credit for that. My muscles are accustomed only to swimming."

"I'll take that as a compliment." She stood too. "See you tomorrow at three."

"You'll hear from me before then." His expression turned serious. "It's a good bet that something shady is going on here. I wouldn't mention it to anyone you don't trust one hundred percent."

That was pretty much her motto for life nowadays. She nodded. "Only Alice knows about this from me." Although she might talk to her friend Natalie. Nat owned the Mane Attraction hair salon and knew more about what was going on in Cofferwood than even the police chief. And she was totally trustworthy.

"Excellent." He smiled, his eyes glinting behind the glasses. "Maybe you should walk me to the door in case the muscles you've tortured can't hold me up."

The hollowness was banished by a wave of pleasure. He wanted her company a little longer too. She gave him a scan up and down. "I think catching you would be a job for Ramón, not me."

"You are stronger than you think." He moved to her side and put his hand against the small of her back to nudge her forward. The casual touch vibrated into the marrow of her bones while his words zinged around in her brain.

He saw her as strong, but he meant physically. He didn't know who she really was.

Chapter 4

"Yo, Leland!"

The boom of Tully's voice dragged Leland out of his focused probe into the data traffic at Work It Out. He spun his chair around to see his partner, arms crossed, hip hitched against a workstation.

"No need to shout," Leland said, tamping down his irritation at being interrupted.

"Are you kidding me? I tried twice at normal volume and you didn't even twitch." Tully nodded toward the monitor Leland had been engrossed in. "Is that the Mentix data theft you're working on?"

Guilt jabbed at Leland, an emotion he rarely felt at work. He'd pushed the high-profile Mentix project down his list of priorities, partially because the traffic problem was more interesting and partially because he wanted to have an answer to share with Dawn. "No, this is a Small Business Initiative project. The gym in Cofferwood."

"I thought they got that problem fixed."

"Another rose up in its place. An even more interesting one."

"Uh-oh, I recognize that expression. You've gotten hooked on a puzzle." Tully snagged a wheeled chair with the pointed toe of his cowboy boot and rolled it over so he could sit beside Leland. "What's up?"

Leland watched his partner stare at the monitor with its scrolling code as though Tully could actually interpret any of it. "Tell me what you see," Leland challenged, knowing his colleague wouldn't have a clue.

"A shitload of meaningless mumbo jumbo." Tully grinned. "I was trying to look interested in your problem."

"You failed." But Leland's irritation had faded. "Someone has turned all the cell phones connected to the gym's Wi-Fi into an almost untraceable node for the dark web."

"But you traced it because you're that good."

"No, I traced it because I was pointed in the right direction by a concerned citizen."

"So what do you do about it?" Tully glanced at the screen again.

"Monitor it. Pick it apart until I can figure out why. Make sure it's not being used for something illegal." Not to mention, the longer he monitored it, the more training time he would get with Dawn. He massaged one of his aching thighs. She was damned good at her job.

Tully rolled his chair away from the monitor. "How come I never get any SBI assignments?"

"Because most small business owners aren't threatened with actual bodily harm. Not enough money involved."

His partner's expression turned grim. "You'd be surprised by how little money it takes to tempt people into violence."

The word triggered a chill in Leland as he pictured Dawn with her well-honed body and glossy ponytail. He hadn't lied when he'd said she was strong. She was an expert in self-defense, but the dark web was by definition a lawless place, which meant their project might get dangerous.

Leland resolved to proceed carefully for Dawn's sake. "Did you come here to discuss something with me?" he asked.

"Hell, yes!" Tully's face lit up. "We're Derek's best men so that means we have to plan a bachelor party."

Leland winced. He'd forgotten about that particular responsibility. Or maybe he'd hoped to avoid it. "You plan it. I'll pay for half."

"No way, bro. You're part of this. I need input."

He recognized Tully's insistence for what it was: an attempt to drag him away from what his partners viewed as his unhealthy devotion to work. He hated social events of any kind, and he was less in the mood for them now than ever before. A bachelor party, even for a man he considered more than a brother, sounded like the worst kind of torture. Leland would be a fish out of water, the same way he always had been among the privileged kids at his private school. Some things never changed. "Tully, I suck at that kind of stuff."

"No, you just *think* you suck at it." Tully tilted the chair back. "Vegas is too obvious, and he's traveled to all the usual places in Europe for work. We need something out of the ordinary. What do you think of a white-water rafting trip in Idaho?"

"Well, at least there wouldn't be any strippers." Leland considered the idea and thought maybe it could work. Weirdly, he had a vision of Dawn in the bow of a raft, a paddle clenched in her strong, slender hands, her face lit with exhilaration as she steered past jutting rocks and through frothing waves. There was one issue with Tully's suggestion, however. "Has Derek ever expressed any interest in white-water rafting?"

"He's never expressed an interest because he hasn't thought about it. It would be a great bonding experience."

Leland had never thought about it either. Rapids and computers weren't compatible. "Have *you* ever been white-water rafting?"

Tully's eyes lit up. "Yeah, in Alaska last year. It's a rush and a half when you hit Class V rapids and the water just picks your raft up and hurls it down the river." He rolled his chair forward and air paddled. "You paddle like hell and you'll still get dumped. The water is colder than a polar bear's butt on an ice floe, which motivates you to get back in the raft pronto."

Maybe the water in Idaho was warmer than in Alaska. "I'd be useless at planning the expedition." Yet Tully's enthusiasm had transmitted itself to him, especially because then the "party" wouldn't be a social occasion. Also, while he was genuinely happy that Derek had found the love of his life, Leland knew it would change the dynamic among them. One last time with just the three of them working together to get their raft through Class V rapids would be a trip to remember.

"I know a real good guide outfit to set it all up," Tully said. "Now we have to decide if we should tell him ahead of time or keep it a secret until we get him on the plane."

Leland didn't remember agreeing to the idea, but it was growing on him. However, he knew how much he personally hated surprises. "We tell him ahead of time."

Tully stared at the ceiling for a long moment before he shook his head. "Nope, we surprise him. We'll tell Alice, though. She can keep a secret and she'll organize whatever he needs to take without him having a clue."

"If you've got all this figured out already why did you come in here and interrupt me?" Leland made his tone as dry as dust.

"I needed your valuable input." Tully grinned and stood up just as Derek walked in.

"You look guilty," Derek said, his gaze moving between his two partners. "Conspiring against me?"

"Just planning your bachelor party." Tully clapped Derek on the shoulder. "How many strippers did we decide on, Leland?"

"Twenty-five, I believe," Leland said.

"Thank God I don't believe either one of you." Derek sat in the chair Tully had vacated. "Leland, I hesitate to tell you this, but we just got the RFP from Fincher. The deadline's a bear . . . end of next week. Have you got time or should I tell them we're not going to respond? It's a nice piece of business but we can easily say no if you're swamped."

"Leland never says no nowadays." Tully threw a warning frown at Derek. "So I'll say no for him. He's got a full plate and I just found out he's also working on an SBI project."

Leland cast his best look of disdain at Tully. "I can manage an RFP without any problem." His plate was overflowing but he'd work more hours. If he was exhausted enough, he could sleep through the night. Otherwise he would lie awake in the dark, swamped by waves of grief and regret.

Derek gave him a searching look. "It's a short deadline for such a complex RFP."

Leland raised his eyebrows. "Have I ever missed a due date?"

"That doesn't mean it's okay to kill yourself doing it," Tully said. "Let this one go, partner."

"You're determined to annoy me today," Leland said.

"I'll send you the RFP and you can decide after you read it." Derek nodded toward the computer monitor. "Is the SBI project the one at the gym where Alice goes to work out with her friend Dawn? She told me the data traffic picked up again, only on cell phones."

"Indeed it has. There's something very strange going on in Cofferwood, New Jersey. Who'd have thought?" It was odd, but hearing Derek mention Dawn's name gave Leland a little kick of pleasure, as though it had brought Dawn into the room with them.

"Well, it got you out of the office for a few hours this morning, so I'm in favor of it," Derek said.

"Amen to that!" Tully exclaimed.

Leland refused to rise to their needling. "I believe I accompanied Derek to a client meeting for an entire half day last week."

"Only because the client insisted on meeting our computer genius," Derek said. "His IT guy wanted to touch you." Derek glanced at Tully. "You should have heard the jargon flying between them."

Tully chuckled before he headed out the door. "I gotta get to a meeting with a client myself."

Derek locked his eyes on Leland before he said in a low, commanding voice, "No strippers. Swear it!"

Leland just smiled.

Dawn had checked her phone between every client, but no email from Leland showed up. She shoved her arms into her jacket with unnecessary force before she stalked into the lobby to head home.

Chad was propped against the front desk, flirting with Tiffany, the nineteen-year-old night receptionist. When he saw Dawn, he straightened and walked over to fall into step beside her. "You look like you've had a bad day. Let me buy you a drink to cheer you up."

He snaked his arm around her shoulders, sending her nervous system into overload. She twisted out of his grasp to face him. "How many times do I have to say no to you before you get the message?"

Chad held up both hands, palms out. "Hey, just being friendly. A beer is all I had in mind."

"Sorry, I'm just cranky." Disappointment over Leland's silence made her irritable and she'd overreacted. "Long day." She waved her hand in apology and jerked open the door.

"Rain check," Chad called out as the door swung closed behind her.

Jesus, the man really didn't quit. However, he flirted with everyone, so she decided it was nothing more worrisome than an exasperating personality trait. It wasn't his fault that his clueless persistence triggered her reflex to knee him in the balls.

She walked the five minutes to her apartment building, sticking to the bright pools of illumination cast by the streetlights. She made sure that the entrance door to the building was locked before putting her key in. Then she scanned the small front hall and staircase before she stepped inside to check her mailbox. Bills and junk mail.

She jogged up the stairs to the second floor, where she keyed in a six-digit combination to open her apartment door. The solid thunk of the high-quality dead bolt sliding back always reassured her. Once she was inside, she disarmed the alarm and then rearmed it the moment the door was closed again. The tension in her shoulders eased and she blew out a breath of relief.

After dropping her gym bag on the table by the door and shrugging out of her jacket, she headed for the kitchen. She had the ingredients for a broccoli-avocado tuna bowl spread out on the granite countertop when her cell phone rang. She glanced at the phone but didn't recognize the number. "Stupid telemarketers," she muttered as she sliced up the avocado.

But a ping indicated the caller had left a voice message. Curiosity got the better of her, so she punched her voice mail button.

"Dawn, it's Leland. I hope you don't mind that I called in a favor to get your cell number from Alice. She thought it would be all right with you since we're working together now." Leland's honey-smooth drawl seemed to stroke over her skin. "Please give me a call when you have a free moment."

So they'd escalated from email to phone calls. That seemed like a good sign. Her stomach grumbled as she debated whether to respond immediately or eat first. However, the thrill of hearing Leland's voice won out. She settled on her sofa, added Leland's number to her contacts, and hit the call button.

He answered after the second ring. "I appreciate the quick return call. Sorry to bother you so late, but we need to talk about things that should not be put in writing."

So he hadn't just wanted to hear the sound of her voice. She slumped back against the sofa cushion as her little fizz of excitement died a sad death. Following his lead, she stuck to business. "Sounds sinister. What did you find?"

"The phones are definitely being used as a dark web node. It makes for a very secure node since it's scattered through multiple devices. Which is clever but also illegal because their owners haven't given permission to use their phones for this purpose." By the time he finished, his drawl had nearly disappeared.

"Not to mention that the customers grouse about the high data drain. But who the hell is doing it? And why?" she asked.

"I'm digging in to see if there are any known hacker signatures on this, but so far, no luck. That's why I called. You know the people at the gym. Does anyone come to mind who would demonstrate this level of technical sophistication?"

Dawn choked on a laugh of disbelief. "At the gym? No one. I mean Vicky is the gym's so-called IT expert and it took her a week to get the Wi-Fi fixed. She hates to use a keyboard because it messes up her fancy manicure. Ramón can't even find a document on his computer five minutes after he saves it. As for the rest of the staff, I can't think of anyone, except a couple of video gamers. Maybe they'd be computer savvy enough to do this?" She considered whether Josh or Ripley would be surfing the dark web. "Nah, I don't see them getting involved in dirty stuff, even if they had that kind of smarts."

"It could possibly be a gym member," Leland said. "However, they would have to get access to the router to set this up. Do you have any new staff members?"

Dawn sat up straight. "Chad?" She didn't like him because of his refusal to take no for an answer, so it seemed unfair to put him on the list of suspects. But he *was* new.

"Who is Chad?"

"A new trainer. But he can't be a computer wizard. He's one of those backslapping ex-jocks, still riding on the glory of his high school football career. He speaks in sports clichés."

"That's a scathing condemnation. I find it in my heart to feel sorry for him."

"Trust me, you shouldn't. He thinks he's hot stuff."

"It could be a facade meant to disarm those around him."

Leland sounded as though he knew something about facades, which made Dawn wonder about his. She got daring. "You mean like that southern accent of yours that comes and goes depending on what you're talking about?"

He gave a little huff of amusement. "Northerners tend to think speaking slowly means thinking slowly. It's often too late when they learn they're wrong."

It was a tantalizing glimpse into the man behind the computer genius. Alice had once said that Leland looked like a preppie pretending to be a nerd. The T-shirts and jeans couldn't entirely counteract the cleanly defined planes of his jaw and cheekbones that screamed blue blood. Not to mention his smooth accent, precise word usage, and last name for a first name. Which was facade and which was Leland Rockwell?

"I'm not seeing Chad as evil genius but let me talk to him. Maybe there's more there than I think." She grimaced at the thought of deliberately seeking out Chad because he would interpret it the wrong way. "I haven't spent that much time with him because he's a jerk."

Leland's chuckle was like the smoothest bourbon, dark and sexy. "You don't pull any punches. I like that about you."

His words soaked into her as though she'd taken a gulp of the liquor, loosening her muscles and firing a glow in her belly. "Honesty between partners."

"I suppose you could call us partners." He sounded as though he wasn't sure if that was a good thing or a bad one.

"I didn't mean we're like you and your KRG partners. Just that we're working together."

"You definitely don't want to be like Derek and Tully. They're both pains in the ass." His tone was dry.

"You and your partners appear to be pretty solid with each other." Dawn had watched the three men at Alice and Derek's engagement party. They seemed more like brothers than business partners, ribbing each other but with affection. Like her family had done when they were all kids. She missed it now that they were grown and scattered around the country. She felt like an outsider anyway, although that was her fault, not theirs.

"Derek and Tully aren't your average partners. We've been all over hell's half acre together, which creates a certain bond."

"I hear you." Revealing a painful secret also created a bond. That's why Alice and Natalie were so special to Dawn.

"Speaking of Tully, he reminded me that we need to be careful." Leland's tone was serious. "If Chad is running an illegal operation on the dark web, he won't want to be found out. That could make him dangerous if he gets suspicious of you. Point him out to me and I'll strike up a conversation with him."

"Won't that make him suspicious of *you*?" She was torn between being offended that he thought she couldn't be subtle about her probing and being gratified that he was worried about her.

"I don't work with him, so I can avoid further contact if necessary."

"That doesn't make sense. He could still come after you." Chad was a big, burly guy. Not that Leland was any slouch when it came to body tone.

"I have Tully on my side."

His partner was ex-FBI, so that made sense. "Fine. You talk to Chad. You know a lot more about computers than I do anyway." That was the real reason she was backing off.

"You're much more amenable to reason than my other partners." He sounded surprised but in a good way.

She coughed out a laugh. "It doesn't happen often, so don't get used to it."

"That's a shame. I was going to invite you to join our meetings so I have an extra vote on my side." His voice had gone honeyed again.

"You're drawling so you must be trying to disarm me."

"I gave away my secret and now you're going to use it against me. I should have known better."

He was definitely flirting. She relaxed into the corner of the sofa and stretched her legs out. "Jersey girls are tough that way. Not like the New Yorkers you find so easy to fool."

"I would never attempt to fool you. We're partners, remember?" A ridiculous thrill zinged through her at his acceptance of her designation. It turned to equally ridiculous disappointment when he continued with what sounded like regret in his voice. "I have to get back to work. I'll see you tomorrow for our next training session. Don't hurt me too much."

Before Dawn could respond in kind, he had disconnected. Dawn looked at the time on her phone. He was getting back to work at nine forty-five at night? She knew why she put so much time in at the gym; it was her sanctuary. But what kept Leland at the office so late?

She hoped she'd get the chance to find out. After all, he'd been honest about how he used his accent. And he'd flirted with her until duty called.

She sighed and forced herself to consider Chad instead. Would a dark web criminal pester a coworker to go out with him? Wouldn't he want to fly under the radar rather than annoy her? She just couldn't imagine Chad being either a computer wizard or a criminal mastermind. He'd have to be a really skillful actor to make himself seem like such a dopey jock to cover his real self.

Although maybe criminal masterminds were smart enough to seem dumb.

She rubbed her temples to stop her mind from spinning in circles. She would see what Leland thought of Chad tomorrow.

Even better, she would see Leland tomorrow.

Chapter 5

When Leland walked through the gym's entrance doors, the afternoon sun caught him in its warm light, painting his hair gold, highlighting his broad swimmer's shoulders, and tracing down his long, long legs. Desire slid through Dawn like warm molasses, thick and sweet. She continued to lean against the reception desk, partly to have the pleasure of watching him walk toward her with that delicious smile curling his lips and partly because her knees had gone weak.

"You're early," she said, still gripping the edge of the glass countertop. "I like an eager client."

The sun flashed off his glasses as he shook his head. "Well, darlin', you mentioned I should warm up on the treadmill before we get started. I do my best to follow my trainer's instructions." The slow southern drawl was out in full force.

Delight tickled through her.

"Besides that," he continued, "I figure the sooner we begin, the sooner the torture will be over."

"Hmm. Not the attitude I was hoping for." She flipped her ponytail over her shoulder and gave him a slanting smile. "For that you'll get an extra five pounds on the barbell."

"But I used my slowest southern accent on you." He raised his eyebrows. "It's supposed to charm you."

"I'm immune." But she wasn't immune to the dancing imp of mischief in his blue eyes. That charmed her right down to her toes.

"I'll have to resort to different methods, then." His voice dropped to a rough purr that rippled over her skin.

"Okay, where's my next victim?" Chad's booming voice ripped through the delicious cocoon that seemed to envelop Dawn and Leland.

She squeezed her eyes shut briefly in disgust before she remembered that Leland needed to talk to the other trainer. Her eyelids snapped open and she moved close to Leland to murmur. "The blond guy who just walked up to the reception desk is Chad."

The fun vanished from Leland's eyes as he cast a sharp glance in Chad's direction. "Got it."

"You can ask Gina at the desk about that," Dawn said, raising her voice and hoping Leland could come up with a plausible question. After all, he was a genius. "I have to check on one thing before we get going. I'll see you at the treadmill."

Leland smiled and nodded to Dawn. "Thanks. I'll get a good sweat going before you arrive."

She could see his brain shifting into high gear as he started toward the unsuspecting Chad. She wished she could stay to eavesdrop on the conversation. Watching Leland use his impressive brain to run circles around the annoying trainer would be a treat and a half. However, she didn't want to screw up the investigation, so she strode toward the door to the locker rooms as though she had a real purpose.

Several minutes later, she found Leland running at a brisk pace on one of the treadmills. "Don't overdo it," she said, enjoying the way the muscles in his calves flexed with each stride. "I have big plans for you."

He stumbled slightly and muttered something under his breath.

"I missed that. What did you say?" Dawn asked.

"For my ears only." Leland slowed the treadmill. "I'm trying to loosen up all the stiff spots you left me with."

Dawn waited until he was looking her way before she scanned down his body. "Your stride looks pretty fluid to me."

"If only you knew," he said, dropping his speed to a walk. "Let's get this over with." He sounded like he was speaking through gritted teeth.

He'd been happy to flirt before. Why was he suddenly in a rush? Maybe she should drop the intensity a little. "You know I was kidding about the extra weights, right?"

"Do your worst," he challenged.

After a quick warm-up, she moved into the strength section of the day's program. She could use spotting him as a way to hold a private conversation.

As he stretched out on the weight bench, she picked up two twenty-five-pound dumbbells from the rack and moved to the end of the bench where his head lay. When she looked down at him, he smiled, his eyes gleaming behind the lenses of his glasses and deep creases bracketing the corners of his mouth. "You're going easy on me, aren't you?" he asked, holding up his hands for the weights.

That smile hit her like a sucker punch to the gut. "I . . . what? No." Except the heat it brought spread through in a delicious wave. "Maybe."

"Don't go easy. I like a hard workout." He took the weights and held them up straight-armed, his lips still curled into that teasing smile. "What next?"

She had to pull together her scattered thoughts. Were they back to flirting? "Skull crushers. Bring the weights down beside your ears and then back up, elbows in tight. Don't straighten your arms all the way at the top, to get the maximum benefit. Okay, start." She knelt in spotting position, which brought her down almost to the level of his head. "What did you think of Chad?"

"Aha! That's why you're getting up close and personal." He bent his elbows and she held her hands under the weights. Sweat sheened his forehead and his sexy scent tantalized her nostrils again. She resisted the urge to breathe him in.

"Is Chad a criminal mastermind?" she asked more sharply than she meant to.

"He's not a computer expert, unless he's very good at playing dumb. But I wouldn't count him out. There's a certain shrewdness behind those sports clichés. By the way, he told me I was training with the best in the gym." Leland's gaze locked on hers as he pushed the weights upward. "You."

"Chad said that?" Dawn was stunned. "He generally tries to lure my clients away from me. Maybe he's using some kind of reverse psychology on you."

"Which could support my theory that he's not as unsophisticated as he lets on. I told you I was always right."

"I was kidding. Watch the elbows there. You're flaring out slightly." Dawn put her hands against the outside of his elbows as he bent them again since he didn't really need spotting with twenty-five-pound weights. The feel of his skin sliding against hers sent a tingle racing up her arms, but she didn't pull away. "So you think Chad could be involved in some aspect of this dark web thing?"

"I don't know," Leland said, his voice tight with effort. "The timing is suspicious. But we're still looking for a computer expert."

"I'm going to talk to my friend Natalie. You might remember her from Alice and Derek's engagement party."

"Blonde, well groomed," Leland huffed out.

"You got her." There was a little twinge of pique that he'd noticed Natalie's grooming.

"I'm not clear on why she would be able to pinpoint the computer expert."

"Right. She owns a hair salon here in Cofferwood and she trains at the gym. She pretty much hears everything about everyone at the salon and she knows all the gym's staff. Not to mention that she's a great judge of character."

"I think the fewer people who know about our project, the better," Leland said.

"She's totally discreet."

He gave her a sardonic look. "Except when you ask her not to be."

"That's different. We're friends and I'm just as discreet as she is. Okay, you're done." Dawn curled her hands around the bar of the weights so her palms met the backs of his fingers. She'd done the same thing with a hundred other clients, but never had she felt such a shock of awareness. She had to remind herself not to drop the weights on Leland's head as he released his hold. Something made her look down, and she saw the same awareness in his eyes. Heat flashed through her and she almost staggered as she stood up.

"Um, let's get to the lower-body work." She winced as the unintentional double entendre of her words sank in. Or maybe it was her primitive subconscious being quite deliberate and enthusiastic.

His lips quirked into a half smile. He must have had a similar thought. She stalked over to the weight rack and slotted the weights into place, closing her eyes for a moment to calm herself.

"What new torment are you dreaming up for me?" His deep, slow voice sounded as though he was murmuring directly beside her ear. When her eyes flew open, the mirror showed that he stood right behind her, watching her in the reflection. She had an intense desire to press herself back against his sweat-darkened gray T-shirt and hope he would wrap his arms around her.

"Traveling lunges," she blurted out, even though she had no memory of including them in her plan for today's session. She sidestepped to get away from the gravitational pull he exerted over her. "With a barbell on your shoulders to challenge your balance."

He blew out a breath and nodded. She managed to get through the rest of the exercises without touching him again, a good thing for her concentration. "Okay, time to stretch," she said, as he finished a series of squats to cool down.

A look of what she could only interpret as pain crossed his face. "If I swear to stretch after I swim, may I skip this part?"

She stiffened as hurt jabbed at her. It was the second time he had tried to dodge her training. Had she overstretched him yesterday? Or was he trying to avoid her touch because he reacted to her physically? The possibility sent heat sizzling through her.

"If you're not going to stretch now, I should add more exercises so you get your full hour in." She put a little bit of seduction in her smile.

He grabbed his sweat towel and scrubbed at the back of his neck. "I need to get back to the office sooner rather than later, so even my swim will be brief." He softened that by giving her a rueful look. "Believe me, I got my money's worth from you. Chad was right about you being the best."

"Thanks." She gave him a tight-lipped smile, still unsure why he was leaving early.

He bent down closer. "Let me know what Natalie says." Then he pivoted and strode toward the locker room.

She refused to allow herself to stand and watch him go, so she grabbed a spray bottle and began to wipe down the weight bench, giving it a hard scrub in frustration.

However, she volunteered to help a newish member program her treadmill so she could keep an eye on the pool. Luckily, she had just saved the program to the machine's memory when Leland walked into the swimming area, wearing a pair of dark-red swim shorts.

Dawn forgot about the treadmill's speed and incline as her gaze traveled over the beautiful planes of Leland's body. She'd guessed at what he looked like under his workout clothes, but seeing him stripped down to bare skin made her gasp in a breath and hold it as desire burned through her veins. She imagined skimming her hands down the ridged *rectus abdominis* of his abdomen, tracing the line of his quads from his thigh to his knee, flattening her palms against the powerful deltoids of his shoulders. His skin would be warm and smooth over the hard press of muscle and tendon.

He stopped on the edge of the pool, tensed for a moment, and then arced into the water in a shallow racing dive, surfacing with his arms already thrusting like a piston-driven engine, perfectly calibrated and propulsive. He cut through the water without apparent effort, his strokes never varying as the wet-slicked, flexing muscles in his back caught flashes of light. She waited for him to resurface after he hit the pool's far wall in a perfect flip turn, taking much too long to emerge from under the water so she could savor the sight of him again.

The alarm on her smart watch sounded, making her jump. Glancing down at it, she saw that her next client was due in ten minutes. Maybe it was a good thing that she had another commitment to drag her away from drooling over Leland.

─

Leland fell into the familiar, mind-freeing rhythm of moving through the water. Except his mind kept taking cues from his body, which was still humming with arousal. He'd seen the baffled look in Dawn's eyes when he'd turned down stretching, but he didn't want to risk the strong possibility that his desire for her would become visible when she put her hands on him. The day before, it had been a near thing. Today the intensity of his attraction had been amplified by nothing more than her proximity during their training session. The few times her skin had come in contact with his, her touch had sent a streak of arousal straight to his groin.

He'd taken a cold shower before putting on his swim trunks, but that had offered only a temporary fix. Now her face, her body, and her voice—rough velvet with a weirdly sexy touch of Jersey accent—clouded his mind with lust.

Summoning every ounce of mental self-discipline he possessed, he focused on the Fincher RFP he'd promised Derek. Tully had been right, damn him! Leland didn't really have time to do it justice. Especially not with Dawn undermining his concentration at every turn.

What the hell was wrong with him?

He hit the wall and flipped feet over head, launching himself in the opposite direction underwater.

He had to stay focused on the job. That's where he knew who he was. That's where people depended on him. Where he didn't have time to think about the hole in his heart.

Although Dawn was proving to be an effective distraction from his grief. Maybe he should go with that. No, he couldn't use her that way. She deserved to be more than a sort of temporary bandage.

He forced himself to work through the next step in solving the mystery of the dark web node. That was what he was here for, after all.

He'd gone as far as he could with his monitoring software. He needed to get into the router itself. He'd been a little surprised to discover that it had the latest security protocol and had been set up so administrative access was authorized only through a physical Ethernet connection. Someone knew their cybersecurity. Which was unusual for a business like Work It Out, a single-owner gym without particularly sensitive data to protect.

That made the dark web activity all the more suspicious.

He'd have to ask Dawn where the router was located, although he would take a guess it was in the boss's office. Getting in there with his laptop was going to be tricky, to say the least. He could ask Tully for help, but he suspected his partner would insist on coming along.

He kick turned and his thoughts inexorably returned to Dawn now that her name had floated across his consciousness again.

One more lap, during which he would allow himself to fantasize about peeling her exercise clothes off and running his hands over her naked skin.

Then he had to get back to work.

Chapter 6

"Nat, I need your opinion about something." Dawn bit into a fried zucchini stick, a specialty at Winenfood that she allowed herself to indulge in no more than once a month, even though she and her friends generally met at the local bar once a week.

"And I thought you'd invited me out for a drink for the pleasure of my company," Natalie said, her slim fingers curled around the stem of her Manhattan glass. She had her short blonde hair smoothed back into a sleek, sophisticated style and wore a simple white cotton blouse that she had somehow turned into a fashion statement by adding a couple of delicate silver necklaces.

"I thought people were flattered when you asked their opinion." Dawn took a swallow of her Stella Artois.

"An opinion is like advice. Everyone thinks they want to hear it until they do."

Dawn nodded. Natalie was smart that way. Maybe it was because she owned a hair salon and heard more about her customers' lives than she really wanted to. Or because she was about ten years older than Dawn and had survived some tough experiences in her life. That's what had made her trust the other woman almost from the start.

"Well, I really want to hear your opinion about this." She told Natalie about how Leland had discovered the dark web activity at the gym. "So who at the gym do you think might be capable of doing something illegal on the internet? And what would it be?"

Natalie gave Dawn a searching look. "Why are you getting involved in this?"

Dawn frowned in surprise. She'd never questioned her motivation for searching out the truth. "Because something criminal is going on at the gym. Because the customers are complaining and I don't want Ramón to lose business because of it. Because it's not right and I don't want to back away from a situation like that ever again."

"Why don't you just call the police?"

"Leland's an expert on this stuff and says that the bad guys will just move the node if the police get involved before we know what's going on."

"I can't help remembering what happened when Alice tangled with some bad guys." Natalie rotated her glass by the stem. "Haven't you had enough violence in your life already?"

If anyone else had said that, Dawn would have been furious, but Natalie genuinely worried about her. "Now I know how to handle myself."

Natalie gave her a tight smile. "You tell us in every self-defense class that a gun changes everything. Or a knife. Or more than one attacker."

Dawn flinched at the last one, but she had techniques to deal with that now. "I have no intention of getting myself into a situation where I need to defend myself. Leland is the one who's doing the hacking."

"That's another thing. You don't have permission from Ramón or Vicky to mess with their Wi-Fi. So you're getting in their business without their knowledge."

"Ramón just defers to Vicky and she thinks the whole thing doesn't matter. I tried to talk to her about it, remember?"

"Yes, you told me." Natalie looked away across the bar for a long moment before she took a sip of her drink and swallowed. "The whole situation worries me."

"Me too. Help me figure out who's behind it so we can call the police."

"You're like a dog with a bone."

Dawn grinned. "My mother used to tell me that. I take it as a compliment."

"I'm sure she didn't mean it as one," Natalie murmured.

Dawn set down her beer. "Ramón got me out of the dark, scary place I was stuck in. Maybe I can repay him in some small way."

"All right, let's look at the suspects," Natalie said with a sigh. "Who's on your list?"

"Pretty much everyone except Ramón and Vicky. I was hoping you might narrow it down since you know most of the staff and most of the customers." Dawn paused before she decided to say it. "I think the new guy, Chad, is involved somehow. He gets hired and we start having problems with the Wi-Fi almost at the same time."

Natalie tapped her martini glass as she thought. "Why are you eliminating Ramón and Vicky?"

"Seriously?" Dawn nearly dropped her zucchini stick. "Because Ramón is a good guy and Vicky can barely type without breaking a nail."

"Ramón was once a successful boxer. He has the capacity and will to hurt people."

Dawn shook her head so hard her ponytail smacked her in the face. "Not anymore. He's done with that life. No way he's involved."

"Also, don't let Vicky's big hair and highly decorated nails fool you," Natalie said. "She's a lot smarter than she appears."

"I know. She's the one who runs the gym's finances. But she and Ramón are joined at the hip. If Vicky was up to something, Ramón would know."

"And he would protect her because he worships her. Just keep that in mind."

"No accounting for taste," Dawn said to lighten the mood. "Do you really think they're the ones doing this?"

"I'm just saying you shouldn't rule them out. However, I'm with you on Chad. He's another one who might be concealing his true self, in this case, behind that jock facade. I can't get a good read on him."

"What about Josh and Ripley? They're heavy-duty gamers, so they've got the computer chops."

They ran through everyone Dawn could think of at the gym and eliminated most of them, although they kept Josh and Ripley as long shots. Dawn jotted down the short list of possibilities on her phone's notes app.

"Speaking of facades," she said with a casualness she didn't feel, "what do you think lies behind Leland's?"

Natalie sat forward. "Now we're getting to the crux of the matter."

"What do you mean?"

"I mean Leland is the reason you are so involved in this Wi-Fi thing. You've mentioned his name at least two dozen times tonight."

"Because he's the computer expert," Dawn protested before she set down her beer bottle with a thunk. "Fine, I think he's hot."

"He's not your usual type." The innocuous phrase came with a concerned expression.

"He's too smart for me."

"You know I don't believe that."

Dawn had the good grace to be ashamed of her knee-jerk remark. "Sorry. It slipped out." Natalie was always telling her to stop putting herself down about her lack of education. She pointed out that Dawn had a compelling reason for dropping out of college, one that had nothing to do with her intelligence.

"I've spent some time talking with him at Alice and Derek's parties, and I can tell you that he's not just a computer nerd, sweetie, despite the clothing," Natalie said.

Dawn had watched him at those same parties. She'd been impressed with how he treated women with the same respect he treated men. That didn't always happen with people like Leland. "If he's not a computer nerd, what is he?"

"He's a brilliant, driven man who's at the top of his profession. He's got money and power and influence that we can't really comprehend. Those T-shirts, glasses, and jeans are meant to disarm you, to keep you from seeing the ruthless determination to succeed."

"Don't forget his southern drawl," Dawn said with a reminiscent smile. "He admits to using it as a weapon." It certainly disarmed her when he laid it on thick.

"I'm surprised he admitted that." Natalie shook her head at Dawn. "He's not going to let you be in control."

Dawn thought of the play of muscles in Leland's back and shoulders as he swam. She'd seen his raw power and still wanted him. No, she *needed* him, needed the way her desire for him overwhelmed her fear.

"Maybe I'm ready to push myself out of my comfort zone."

"I'm not sure he's the right person to test it with." Natalie's well-groomed eyebrows were drawn down into a frown of concern.

"He's never been anything other than a perfect gentleman." Except for the occasional flash of heat in his eyes, which made her nerve endings dance.

"He wouldn't mean to hurt you. He just wouldn't know." Natalie went still. "Unless you plan to tell him."

"No, God, no! We aren't close like that." Dawn didn't want the straightforward attraction she felt for Leland tainted by her history.

"Be careful, then."

She *was* careful. All the time. Her vigilance and caution helped, but they didn't erase the fear or the shame. Leland made her want more than the circumscribed life she lived now. Her profession demanded that she listen to her body, so she paid attention to the intense physical reaction he evoked in her. He made her want to blast her demons into oblivion so she could feel and act normal again.

But Natalie was right. Wanting to be healed didn't mean she was. Diving into the deep end with a man like Leland wasn't smart. She needed to be able to touch the bottom of the pool at all times for her own sanity. He would sweep her in over her head.

Natalie reached across the table to squeeze Dawn's hand. "Don't look so down. I'm not saying to give him up. I'm glad you feel so strongly about a man for a change. It's a good sign. Just be aware of who you're dealing with."

"You really don't think he's too smart for me?" Dawn wasn't being snarky now.

Natalie rolled her eyes. "How many times do we have to go through this?"

"I know, I know. Being a college dropout does not make me stupid." But it made her uneducated. Whereas Leland was the product of some very fancy schools, according to the bio on KRG's website. Yes, she'd looked him up. Studied the few photos she'd found on the internet, mostly of Leland speaking at tech conferences, a jacket thrown on over his T-shirt. She liked that he refused to wear a suit and tie even then.

"You asked me what I think is behind Leland's facade," Natalie said. "I think he hasn't had such an easy life, despite what it looks like."

"Why do you say that?"

"Because no one works as hard as he does unless he has something to prove. To himself, to the world, to someone important to him. I don't know which."

Dawn digested that. "Maybe we really are kindred spirits in some way. Maybe that's why I'm not afraid of him."

"Kindred spirits?"

Dawn hadn't meant to say that out loud and she flushed. "He said that in an email. I didn't believe it at the time."

Natalie gave her a searching look. "You need to be *very* careful."

Dawn stayed up later than usual that night. First, she reviewed all the possible suspects she and Natalie had talked about and tried to figure out what any of them would want with the dark web. She sat cross-legged on her sofa and listed the names in order of probability on her laptop. She still couldn't bring herself to put Ramón anywhere near the top of the list, but she went ahead with Vicky's name in the number-two slot. She'd never been a huge fan of the Vickster on a personal level. Chad sat at the top of the list, even though Dawn couldn't see him as anything more than a has-been jock reliving his glory days with his clients.

But that was all a pretext for waiting to see if Leland emailed her. There was no reason for him to do so because they would see each other the next day for a training session. Tomorrow was a Friday, which meant most of her clients took the evening off from exercise, heading for bars and other entertainment instead. Evidently, Leland didn't drink or go to movies or sporting events, so he'd taken the six o'clock slot.

By the time her list was finished, she still hadn't heard from him. At eleven thirty, she closed her laptop and drummed her fingers on top of it. He'd turned down stretching with her and left immediately after swimming. She had been with a client by then so she didn't expect him to say goodbye, but he might have given her a wave or something. Now no email. What was going on?

Something Natalie had said nagged at the back of her mind. Her friend had reminded her that at some point very soon, they would call in a law enforcement agency—whether the police or the FBI—and then the project would be taken out of her hands, removing the need for Leland to train with her. He would go back to his corner office in Manhattan and she would be left at the gym in New Jersey. The hollow feeling that left her with made her reopen her laptop.

Maybe Leland was wrong for her, but his presence made her body thrum like a perfectly tuned treadmill going at high speed. Even an email from him sent a thrill of endorphins rippling through her. Honestly, she'd been afraid she *couldn't* feel this way about a man ever again.

She needed to see where this could go while she had the chance.

After typing a brief email to him, she hit "send" and shut down the laptop immediately.

The next morning she braced herself for disappointment before she opened her laptop to check for new email messages. And there it was.

She checked the time it had come in and her breath hitched. One minute after she'd sent hers. He'd made up his mind fast. Was that good or bad? Clicking on the email, she actually closed her eyes before it popped up on the screen. Turning her head, she squinted at it sideways, afraid to see what his reaction had been.

It was brief but sent a shock of delight through her. All he had said was: *Yes.*

She floated through the morning, often having to force her wandering mind back to whatever client she was training. For her lunch break, she took her quinoa bowl out to the picnic table Ramón had set up for the staff in a little patch of grass behind the gym. Her buoyant mood made her want to bask in the gentle caress of the autumn sun.

"There you are!"

Dawn jumped as Vicky's voice broke in on her fantasy about Leland and her in the swimming pool. Naked. "Yup, getting a dose of vitamin D. You should try it. It's good for your health."

Vicky slid onto the bench opposite Dawn. *Could this woman be running an illegal operation out of the gym?* It was hard to believe when you looked at the fake eyelashes, the tan produced by a salon bed, and the fingernails decorated with, yes, leopard spots and rhinestones.

"I wanted to check in with you about something," Vicky said, fluffing her blonde hair. "Have you gotten any more complaints about clients' data usage on their phones?"

Dawn put down her fork. "I thought you weren't worried about that."

Vicky shrugged. "A couple of people mentioned it to Ray so maybe it's more of a deal than I assumed."

"Yes, a few more customers have said something about it." Dawn downplayed the griping because she didn't want Vicky fixing it before Leland figured out what was going on. "Are you going to get your IT guys involved?"

"Maybe I should." Vicky tapped a painted talon on the picnic table. "Don't want the customers unhappy."

"Give it the weekend and see if it resolves itself," Dawn found herself saying.

"Yeah, I'll do that." Vicky slithered off the bench. "Thanks."

Crap, they had a deadline now. Even though Vicky's IT fixers seemed to be inept, once they started messing with the router, it might scare away the dark web people.

She was glad she'd summoned up the nerve to send that email to Leland.

The afternoon seemed to drag by, but finally she was lounging at the front desk, watching the door for Leland's arrival. She wanted to get a read on his mood about her invitation. She was pretty good at body language, and her awareness of him made her almost hypersensitive to his.

The door swung up and she tensed until she saw his smile, heavy-lidded and focused entirely on her. Heat seared through her. Even the way he walked—with an almost predatory stride that shrugged off all distractions—made her shiver with arousal.

When he stopped, he was close—very close—so she had to look up to meet his gaze. "I'm glad you emailed me," he said, his drawl soft as velvet.

She swallowed. "Me too. It's good that you were free."

A shadow of guilt crossed his face. "I made myself free."

Pleasure flushed her cheeks at the admission that he'd made room in his loaded schedule for her. "Let's get you warmed up on the treadmill."

"I meant to come early for that but work got in the way. Does a brisk three-block walk from the limo count?" He fell into step beside her and she swore she could feel the stir of air around him brushing over her skin.

"How about I work warming up into your session so you can skip the treadmill? I'll meet you in the training room." She veered off to pick up her tablet while Leland dropped his gym bag in his locker. As she walked away, she let the grin she'd been suppressing pull the corners of her mouth up. However, she stopped herself from doing a dance step across the gym floor.

She'd gotten over the grinning when Leland joined her where she'd set up for their session. But the hot look that still smoldered in his eyes stroked delicious tingles over her skin. The next hour was going to be the most exquisite kind of torture. Then who knew what would happen afterward?

Starting him with some easy sidesteps and lunges, she moved in closer and lowered her voice. "There's been a development in our project." One that made her impulsive dinner invitation even more timely.

The gleam in his eyes flickered out. "And you decided it would be better to discuss it elsewhere. Hence, dinner away from the gym."

He'd gotten it backward but should she tell him that? "That's not the reason for dinner."

He straightened from his lunge, his brows drawn down in puzzlement. "Is the development positive or negative?"

"It speeds up the timetable. *That's* the reason for dinner." She gave him a smile that held all the sexual interest she felt.

He answered her smile with a slow curve of his lips, all the focused intensity alight in his eyes again. "Ah, *that* timetable has sped up as well."

He understood. Maybe it was good to hang around with a smart guy. You didn't have to spell things out for him. It saved some embarrassment. Although she'd only asked him if he'd like to have dinner after their training session, so it shouldn't be that big a deal. It just was, somehow.

"Are you going to swim afterward?" she asked.

He shook his head. "No time. I've got to get back to the office after we, er, *eat*."

She ratcheted up the intensity level of his workout just a little so he was huffing by the end of it. He braced his hands on his knees. "Is this to make up for my lack of swimming?"

"You don't want to lose ground," she said with a grin.

He narrowed his eyes at her before he grabbed his sweat towel and mopped his face and neck, using one corner to wipe off his glasses. His T-shirt was dark with sweat and clung to the pecs and abs that his swimming had honed to underwear-model perfection.

She must have been staring because when she glanced at his face, his eyes burned hot. She quickly turned to put away the BOSU ball he'd been using. "If you're not swimming, I really need to stretch you," she said. It was her job and she had to do it.

He draped his towel around his neck and grabbed his water bottle. "Anything to lie down and rest." Tilting his head back, he lifted the bottle to his lips, drawing Dawn's eyes to the movement of muscles and tendons in his throat as he swallowed. He had a slight scruff of whiskers at this hour, and she longed to run her fingertips over it to test the texture of skin and hair.

"I wasn't that hard on you," she scoffed before she spread out a gym towel on the mat.

"It's cumulative," he said, lowering the bottle. "I was stiffer this morning than any one before."

"The second day is always the worst. You'll be better tomorrow, I promise." She waved him down onto the mat, enjoying the fluid way he crossed his ankles, bent his knees, and lowered himself onto his butt. No balance issues there. He lay back and she let her gaze skim over the full length of him. He'd stripped to his shorts for this session so she could see the way his skin outlined the powerful muscles of his thighs and calves. "For a computer geek, you're in surprisingly good shape."

He chuckled, a deep, rich baritone sound. "I learned early that if you want your mind to function at peak efficiency, you have to make sure its container is also in good shape."

"The mind-body connection." She nodded.

He ensnared her gaze with his. "It's key for multiple objectives."

There was no mistaking the undercurrent in that statement. "Bend your right knee," she said, pretending she hadn't noticed.

He moaned and closed his eyes when she pressed against his leg to deepen the stretch. "Heaven and hell all in one," he said. "More."

"Breathe in and then let it out." As he exhaled, she pushed, feeling his body relax enough to stretch that little bit farther.

He moaned again, a melodious rasp, and she couldn't help speculating how he would sound in the throes of something more than a stretch.

"Okay, straighten now." She shifted her weight off his shin and wished she had a sweat towel to wipe off the perspiration she could feel popping out on her skin, perspiration that was brought on by nothing more than her indecent imagination.

Yup, her job was sheer torture.

After she'd showered and changed, Dawn walked into the gym lobby. Leland was there, chatting with Chad again. Dawn's eyebrows rose because Chad didn't generally train late on Friday or Saturday. Since most of his clients were sports crazy, they spent their weekends at games or at bars watching games.

"Dawn, honey," Chad said, making her teeth grit at the patronizing endearment. "Lee and I were just talking about what a tough workout you gave him. I told him, 'No pain, no gain.'"

Dawn stopped herself from rolling her eyes but she couldn't resist saying, "He gave one hundred and ten percent."

Chad slapped Leland on the shoulder. "That's what I'm talking about, man. Hey, you two want to go have a beer at Arthur's? The Jets are playing tonight and the screen there is ginormous. You almost feel like you're at the game."

"Thanks, but I've got to get home," she said without offering a further excuse.

"I have to get back to my office," Leland said, his smile regretful. "Big project due next week. But let me take a rain check, if I could."

"You got it, buddy." Chad gave his shoulder another slap.

"It's dark so I'll walk you to your car," Leland said to Dawn.

"No car," she said. "I live close by so I'm good."

"I'd be glad to walk you home then," he said.

"Thanks but no." She didn't want Chad to wonder if they were anything more than trainer and client. And she would never allow a client to come with her to her apartment building. "See you tomorrow."

Leland accompanied her to the door and held it for her. "Till tomorrow."

She turned toward her apartment because she figured Chad might remember which way she usually went. Leland took the hint and turned in the opposite direction.

A moment later, a text pinged into her phone: Wait just around the corner two blocks from the gym and I'll pick you up.

She texted back a brief agreement and slowed her pace so she wouldn't have to loiter for too long. She preferred to keep moving when outside alone, even in a safe neighborhood like this one. She knew how quickly a peaceful situation could turn ugly. The sun had dropped behind the brick buildings that lined the street, casting shadows on the sidewalk while the sky turned deep blue.

Reaching the corner, she sauntered slowly down the cross street and stopped to admire the flowers in the window of a closed florist's shop. A flicker of movement caught her eye, and she turned to see Chad striding across the street she'd just come from. If he was planning to go to Arthur's, he should be headed for the gym's staff parking lot to get his car. He was going in the opposite direction. She frowned and moved into the shadow of a sidewalk tree as she watched him until he walked out of her view.

Maybe he'd changed his mind when he couldn't find company to watch the game with. Or maybe he was up to something nefarious. She shook her head. She just didn't buy Chad as a criminal genius. Maybe the heavily muscled sidekick for one, though. That made her shoulders tense up.

She nearly shrieked when a limousine stopped at the curb beside her and the door swung open. Leland got out and extended his hand for her gym bag. "Did we fool Chad?" he asked.

"I don't know but he didn't appear to have seen me." She passed him her duffel but pretended not to notice the other hand he held out to help her into the limo.

Leland slid onto the leather seat beside her and placed her bag beside his on the expanse of carpeted floor in front of them. He stretched out his long legs, now encased in his usual jeans, and crossed them at the ankles. He had changed shoes to a pair of black sneakers that she happened to know cost more than $1,000. Her job wore out sneakers fast so she was always browsing the latest styles. "What do you mean he didn't see you?" he asked.

"I just saw him on foot, headed away from where his car should be parked in the staff lot. He probably changed his mind about going to the bar since he couldn't convince anyone to go with him."

"That's certainly plausible." Leland went silent for a moment. "You shouldn't be involved any further in this matter."

"You're thinking of what happened with Alice and Derek." Thank God Alice had paid attention in the self-defense class Dawn had talked her into joining.

"It's difficult not to." He drummed his fingers on his knee for a moment. "Where shall I tell the driver to go?"

"Oh, right." She raised her voice. "We're going to Carmella's. It's on the corner of Broad and Belleville."

The driver nodded and the limo slid away from the curb.

"Italian?" Leland asked.

"We're in Jersey so, yeah, Italian." Carmella's was a real throwback with red-and-white-checked tablecloths, candles set in Chianti bottles coated with wax drippings, Frank Sinatra crooning in the background, and Carmella presiding over the kitchen with a Neapolitan accent and an iron hand. Might as well show Leland the kind of folks she came from.

"Time for some carb loading?" he asked. She had angled herself into the corner of the seat so she caught a flash of smile in the dim illumination cast by Cofferwood's streetlights.

"No, I just like Carmella's lasagna."

His smile disappeared. "What moved up the timetable for our . . . research?"

"Vicky decided to pay attention to the problem. I talked her into delaying a visit from her computer geeks until Monday. They're not very good but I figure they still might gum up the works."

Leland muttered something that sounded like a curse. She could read tension in the clench of his jaw and the rigidity of his shoulders.

"You don't have to deal with this," she said. "Vicky's guys will chase away whoever it is and the gym's tech will go back to normal. I only got involved because Ramón has been very good to me, and I don't want to see anything damage the gym's reputation. It's not a problem as long as the dark node moves somewhere else."

He shook his head, making his lenses flash with reflected light. "This has a criminal stench and I can't walk away from that. But you can." He turned toward her. "Let me work on this by myself. I'll bring Tully in on it as soon as I have something more concrete. He'll know who to contact in law enforcement, if necessary."

"How are you going to get something more concrete?" She crossed her arms and shot him a challenging look.

He shifted on his seat. "Where is the router for the gym?"

"In Ramón and Vicky's office. I have plausible access. You don't."

The limo glided to a stop. "We're here, sir," the driver said.

Dawn had forgotten all about the third person in the car. But then she didn't spend much time in limos. In fact, none since her high school prom. How much had the driver heard? Could he be trusted?

Leland looked pissed but not about the driver. "You are not going into that office on a spying mission." His tone held no trace of southern charm. "I'll find a way to get in alone."

"You've got only two days to do it, so that's not realistic." She reached for her gym bag.

"Are you bailing on our dinner?" She heard disappointment, sending her heart into a flutter.

"No, I've got the wine in my duffel." She unzipped it and pulled out two bottles of Barolo that she'd splurged on big-time. If Leland wore $1,000 sneakers, he wasn't going to be happy with Two-Buck Chuck wine. "Around here, it's BYOB in most restaurants. It's a good thing because you can afford better wine with your meal."

She winced as she realized how meaningless that would be to Leland.

He took the bottles from her, turning one to read the label. "I'm more of a beer drinker but I've heard of Barolo."

Shock made her stare. He didn't drink overpriced wine on his expense account? "Don't you have to take clients out to dinner and stuff?"

"Not if I can avoid it."

Her perspective on him tilted.

She suddenly noticed that the driver had already opened her door and stood patiently waiting for her to get out. "Sorry," she muttered, scrambling sideways.

She remembered to make sure her feet were on level ground before she stood up. She wore black ankle boots with high stiletto heels, which required more attention to balance than her standard foot attire. She smoothed her hands down the front of her slim-cut jeans and checked that her black silk blouse was still buttoned up so that the lace edge of her bra didn't show. The silk was so slippery that the buttons had a tendency to slip out of their holes at inopportune moments. However, she had decided to risk it since this was her first dinner with Leland and she didn't have a lot else fancy to wear.

She watched him stride around the limo with a bottle of wine in each hand, the muscles that she now knew so well outlined by his dark-blue T-shirt. The way light slid over the fabric made her think that he hadn't bought it in a three-for-nineteen-dollars deal. "What kind of beer do you like?" she asked.

He stopped. "I'm good with wine. I should get more familiar with it anyway."

"I'm just curious about the beer."

He opened his arms to his sides in a gesture of apology. "I hate to admit it but I'm happiest with a Budweiser."

"Huh," she said. "Maybe we *can* be friends."

Chapter 7

Friends. The word felt like a smack of cold water in his face. He'd thought . . . no, he'd been sure that Dawn wanted more than that. God knows, he did. Their training sessions had ratcheted up his desire for her to the point where even the brush of her ponytail sent a jolt of arousal to his balls.

Shifting a wine bottle to the crook of his arm, he held open the door to the restaurant and let his gaze linger on her back as she walked in front of him. Tonight she'd left her hair loose, the first time he'd seen it that way. The straight dark fall of it gleamed like satin as it swung slightly with her movement, and he wanted to feel it sifting through his fingers. He followed her tresses down to where they ended above her waist and then allowed his gaze to rove over the swell of her butt. He wanted to toss the wine bottles away and fill his palms with those delicious curves before he pulled her back to settle against his now hardening cock.

Somewhere through the haze of his lust, he heard the hostess greet Dawn like an old friend, tell her the table was ready, and to come this way. He tore his eyes away from the sway of Dawn's hips, so delectably wrapped in the tight denim of her jeans, and glanced around the packed, candlelit restaurant as they walked toward the back corner. Servers dressed in white shirts and black trousers sped between tables with food-filled white china plates lined up on their arms. Conversation and laughter filled the room without being overpowering. A smooth male voice sang something vaguely old-fashioned that blended with the clink of silverware and glasses. The kitchen door swung open and a spate of fast-paced Italian spilled out.

He felt an unexpected sense of ease here. Maybe it was the aroma of hearty cuisine and the rhythm of a foreign language that almost sounded like the Spanish his mother had spoken.

The hostess put the menus on the checked tablecloth. Leland plunked down the wine bottles so he could pull out the chair for Dawn. He wanted the excuse to get close enough to inhale her scent through the admittedly mouthwatering smell of the food. He bent as she sat and filled his lungs with her. His cock twitched.

As he settled in the chair across from her, Dawn leaned forward. "I asked for a corner table so we could talk without worrying."

"Let's put aside the espionage for now," he said. "I'd like to focus on something pleasanter."

"Carmella's food is more than pleasant. It's fantastic."

He decided to take a risk. "I meant you."

She looked down at the closed menu lying on the table. Her skin glowed golden in the candlelight and his fingers itched to feel the texture of it.

It took her a long moment but she finally lifted her gaze to meet his, the dark pools of her eyes catching the flicker of the flame. "As long as I can focus right back on you." The huskiness in her voice licked through his veins.

Not friends after all. He let his lips curl into a satisfied smile. "That's a condition I can agree to."

He saw her take a deep breath, the swell of her breasts lifting the black fabric of her blouse. "So tell me where you grew up," she said. "Somewhere down south, it sounds like."

A shock of surprise made him straighten in his chair. He hadn't expected a question reaching back into his childhood. None of the other women he'd dated had been interested in more than his current status as a successful businessman. Maybe that was why those relationships hadn't lasted.

"I grew up in Atlanta, Georgia." Short and revealing nothing.

"That explains the sexy southern drawl." She gave him a provocative little smile that stroked right down to his gut. "Where did you go to school?"

Relief surged at the interruption as a server walked up with a corkscrew to open the Barolo. Dawn called the waitress by name and asked about her baby while Leland debated how brief he could continue to keep his answers.

As soon as the server left, Leland said, "I went to public school until the ninth grade. After that I attended Burnes-Fielding Academy." He lifted the glass and took a sip, rolling the Barolo over his tongue while he culled some memories of a wine-tasting class he'd taken while at business school. "I detect notes of oak, tannin, and leather, but mostly fermented grapes."

Dawn wrinkled her nose. "Why would anyone want wine to taste like leather?" She swirled the garnet-colored liquid in her glass before she took a sip. "I'm with you on the fermented grapes, but really good ones." She set her glass down. "Did you live at Burnes-Fielding Academy?"

His attempt at diversion hadn't worked. "Fair is fair. You have to tell me where you went to school."

Her gaze flicked away and back so quickly that he almost missed it. "Public school all the way. My family lived a couple of towns over from here and the public schools were good there. The regional high school was only okay."

"Bigger isn't always better," he said.

"It was a financial thing for the towns around here," she said with a shrug. "The property taxes just couldn't support a local high school. What about Burnes-Fielding?"

"It was a private day school so I didn't live there." He'd had to take two buses to get to and from school, leaving at five thirty in the morning and returning home at six thirty in the evening. His mother had seen him off with a brown-bag lunch every morning, but she was often still working one of her three jobs when he got home in the evening.

"Did you have to wear a uniform? I always thought that would be weird."

"A very ugly tan blazer with the school's crest on the pocket and an even uglier brown, gold, and maroon tie. Whoever picked the school colors should have been forced to wear them for the rest of their lives." A memory surfaced of his mother singing along to Spanish pop music on the radio while she ironed the white shirts he had to wear with the god-awful blazer.

Dawn laughed, the music of it surprising him since she didn't laugh often. "At least you all looked equally terrible in your ugly blazers."

Yet somehow they hadn't. The rich boys, most of whom had been at the academy since pre-K, had polo ponies embroidered on their shirt pockets. Some even had their initials sewn onto the cuffs in elegant block letters. Their navy trousers were from Brooks Brothers. His were from the local thrift store. "I added black-rimmed nerd glasses to complete the ensemble, so I earned the worst-dressed prize." He said it in a light tone, passing off the remembered pain as a joke.

Not light enough, because Dawn reached across the table to touch the back of his hand. "High school is hard on everyone. I was a metal mouth myself. Even worse, I had brothers who called me Train Tracks. On the other hand, they'd beat up anyone else who called me that."

"How many brothers?"

"Two. And three sisters." Dawn gave him a slanted smile. "My mother didn't figure out that the rhythm method doesn't work until after I was born. Then she wised up."

"I envy you," he said. "I'm an only child." Raised by a hardworking single parent. It had been lonely, so he'd sought companionship within the cyberworld on the school library's computers. He couldn't regret it since it had led him to where he was.

"You ready to order?" The server's question made him start. Neither of them had opened their menus.

He looked at Dawn. "Whatever you recommend. The lasagna?"

She nodded and rattled off a list of Italian dishes while the server scribbled on her order pad and departed.

"That sounds like a lot of food," he said.

"You've earned it." She gave him a sideways look over the rim of her glass. "I worked you hard this week."

"So you admit it."

"I knew you would thrive on a challenge."

That was gratifying. "I'd like you to continue to train me, even after the data problem is resolved." When had he made that decision?

Her eyebrows rose. "You're going to trek out to Jersey on a regular basis?"

"I was hoping you would come to the city," he improvised. "I'd provide transportation and pay for your travel time."

She sat back in her chair. "You don't need to go to so much trouble and expense. There are plenty of excellent trainers in Manhattan. I could even recommend a couple."

"I've tried other trainers." A lie. "I like your style and I can afford to indulge myself for the benefit of my health."

"You've only worked with me for three sessions so I'm not sure you know my style."

"Okay, I like you and I trust you." Odd how true the latter was.

She raised her glass as though toasting him. "Thanks. I like you too. We'll discuss it once the issues at Work It Out are resolved."

The server appeared with a large platter and a basket of breadsticks. "Your antipasto." She looked at Dawn. "Shall I tell you what's on the plate?"

"No, I've got this," Dawn said. She pushed the platter closer to Leland and began pointing to the various foods artistically arranged on a bed of dark-red radicchio leaves. "Soppressata, olives, fresh mozzarella balls, figs, roasted red peppers, provolone cubes, prosciutto, Genoa salami, artichoke hearts. And don't miss the breadsticks. They're the best." She pulled one from the basket and bit down on it with a crunch, closing her eyes as she chewed.

He followed suit. The flavor of garlic and olive oil exploded in his mouth, along with the delicious, fresh crispness of the bread. He understood why she closed her eyes to concentrate on the first bite.

"You're right," he said. "The breadsticks are superb."

She opened eyes that held a wicked glint. "I'm always right."

"Why do I feel that there's an extra meaning there?" Something nagged at his memory.

"Because that's what you said to me in one of your emails."

He gave a wry grimace. "Obviously, I was joking."

"Were you?" She tilted her head so her hair slid over her shoulder, her expression provocative.

"God, yes. I'm not that big an ass."

She gave a little choke of a laugh. "You aren't an ass at all. Just sure your opinion is the right one."

"If you're referring to my desire to keep you away from the dark web, I will not apologize for it. Otherwise, I am very flexible, as you have pointed out during our training sessions."

He heard her breath hitch slightly and then she nudged the platter toward him again. "*Mangia!* This stuff is good."

"What should I eat first?"

She frowned at the platter for a moment before picking up a piece of fig and wrapping it in a slice of prosciutto. "Sweet and salty," she said, offering it to him. "My favorite combination of flavors."

When he took the morsel from her, their fingers brushed and he felt the sparks run up his arm. For a moment, their gazes tangled across the table, fanning the sparks into something hotter. Then she pulled her hand away and dropped her eyes to the platter, grabbing a cube of provolone.

So she'd felt it too. He smiled to himself and popped the fig and prosciutto into his mouth. Again, the tastes burst over his tongue and he found himself groaning in appreciation.

"Told you," she said, grinning at him. She picked up a piece of roasted pepper, a cube of provolone, and a slice of soppressata, wrapping them together and holding the little package of food out to him. Her fingers gleamed with the oil the pepper was bathed in, and he wanted to taste it on her skin.

He kept his hands flat on the table and inclined his body toward her. Her eyes widened and he thought she would draw back. Then she bent forward and brought the morsel to his mouth. He took it from her, flicking his tongue over her fingers to lick the oil from them.

Her breath hissed in sharply, but she let him savor the texture and taste of her skin before she took her hand away. He chewed the delicious bite but his attention was all on the woman across the table from him. He could see the accelerated rise and fall of her breasts. He wanted to unfasten the white buttons gleaming against the black silk of her blouse and suck on her breasts the way he'd sucked on her fingers.

"Shall we request that our lasagna be boxed up to go?" he asked.

⌒

This was the question Dawn had both wanted and dreaded. Leland's blue eyes blazed with the same intensity of arousal that she felt. Her gaze skittered over the defined swell of muscles under his T-shirt, the determined line of his jaw, and the strong, tapering fingers she'd seen clenched around dumbbells. Add to that his formidable intelligence and the aura of confidence his success gave him. Nat was right. He was a powerful man; she would not be able to control him the way she had others.

Panic tightened her throat so she pictured Leland at one of Alice and Derek's parties, his head bent while he listened with respectful attention to Natalie discussing her salon's business. She reminded herself that he had volunteered to put his computer genius at the disposal of a local gym just because Alice had asked him to. She closed her eyes to replay the delicious slow drawl of his voice, soothing her with its honey.

Her throat eased enough for her to open her eyes and rasp out, "Lasagna to go works for me."

Because she might never have this chance again.

Her reward was a smile from Leland that was so hot it practically scorched her. He lifted his hand and instantly conjured up their server despite the crowd of customers.

She busied herself with stuffing the cork back into the open wine, although what she really wanted to do was take a long swig directly from the bottle. Dutch courage, they called it.

Yet her body hummed with anticipation. One of Leland's hands lay on the tablecloth, and she imagined how it would feel skimming over her bare skin, cupping her breast, gripping her thigh. Heat flared in her belly, banishing her fear. For now.

When she raised her head, she found him watching her, the heat in his eyes matching hers. His smile was pure lust and she felt an answering curve in her own lips.

"Sorry you're not feeling so great, Dawn," the server said, setting a large brown shopping bag on the table. "Carmella gave you some biscotti for tomorrow morning to dip in your coffee. She hopes you feel better by then."

"Please tell her how much I appreciate that," Dawn said. She hadn't even heard Leland make up an excuse for why they were leaving early.

He pushed back his chair and came around the table to hold hers as she rose. She could feel the desire vibrating between them through the air. It made breathing something she had to think about. She grabbed the open wine bottle while he picked up the take-home bag and the untouched bottle, all in one hand. His other hand was on the small of her back, the firm pressure of his palm sending a streak of sensation to coil between her legs. God, she wanted him to touch her there where yearning pulsed. She could almost feel his long fingers sliding into her.

The limo glided up just as they exited the restaurant.

"How did the driver know?" she asked as Leland opened the car door.

"I sent a preset text message. No need to even look at my phone to do it."

"I thought he was a mind reader or something." She slid across the leather seat so Leland could fold himself into the space that suddenly seemed smaller than before. He set the bag on the floor, took the wine from her, and slotted both bottles into holders in the limo's side console. The privacy screen between them and the driver was already raised.

"Your place, my place, or a hotel?" he asked, taking her hand and raising it to brush his lips over her knuckles. "Wherever you prefer is fine with me."

"My place." She felt safest on her own turf.

"Good. I don't want to wait much longer." He turned her hand to kiss her palm, his warm breath sending a shiver through her. "What's the address?" he asked, pushing the intercom button on the console.

"Right. The driver isn't a mind reader." She rattled off her street address and the driver confirmed that he'd heard it.

Leland settled back onto the seat beside her. She liked that he sat close enough that their bodies grazed against each other from shoulder to knee, yet he didn't crowd her. Instead he twined his fingers with hers and rested their joined hands on his thigh. "Would you like a glass of wine en route? The limo is equipped with appropriate glassware."

"We'd have to chug it because my apartment is about five minutes from here." There was a nervous quaver in her voice that she couldn't quite suppress. She hoped he hadn't heard it.

"A most convenient commute." The Georgia honey was deep and thick in his voice now. It seemed to slide through her, rich and sweet and sexy.

"That's why I chose my apartment. Easy to walk to and from the gym." Nerves were beginning to tighten her chest.

He stroked the back of her hand with his thumb. The tiny friction sent a ripple of sensation skimming through her. She needed more to keep the fear at bay. She pushed up from the seat and swung her leg up and over his thighs so she knelt on his lap, facing him. He released her hand so he could wrap his fingers around her waist to steady her.

"No use wasting those five minutes," she said before she cupped his face and brought her lips to his.

Oh my God, the man knew how to kiss. He found the perfect angle for their mouths and took full advantage of it. His lips were warm, firm, and delicious. When he drew her bottom lip into his mouth with gentle suction, she moaned and rocked her hips into the erection she could feel through his jeans. His grip tightened on her waist as he tilted her hips to press against him in exactly the right spot to make her arch and gasp.

She jerked in surprise when the driver's voice announced that they had arrived.

Leland smiled into her eyes in a way that sent extra heat surging through her. "We could just stay here."

"The driver would make me self-conscious," she said, shifting off his lap. And the space was too confined.

Leland swung the door open and climbed out first, reaching back in to help her. She decided the lasagna and wine could stay in the limo. She didn't want to risk losing the scorching arousal that overwhelmed every other feeling at this moment.

As always she had her keys in her pocket, her free hand already curled around them. It was pure reflex. At least she could skip her customary scan of the entrance hall and the staircase as she led Leland into her building and up the stairs. When she keyed in the combination for the dead bolt, she felt him brush against her back, making panic flicker briefly. She shoved it down and pushed open the door, turning off the beeping alarm.

She glanced up to see his eyebrows raised, but he made no comment about her array of security measures. Instead he closed the door behind them and pressed her against the wall in her foyer, his fingers curving around her head so that he could angle it for a kiss. She tried to lose herself in the pleasure of his mouth, but the feeling of being trapped began to build. She used a modified self-defense move to spin them both so that their positions were reversed. He broke the kiss to look down at her with a slight frown. She didn't want to answer the questions she could see forming in his brain, so she drew his head down again to meet her lips and bent her knee up against the wall to lever herself against his hard cock. The distraction worked on both of them as he cupped her bottom, his fingers digging into her buttocks to pull her in tight to him.

"I want your breasts," he said against her lips. "Where's your bedroom?"

"Let's sit on the couch the way we did in the limo," she said. "I liked that."

"No argument here." He used his hold on her butt to lift her feet off the floor. She wrapped her legs around his hips, opening herself further to the exquisite pressure against the V of her thighs. Every step jostled them together, spinning ropes of yearning through her.

"Yes, oh, God, yes!" she gasped as he walked.

And then he turned to drop down onto the couch, staying toward the front edge so her legs didn't slam into the back cushions. She unhooked her ankles from behind his back and scrambled up to plant a knee on each side of his thighs. This was a position she felt confident in.

She laid her palms on either side of his face and hooked her fingers around the temples of his glasses. "How badly do you need these?"

"In this kind of situation, I work mostly by touch." His smile was sin personified.

"A good strategy." She gently lifted the glasses from his face, the tortoiseshell temples warm from where they had lain against his head. She felt a strange urge to bring them to her cheek to soak in his body heat indirectly. Instead, she folded the temples in and placed the glasses on the console table behind the sofa. "Now I don't have to worry about breaking them."

The flame in his eyes burned even brighter. Or else it seemed easier to read his emotions without the mask of his glasses to conceal them.

The moment she settled back over his lap, Leland's fingers were at the top button of her blouse. "One part of me wants to take it slow and the other part wants to rip open your blouse so the buttons pop off," he said, his accent edged with huskiness.

"Not too slow," she said, "but I'd appreciate keeping the buttons intact."

He flashed her a quick, feral smile before he unfastened the first three buttons, pushing the blouse aside to expose the black lace of her bra. Her nipples were already taut, outlined by the fabric. He circled his thumbs over them and she felt an electric charge jolt through her body.

"More," she begged.

He bent to suck at one breast through the lace while his thumb brushed over the other one.

"Leland, yes!" She arched into him for more pressure, more heat, more sensation.

He came close to ripping the rest of the buttons off as he pulled her blouse open and jerked it down her arms—with her willing help—before tossing it away. He flicked open the clasp of her bra with deft fingers and yanked it off as well.

Then he stopped and simply looked at her, his hands cupping her rib cage without touching her breasts. She had a brief impulse to cover herself, but his gaze was hungry and stoked an answering desire in her. She shocked herself by sliding her hands under her breasts and lifting them for him.

The groan that tore from his throat was pure animal lust, and she reveled in it for the split second before his mouth fastened on the bare skin of her nipple, sucking, nipping, flicking, and driving her arousal higher. She threaded her fingers into the brown silk of his hair, loving the feel but also keeping his head where she wanted it.

She lost track of time and space as his mouth and hands spun lightning and liquid heat through her body, all of it sliding into a single focus of longing between her thighs. And suddenly she could wait no longer. She needed him there, filling her, finishing her.

"Do you have a condom handy?" she asked.

He took his time releasing her breast from his mouth, licking the tip before he drawled, "I do."

She smiled in relief. No breaking the mood to dash to her bedroom for protection. "Let's use it."

He curled his fingers around her shoulders and held her still. "What's the hurry?"

"I'm going to explode if I don't come right now."

"Oh, darlin', I can make you come whenever you want." A confident smile curled his lips.

"I want to come with you inside me."

"We can arrange that." His fingers were at the button of her jeans, flicking it open, pulling down the zipper, helping her stand to shuck off the denim and her boots. But when she started to shove down her panties, he seized her wrists. "This is *my* job."

Leaning forward, he dropped her wrists at her sides before slipping his index fingers under the lace circling her hips. He bent further and pressed a kiss on each hipbone, his touch sending shivers reeling over her skin. When he moved lower and flicked his tongue against the lace between her thighs it was like setting a match to dry tinder. Her insides seemed to burst into flames.

"Hurry," she urged, even as she rocked her hips against his mouth.

He blew out a breath and began to drag her panties down her legs. Her knees felt weak so she clutched his shoulders for support. As soon as her panties hit her ankles, she stepped out of them and kicked them away.

"I want to taste you," he said, one of his hands splayed over her bare butt to brace her, while his other slid between her thighs to open them slightly.

"I don't know if I—"

But his tongue was already there, lapping at her clit and then thrusting inside her. Her muscles spasmed once before she could control them. "Leland, you need to stop or I'm going to come."

"That was enough . . . for now," he said. He reached into his back pocket to produce a foil envelope, which she took from him and ripped open with her teeth.

While she waited, he unbuckled his belt, unfastened his jeans, and shoved his briefs down far enough to release his cock. The muscles inside her gave a little quiver of anticipation at the sight of him, and she stroked down the length of his erection for the sheer pleasure of it.

He moaned and pushed into her hand. A snap of panic hit her and she snatched her hand away to remove the condom from its envelope. She rolled it onto him to remind herself that she was in control.

He moaned again at her touch and curled his hands around her hips, balancing her as she knelt on the couch over him. She positioned him between her legs and bent her knees so that the tip of his cock pushed into her, sliding in easily because she was so wet with anticipation. Still the fear rose into her throat so that she had to focus on breathing in and out.

When he dug his fingers into her hips and pushed her down further onto him, her throat tightened. But she was not going to let her past ruin this. She lowered her mouth to his, seeking comfort in the searing kiss he lavished on her.

His kiss fanned her need high again so that she wanted all of him inside her. She surged downward on him, reveling in the stretch and completion as he filled the hollow ache inside her. They groaned into each other's mouths at the same time and began to move.

She lifted and fell. He thrust and withdrew. Their rhythm synchronized and accelerated until she could do no more than hang on to his shoulders and feel the coil of her desire tighten into a scorching pinpoint of wanting. His grip on her turned to steel as he held her just above him so that he could drive in deeply and hit her clit at the same time.

Her climax exploded so that she arched back and shouted his name, her fingers digging into the swell of his deltoids. Her muscles clenched around him so hard that she felt tears squeeze out of the corner of her eyes at the intensity of the release.

"Oh, yes, Dawn, darlin'!" he shouted as her orgasm triggered his.

She felt him pumping through the cadence of her own grip and release, saw his head thrown back against the sofa cushion, his eyes glittering beneath half-closed lids. His hips bucked up from the couch, seating his cock even deeper and setting off another shudder of pleasure within her.

They stayed locked together until both had wrung every ounce of satisfaction from their joining. Then he lowered his hips and slipped out of her while she sagged forward to rest her forehead against the back of the couch. Her sensitized breasts brushed against the soft silk knit of his T-shirt so that another warm shiver rippled through her.

"Are you cold?" he asked, wrapping his arms around her bare back.

She gave a weak chuckle. "Are you kidding me? After that? I'm just coming down from the high."

In more ways than he knew. Triumph shimmered through her. She'd had sex with Leland and enjoyed it. Relief and maybe even joy tumbled in her chest along with pure physical satisfaction.

"Yeah," he said. "That got intense."

She couldn't see his face and couldn't read his tone so she sat up. His eyes were closed, his face slack with satiation. "Is intense good?" she asked.

His eyes stayed shut but his lips curled in a way that made her relax. "Intense is real good, darlin'."

She slumped forward again, savoring the afterglow while he held her. Her skin cooled and she felt goose bumps rise on it. Still, she didn't want to move.

"I need to get rid of this condom," he said into the contented silence. "And maybe we could move to your bed for comfort's sake. Not that I won't always have fond memories of this sofa."

Tension tiptoed down her spine. Lying down on the bed with him might be a problem. She mentally squared her shoulders and reminded herself that this was Leland. They'd already had sex and it was fine. More than fine. Fantastic.

She sat up on his lap and realized that she was naked while he was fully clothed. Another tremor of nerves hit her. "There's a bathroom through there. First door on the right." She pointed toward the hallway. "When you're done, my bedroom is farther down the hall to the left."

He kissed her shoulder, his lips warm against her chilled skin, before he gently shifted her off his lap and onto the cushion beside him. She grabbed a throw pillow and hugged it to cover herself as he stood, his height suddenly intimidating.

He bent to lay his palm against her cheek, his gaze soft. "I'll meet you in bed."

Most of her worries dissolved under his gentle touch. *This was Leland.*

Leland stood in the bathroom and frowned down at the alarm app on his cell phone. He wanted to spend the rest of the night in Dawn's bed but the Fincher RFP hung over his head. He tried to calculate how long he could allow himself to stay with her before he would need to get back to work.

But his brain refused to do the math because all it could think of was the sight and sound and feel of her moving over him and with him and around him. His cock stirred as the images replayed through his mind.

He groaned and typed in 12:00 a.m., the first time that shoved through the haze of desire. Maybe it was the wrong hour but he couldn't afford to sleep all the way until morning. Especially since he wanted to make love to her again, this time slowly and thoroughly.

Not that he had any problem with fast and intense, but he looked forward to exploring her beautiful body, to learning where she most enjoyed being touched, to tasting her fully.

He shoved his phone back into his jeans pocket and headed for Dawn's bedroom, doing a quick once-over of the photos she'd hung on the walls of the hallway as he passed them. They were clearly her family through the years. One made him stop to take a closer look because it was a younger Dawn—maybe fifteen or sixteen years old—with her siblings. They wore matching red T-shirts from a bar and had their arms slung around one another's shoulders while they laughed into the camera. He examined Dawn's face, trying to figure out what made her look so different in the photo than she did now. She was beautiful then too, with her sleek dark hair, smooth olive skin, and generous mouth, but her eyes held a different expression somehow.

He puzzled over it as he walked into her bedroom, a surprisingly large space done in serene shades of green. She sat up in the bed, the moss-green quilt tucked up under her arms to cover every part of her except her head and shoulders.

The difference struck him then. In the photo, her eyes were unshadowed. Now they held a watchfulness that reminded him of Tully when he was in full FBI mode, constantly scanning the surroundings. That was part of what gave the impression that Dawn held herself under tightly coiled control.

He had wanted to break through that control and she had certainly been passionate in their lovemaking. But he'd still sensed that she hadn't let go entirely. Something held her back from giving herself wholeheartedly to the moment.

Yet he felt he hadn't earned the right to ask her why. That bothered him. He didn't believe in purely sexual encounters and this didn't feel like one. He liked her, respected her, and trusted her, but he had all those feelings without really knowing her.

"You look like you're thinking about work," she said, tucking the quilt more securely under her arms.

Her utterly false interpretation of his thoughts surprised a laugh out of him. "I can assure you that all I was thinking about is how beautiful you look with your hair loose over your bare shoulders."

Her smile was shy, an expression he wasn't accustomed to from her. "Thank you." The shyness disappeared. "I was thinking that you have too many clothes on."

"Shall I fix that or would you like to do it?" he asked.

"I'd like to watch you fix it. Slowly." She settled back against the upholstered headboard as though she were ready to watch a movie.

"Can I get you some popcorn first?"

She chuckled. "I was thinking I should get some dollar bills. Can you dance?"

"Not at all, but I'm pretty good at undressing." He toed off his sneakers and peeled off his socks. She sat up straight to look at his feet. "Nice arches," she said.

"Seriously? You care about my arches?" He stared at his feet, having never considered whether they were arched or not.

"It's a professional thing. I had to study anatomy. I admire a nicely curved medial arch."

"I'll keep that in mind. I'm sure I can find a way to use it to my advantage."

"Just to be clear—I do not have a foot fetish." She sat back again and eyed him up and down. "Are those clothes ever coming off?"

He turned his back to her, crossed his arms, and began to pull his T-shirt up his torso. She gave him a catcall as the shirt cleared his shoulders and a genuine laugh bloomed in his chest. He ripped the shirt off and swung it around over his head like a stripper before slinging it into the corner. Then he curved his arms down in front of his thighs, made fists, and flexed the muscles in his back.

"Okay, for that you get a five-dollar bill," she said.

"How about for this?" He spun around and lifted his fists and elbows above his shoulders in imitation of a body builder. Her gaze was warm with appreciation and he could almost feel it travel over the muscles he tightened. Strange, but he was only this aware of his body when he was with Dawn. When he swam, his movements were automatic, and the rest of the time he lived in his head and his computer monitors.

"Ni-i-i-ice," she said as he curled harder. "Another five for sure."

"I'm keeping a running total," he warned.

"Don't you need your computer to do that?"

"My brain isn't that enfeebled yet."

"Oh, you are not in the least bit feeble." She injected a world of dirty innuendo into her comment.

Her voice stroked right down to his cock. He dropped his hands to the button on his jeans, flicking it open and pulling the zipper down just an inch. "You have to pay in advance for this part."

"That's the one *part* I've already seen," she said with a lascivious smirk. "But I'll pay to see it again. Ten bucks."

"I'm insulted." He put his hands on his hips.

"Do you think I'm made of money? I have to save some for the rest of you."

"When you put it that way . . ." He dragged the zipper down at a snail's pace.

"Is this going to take all night?"

"I'm building anticipation."

She made a show of yawning.

He hooked his thumbs into the waistband of his jeans and shot his hip out to one side. "Do that again and I'm leaving these on."

"Oh, fine," she said, her eyes gleaming with amusement. "I'll pay you twenty to take them off."

The laughter rumbled up again and he realized that he was having fun. When was the last time he'd done that?

He wouldn't have expected it from Dawn either. She was so intense about her work, so controlled in her interactions with him. He'd never seen a playful side to her until tonight.

Now he wanted to touch her so he stripped off his jeans and boxer briefs at the same time before he started toward the bed.

"Wait!" She held up one hand. "I want to get a chance to look first."

That sent a jolt of arousal straight to his cock. She gave him a hot smile as she saw it stir and harden. Which made it harden more.

"Thanks for giving me an especially good view," she purred. "I'd like to see the back now."

"If this is your idea of foreplay, it's working." He turned, savoring the knowledge that her gaze was roaming over his body.

But he needed more so he pivoted again and closed the distance to the bed, climbing onto the foot and stalking up to her on his hands and knees. He planted a hand on either side of her hips and brought his mouth to hers, tracing her lips until she opened them to him, the sweetness of her blazing through him like hot molasses.

He felt her small hands on his shoulders. At first, she smoothed them over his skin, the touch twisting desire inside him. Then she began to press against him, pushing him away from her. He eased back without breaking the kiss. But he wanted to feel her breasts against his bare chest, so he rose onto his knees and gripped her upper arms to pull her up against him, the quilt falling away from her as he lifted.

When he leaned into her so the deliciously hard points of her nipples brushed against him, her fingers dug into the muscles of his shoulders and she gasped into his mouth. That could have meant that she was as aroused as he was, but it didn't feel that way.

Once again he eased back, this time releasing her mouth as well. "What is it, darlin'? What's wrong?"

"Nothing. I was just losing my balance." But a flush of some feeling that wasn't sexual colored her neck and cheeks. "Let me just shift around so I'm on a firmer part of the mattress." She scrambled away from the headboard to kneel almost behind him. "That's better. I'm not going to keel over now."

"I wouldn't have let you fall," he said, moving to face her.

"No, you wouldn't have." She threaded her fingers into his hair on either side of his head, making his scalp tingle. Then she pulled his head down so she could sear a kiss onto his lips.

He wrapped his arms around her back and crushed her against him from knee to shoulder, feeling the swell of her breasts, the push of her hip bones beside the flat, satin plane of her belly, the length of her thighs, and finally the hot, wet silk between her thighs as he slid his semierect cock against her.

As he flexed his hips, she arched and gasped again, but this time it was pure arousal. He could smell it and hear it in the tiny moans catching in her throat. He wanted to taste that so he ran one hand down her back, over the curve of her buttock, and down between her legs, finding his way inside her from behind. His finger easily slipped into the liquid heat of her and she moaned louder, then mewed a wordless plaint when he withdrew it. He pulled his head away from hers and brought his finger to his lips, sucking the salty, erotic flavor of her from his skin.

"Oh!" she said, watching him through half-shut eyes. "That's hot."

"That is only the beginning of what I'm going to do." Some instinct made him state his intentions out loud. "I want to lay you back on the bed and taste you directly."

Her lids fluttered and she nodded before letting him lower her to sit and then lie back, unfolding her legs to rest her feet on either side of his thighs. He stayed up on his knees, savoring the sight of her hair spread over the quilt, her taut nipples, and the spread of her thighs so that he could see a glisten of moisture between them.

He bent slightly to palm her breasts, rolling the nipples between his fingers. She sucked in a breath but something flickered in her eyes that wasn't pleasure. Then she lifted her hips in an invitation and his attention was drawn lower, making him skim his hands down her torso until he could curl his fingers around the lushness of her buttocks and bury his face between her thighs.

Chapter 8

When Leland's mouth touched the aching spot between her legs, his touch shot sparks through her like a downed electrical wire writhing on a wet sidewalk. She slammed her eyelids shut and let herself fall into the sensation. He flicked at her clit with his tongue, then plunged it inside her, then told her how delicious she tasted and did it all again. He had an unerring sense of when she was about to crest into orgasm, her body poised in exquisite anticipation of his next stroke. Instead he would kiss her gently on the inside of her thigh, a lovely thing but not what she needed to go over the edge.

He wound her insides into a coil of unsatisfied wanting until she was about to beg him to finish the job. Before she could open her mouth, he'd rolled on a condom, knelt and pulled her thighs up over his hips, and driven his cock deep inside her. Where he stayed motionless while her entire body down to her toes convulsed in one shrieking, nuclear orgasm. All sensation wrapped around the hard length of him, filling her before it tore through her in a clench and release so violent she thought she might pull an internal muscle. She grabbed fistfuls of the quilt to anchor herself while she arched up and gave herself to the waves of pleasure crashing through her.

When her muscles went limp, he still held her up, and now the rigidity of his erection felt even more sexy in contrast to the melted, liquid softness of her insides. She nudged herself against him in word-less encouragement.

"Are you sure you're ready?" he asked with a husky undertone to his drawl.

"Oh, yes," she said, "but there won't be much friction."

The sound he made was somewhere between a chuckle and a groan. "Friction will not be necessary."

He pulled back and thrust in, the motion rippling across her sated nerve endings like a warm sea. He did it again and once more and then his fingers were digging into her butt and his head was thrown back and his cock pumped inside her while he shouted her name toward the ceiling. Seeing the cords of his neck stand out and hearing the hoarse-ness of his voice and feeling the hard grip of his hands on her skin gave her a new and welcome sense of her own power. She had evoked this primitive reaction in a man who seemed always in control of himself.

And then his grip eased as he lowered her hips, sliding out of her and letting his head fall forward while he sank back to sit on his heels. His chest rose and fell in great gasps.

She let a smug little smile curl her lips. Tomorrow her upstairs neighbor might tease her about all the noise, but she was proud of mak-ing Leland yell in the throes of passion.

He lifted his head and pushed his damp hair back from his fore-head. "I can't believe your bed didn't collapse under the force of that explosion."

She let her smile widen. "Two explosions, mine and yours."

"Whatever you paid for this bed, it was worth it." He ran his palm down her splayed thigh, giving it a pat before he climbed off to get rid of his condom. When he returned, she was still sprawled with her head pointing away from the headboard, too wrung out to want to move.

Without a word, he slipped his arms under her and lifted her off the mattress. She squawked in surprise but relaxed in his grasp when she realized how erotic it was to have the wiry strength of him supporting her while their naked bodies touched in interesting ways.

It was a short experience since he simply walked around to the other side so he could reverse her position and deposit her on the bed again. He nudged her over and lay down beside her, his weight compressing the mattress as he pulled the covers up over both of them.

She braced to fight the clutch of panic when he came up on his elbow and loomed over her to press a kiss on her mouth, but the mild flutter in her chest was banished by the warmth of his lips on hers. He looked down at her. "You are one amazing lady."

His eyes held admiration and heat. His voice brushed over her like velvet. His words she discounted because he'd just had an orgasm. "Thank you," she said nonetheless. "I think we were mutually amazing."

He laughed, a deep rumble in his throat. "It does take two to generate that level of mind-bending pleasure."

Mind-bending. She liked that because his brain was so powerful. It was saying something that she'd bent it.

He kissed her again, a soft, tender exploration. She answered it with the same slow, mellow mood. They hadn't had the patience for this earlier. She nibbled along the strong line of his jaw, feeling the scruff of his late-night beard against her lips.

He touched his forehead to hers with a rueful sigh. "Darlin', I wish I could keep this up but I have to get some sleep. I'm not in the same peak condition you are."

"If I keep training you, you will be," she teased.

"Which kind of training are you talking about?" His smile was slow and sexy.

"Whatever kind motivates you."

"How about you not wearing any clothes while you train me? That would get my heart rate skyrocketing."

"I'll have to ask Ramón if he'll allow that."

He laughed and lay down fully, snaking his arm around her waist to spoon her up against him. She no longer worried that she would react badly, even when he tucked his hand under her hip, its weight caging her to keep her pressed back against his hard, hot body. She reveled in the solidity of his chest and thighs against her back and legs, the way his cock nuzzled against her buttocks, and the whiffle of his breath across her hair.

His breathing deepened and slowed while his arm relaxed over her waist as he slid into sleep.

But she didn't want the oblivion of sleep. She wanted to stay awake to the wonder of Leland's presence enveloping her in a way that made her feel safe, not threatened.

Yet the question of why she felt that way nagged at her. Natalie had pointed out that Leland with his brains and success and confidence was more likely to trigger the opposite effect. Yes, Dawn had controlled their intimacies to a certain extent and Leland had responded to her cues—because he was a smart guy and she'd learned how to manage the situation with a certain subtlety. However, that didn't explain her lying cradled against his big, heavy body without even a small tightening of her throat.

Maybe it was better not to delve too deeply into her reasons. There might be some emotion there that she didn't want to acknowledge. This was supposed to be about sex with a man she had the hots for, nothing more. Smarter to keep it that way.

She shifted in response to her uncomfortable thoughts. Leland responded in his sleep, crooking his knee to rest on top of her thigh, trapping her even more thoroughly.

And she let him.

A shriek of music jolted her awake. But she couldn't sit up because Leland was still wrapped around her, a confinement that sent a spear of fear through her not-quite-awakened brain. "What the—?" She started to shove against his weight but he was already pulling away.

He rolled out of the bed and mumbled, "Sorry, my alarm." He found his jeans, yanked his cell phone out of the pocket, and silenced the music.

"What was that?"

"Nerd music. The original *Star Trek* theme." His grin was charmingly sheepish.

She held the sheet to her chest as she pushed upright, her heart rate settling back to normal. "What time is it?"

"Midnight. I need to get back to the office." He pulled on his briefs.

"The office?! It's the middle of a Friday night. That's called the weekend."

He had his jeans zipped and buttoned. "I have an RFP due a week from today, on top of a lot of other projects."

Guilt poked at her. She'd piled on another one, a job that didn't pay. "Don't worry about the gym. It's no big deal. Vicky will get it straightened out."

The angles of his face hardened and she saw what Natalie had warned her about. This man would always attack a challenge. "There's something not right going on there. That can't be ignored. I'll be at our training session tomorrow."

He yanked on his T-shirt and ran his fingers through his hair, which only made the bed-mussed waves stick out at different angles.

"You can use my brush," Dawn said. "It's on the dresser."

"That bad?" He ducked down to check his reflection in the mirror and grabbed the brush. "Thanks for the loan."

He collected his sneakers and socks before sitting down on the bed next to her. She scooted over to lay her cheek against his back, feeling the flex and stretch of his muscles as he tied the laces. He smelled like clean laundry, a touch of garlic from the restaurant, and sex. She turned her face to inhale more deeply.

"Are you sniffing me?" he asked, a laugh of delight in his voice.

"You smell fantastic." Her stomach grumbled and she remembered that they had skipped dinner. "Good enough to eat."

He reached around and pulled her onto his lap, the covers falling away so she felt denim against her bare bottom. His gaze burned hot. "I want to taste you again." He skimmed his hand over her thigh slowly enough to give her time to stop him.

But his words sent desire pulsing through her. She opened her legs to allow his hand between them, her head falling back as he eased first one, then two fingers inside her and rocked the heel of his hand against her clit. "Leland," she breathed on a long exhale as tremors of pleasure vibrated through her. "That feels so good."

"Yes, yes, it does. So hot, so wet, so smooth." He nipped at the spot where her neck and shoulder met. "So frustrating that I have to go to work. But first . . ." He withdrew his hand and sucked on his long fingers with a lascivious smirk. "So delicious."

"Hey, no fair starting something you're not going to finish." She grabbed his wrist and tugged it back toward her thighs.

"Oh, I'm going to finish it," he said with a low, lewd chuckle even as he resisted her grasp. "I'm just going to let you wonder exactly how for about ten hours."

Joy exploded in her brain. He was coming back!

"You're a tease." She took a small revenge by wiggling seductively against the partial erection she could feel pushing against his jeans.

"Who's teasing whom?" He kissed her lightly on the lips and set her back on the quilt.

"Such good grammar from that fancy private school."

He stood up. "You don't know how hard this is."

"Actually, I do. I was sitting on it."

He groaned and briefly cupped her cheek as she swung her legs off the bed. "Don't get up. I can find my way to the door. And if you walk there naked, the temptation may be too much for me."

She *wanted* to lure him back into her bed—just to curl up against his strength and warmth—but she knew how selfish that was. He needed to go back to solving his corporate clients' issues for heaps of money. Although she had an idea that the money wasn't what drove him—it was the sense of responsibility. He'd made a promise to help them, so he wouldn't stop until he had solved their problem. That certainly applied to the gym's weird issues.

She crooked her finger so he would bend down before she gave him a long kiss that had him seizing her shoulders to bring her in closer. Then he released her and stepped back, her effect on him visible under the denim.

"Work. I have to work." His voice was a rasp. "I've got to go." He spun on his heel and strode out of the room as though the hounds of hell were chasing him.

She fell back on the bed, a delicious lassitude seeping through her arms and legs so that she couldn't force herself to get up to lock the dead bolt and set the alarm. Yet.

Her body hummed with the satisfaction of two fantastic orgasms, but that wasn't what made her hug a pillow to her chest and grin like an idiot. No, the joy bubbling through her was because she'd fallen asleep with Leland's arm locked around her waist, yet she'd only wanted to snuggle closer to him.

She'd been wrong all these years. She hadn't needed a weak, controllable man to feel safe. She'd needed a powerful man who could help defeat her fear. She just wasn't sure how that had happened.

Leland rummaged in the limo's insulated storage compartment to find a container of lasagna. He pulled a fork from a felt-lined drawer of utensils and dug into the still-lukewarm pasta. The first meaty, garlicky bite made him groan with appreciation before he shoved another one into his mouth.

Forget hunger . . . great sex was the best sauce.

He focused on the food, trying not to think about Dawn in hopes that the erection smashed inside his jeans would subside.

However, images of her head thrown back as she came with his name tearing from her lips or the way she'd cupped her breasts and offered them to him or her peaked nipple parting the long, silky fall of her hair kept his cock hard, no matter how he fought to banish them.

"Oh, hell!" he muttered, adjusting the denim in an effort to ease the pressure.

He polished off the lasagna and grabbed a bottle of water from the cooler, sipping it as he sagged back against the seat to analyze the real problem.

Why had it been so hard to leave? Work always took precedence in his life. His mother had held three jobs in order to get him the best education she could. His father's family, who could have spared private school tuition without even noticing it, considered him an unfortunate but minor consequence of a spring-break romance. They pretended he didn't exist.

He didn't care about their acknowledgment, but his mother's life would have been a hell of a lot easier if his father had shown the smallest amount of guts in forcing his family to offer some financial support.

So his mother had dedicated her life to proving that Leland not only existed but was valuable. He owed his success to her. Even more, he owed her his success. He couldn't fail because that would make all her efforts meaningless.

The headlights from other cars strobed through the limo's windows, illuminating the rack of wineglasses, the burnished wood paneling, and the hand-rubbed leather of the seats. Riding in this luxurious car, driven by a man who was paid to wait hours for Leland's convenience, heading back to an office stocked with tens of thousands of dollars of cutting-edge computer equipment purchased for his sole use: This was where all that work had gotten him. And it had been what he wanted.

Until tonight.

He braced his elbows on his knees, lowered his head into his hands, and massaged his temples as a wave of longing swamped him.

Longing for how Dawn had made him feel for a few hours. As though he didn't have to prove anything. As though he could simply be a man who wanted a woman.

And God, he wanted her.

Chapter 9

Dawn had leaped out of bed, filled with energy after a night of sleeping without nightmares. She'd eaten her granola and yogurt with a smile as she replayed various moments of the night before. Slinging her gym bag over her shoulder, she'd walked to her front door and realized the dead bolt wasn't shot home and the alarm wasn't set. She'd fallen asleep without ensuring that her sanctuary was secure.

Stupid. Just because Leland had made her feel safe for a few hours didn't mean her world had changed. Her goofy smile evaporated as reality slammed into her. He'd climbed out of her bed and gone to work in the middle of the night. What did that tell her about his priorities?

That he was a man who kept his promises, who did the right thing by the people who trusted him. That was why she felt safe with him, so she had no right to complain.

She needed to remember that his promises were at a level far beyond hers. Once he had fulfilled his commitment to solving the gym's problem, he would probably go back to breathing the rarefied air of an international consultant, taking her sense of safety with him. After all, there was nothing profound between them. Their connections were sex and an IT problem that would be resolved one way or the other in a matter of days. She shouldn't expect him to stick around.

She punched in the code to arm the alarm and yanked open her door as its beeps counted down the time she had to close it again.

Slamming it shut, she twisted the key to lock the dead bolt and trudged down the stairs, her buoyancy gone like her smile.

But she had her own promises to keep. Maybe her clients weren't giant corporations, but they counted on her for their physical health. Sometimes they even depended on her for emotional reasons, confiding secrets about their marriages or their children's problems because they needed to share the burden and they trusted her discretion. When you worked one-on-one up close and personal on a regular basis, it built a certain intimacy.

That could explain some of what had happened between her and Leland. But not all. She'd never dated a client before this. In fact, she'd considered it bordering on unethical, although Ramón had never specifically forbidden his trainers to get involved with clients. She knew a couple who had, and it had resulted in their losing the clients when they broke up.

The likely outcome of her own relationship sent a chill shivering through her. Although at least she wouldn't have to feel guilty about Leland dropping his gym membership.

However, she walked through the door of Work It Out determined not to let memories of the night before distract her from doing her job to the best of her ability. She owed her clients just as much as Leland owed his.

She mostly succeeded in her goal, sometimes almost forgetting the glow of satisfaction that still permeated her body.

Until something crackled through the air while she was spotting a client through a set of skull crushers. Dawn glanced up to find Leland standing in the door to the weight room, his gaze locked on her.

He wore a pale blue T-shirt that intensified the blue of his eyes and navy shorts so she could see the chiseled muscles of his long legs—the legs she'd felt between hers as he drove into her.

Reality flew out the window, banished by a desire that electrified her nerve endings. She had no idea how he could read that on her face, but she saw heat flare in his eyes before he nodded toward the big space holding the treadmills. She dipped her head in response and checked her watch. Exultation poured through her veins.

He'd come thirty minutes early.

Maybe he wanted to warm up. Maybe he wanted to run programs on his phone to check the data traffic. Or maybe he wanted to see her as much as she wanted to see him.

The possibility bloomed in her chest. Leland had left his job before he absolutely needed to in order to come to where she was.

She floated through the rest of the training session.

"You're in a good mood today," her client commented as he zipped up his gym bag. "Usually you scare me into working hard with that challenging glare of yours. Today you kind of coaxed me into it."

"Which do you prefer?" Dawn was curious for future reference.

He considered that for a moment. "I think Scary Dawn is easier to deal with. I kept wondering what evil plans Happy Dawn was hiding behind that smile."

She laughed. "Next time Scary Dawn will be back, I promise. See you Monday."

She forced herself to clean and stow the mat at a seminormal speed. Then she walked—not jogged—to the treadmill room.

And stopped dead when she saw Leland running, his legs moving like pistons, the cotton of his shirt darkened by sweat down the middle of his back. She wanted to rip the shirt off and lick the salty sweat from his skin.

Not a useful thought.

She closed her eyes to block out the sight until she got a grip on her unruly imagination. Then she walked across the wood floor to Leland's treadmill.

"I'm glad to see you got here with plenty of time to warm up," she said, feeling like an idiot.

He kept running. "I had to force myself not to come any earlier."

She couldn't stop her grin. "I like your honesty."

"I've been thinking about having your hands on me for our training session. I can't decide whether it will be torment or bliss." He brought the treadmill to a halt and scrubbed his face with his sweat towel.

"If it makes you feel any better, I've been debating the same question."

He finally looked at her, his eyes blazing with the same hunger she felt. "I'm going to take a wild guess and say it will be combination of the two."

"Let's get started and find out." She gave him a sideways smile and nodded toward the weight room.

He stepped off the machine and spoke in a low voice. "We need to talk about the gym's router. Since we're on a tight time line I'm going to accept your help with getting into the office. Then you will leave immediately and pretend you were never there."

Right. The reason Leland was at the gym. The haze of lust enveloping them had nearly made her forget about it.

"I meant it when I said you don't have to do this," she murmured as they walked. "It will get taken care of on Monday."

"I meant it when I said that I can't let this go if it's dark web activity that I have the opportunity to stop." His voice was edged with something like anger. "But I won't know until I get into that router."

They arrived in the weight room, where she waved him toward a bench. Once he was in position on his back, she handed him a pair of dumbbells. "Skull crushers, so I can talk while I'm spotting you."

He nodded and straightened his arms above his chest. "You upped the weight."

"It was time." She knelt beside his head, noticing that the shadow of his beard had darkened overnight. Her fingers twitched with the urge to test its heavier texture. "Okay, start."

He bent his arms at the elbow and lowered the weights on either side of his ears while she kept her hands at the ready to support the dumbbells.

"How long do you need with the router?" she muttered as she tilted in closer.

"It depends on the level of encryption. I won't know until I get started." His face was taut with exertion, sweat-curled strands of hair clinging to his temples. God, she wanted to brush them away.

"Better go in late, then, after Vicky and Ramón have left. Around nine o'clock."

He smiled, a drawing back of lips from clenched teeth that spoke of effort and evil intentions. "How much free time do you have between now and then?"

"I've got clients until six."

"Three hours." His smile grew even more lascivious. "Think what we can do with all that time."

Desire jolted through her to curl low in her belly. "Right now you have to do another set of skull crushers."

"I feel energized enough to push out *two* more sets."

She bent lower to lock her gaze with his before she said, "Don't overdo it. You're going to need all your strength for three hours with me."

"Game on," he said with a throaty chuckle.

The next fifty minutes were exactly as Leland had predicted: delicious torment. She made it worse by adding extra little touches that glided along a tempting swell of muscle or a patch of sweat-glistened skin. He retaliated in kind, brushing against her thigh or shoulder when he shifted positions and giving her long stares that made heat singe through her.

When he lay down on the mat for the final stretching portion of the session, she had a moment of madness as she pictured ripping her pants off before she straddled him. She nearly came right then. He must have seen something of her thoughts in her expression because he was back on his feet, standing so close that they were nearly touching, before she even knew what was happening.

"The hell with stretching. We need to go someplace private," he said, his voice a tense rasp. "For our last fifteen minutes."

She'd thought she was aroused before, but his words were like a match to gasoline. "Do you have protection?"

"I was coming to see you, so yes." He patted the pocket of his shorts.

She knew where to take him because one of her fellow trainers had once confessed to having sex with another trainer there. "Fair warning. Where we're going is not romantic and it's not climate controlled."

"If you think I'm going to notice anything but you, you're wrong." He walked along beside her, electricity crackling up her arm every time the backs of their hands brushed.

She led him through the hall, past the locker rooms, to the door that led down a flight of utilitarian cement stairs to the basement. Vicky hadn't spent any decorating dollars there, so it looked like what it was before Ramón had bought it: an old college building that had been neglected for a decade. The cement and cinder blocks were painted dingy gray, and an array of exposed pipes were festooned with cobwebs hung from the ceiling. An undertone of mildew and ancient sweat drifted through the cool air.

None of it dampened Dawn's arousal. She pulled open one side of a set of double doors and stepped into a room filled with a jumble of old football practice equipment, broken treadmills, and obsolete weight benches. As soon as Leland was inside the door, he slammed it shut and thrust his hands down inside the back of her track pants to cup the bare skin of her buttocks.

As he pulled her against his erection, his mouth came down on hers, a hot, hard demand, and she forgot everything except the need to have him filling her. She pulled back from his kiss. "We don't have much time. Get the condom," she commanded.

He laughed, a low, husky growl that vibrated through her. Then he slipped his hands out of her pants and reached into his pocket.

She started to push down her trousers.

"Stop!" he said. "I've been fantasizing about stripping those off you ever since you walked up to the treadmill." He handed her a foil envelope. Before she could do more than accept it, he had hooked his thumbs into the waistband of her track pants and panties and yanked them down to her ankles in a single, swift movement. "Now that was satisfying," he said as she kicked her clothing the rest of the way off.

"My turn," she said, doing the same to his gym shorts and briefs, his cock springing upward as soon as she'd freed it. She wasted no time in rolling the condom over his erection.

As soon as he was covered, he walked her back against a wall. "This looks like the least dusty surface," he said.

When he began to press his body into hers, sandwiching her between him and the wall, she felt her throat tighten and her breath go shallow. She forced herself to inhale slowly, reminding herself that this was Leland as she fought against the panic. Then he bent to grip the back of her knee, dragging it up the outside of his thigh until her hips tilted to meet his cock at exactly the right angle. The lightning charge that shot through her obliterated panic, replacing it with a need so intense that she reached down between them to bring the head of his cock inside her.

"Yes!" he said and drove in and up so deeply that her other foot came off the floor. The sensation of being filled so suddenly started a clench of orgasm. She braced her back against the wall so that she could wrap her legs around his hips, opening and anchoring herself for whatever he wanted to do.

"You . . . are . . . in . . . cred . . . i . . . ble," he said, punctuating each gasp of a syllable with a thrust.

His hands were under her bottom, supporting and massaging while he entered and withdrew faster and faster. She tried to fight off the orgasm that kept threatening to explode before she could fully savor the ferocious pleasure of stand-up sex with Leland. Until he surged hard inside her and worked his hand between them to find her clit. One skillful touch and her entire body convulsed in a paroxysm of release that made it feel as though every muscle screamed its delight individually. At the first spasm of her orgasm, he began to pump within her, his hips rocking so that he hit her clit again and again to multiply the sensations shattering her.

Wordless sounds of pleasure tore from both their throats, reverberating off the hard surfaces around them, wrapping them in a cocoon of lust and satisfaction.

He gave a final push and kept his weight pressed in to hold her as diminishing aftershocks rippled through her. When her body went quiet at last, he sucked in a long breath and blew it out so that it whistled past her ear. She burrowed against his neck, breathing in the delicious scent of sweat and hot sex.

"So that's what an hour of continuous foreplay does for you," he said. "I'd say I'd like to do it again but I'm not sure I would survive the experience."

"At least you don't have to go back upstairs and attempt to stay upright when your bones have pretty much melted."

"Worse, I have to try to think when you've fried every brain cell I have." He slipped out of her and eased her feet to the ground, grasping her shoulders when she swayed.

She glanced at the fitness watch strapped to her wrist. "Shit! I've got to get back to the gym now." She scrambled into her panties and track pants while Leland dealt with the condom and picked up his clothes. "Can you find your way upstairs? We probably shouldn't be seen together anyway."

He raised his eyebrows. "You weren't worried about that on the way down here."

"Because I was crazed with lust." She rose onto her toes and gave him a swift kiss on the mouth. "I'll text you when I'm leaving the gym."

He ran his palm down the outside of her arm. "I'll have the limo park a block or two away from your apartment building to keep a low profile."

She spun away and cracked open the door before she decided to kiss those firm, warm lips again and longer. As she expected, no one was in the dim hallway. She took off at a brisk jog, taking the steps two at a time and arriving for her next appointment breathing heavily but on time.

⌐

Leland rubbed his hand over his face before typing in another set of numbers to see how his changes would affect the RFP for Fincher. His vision blurred for a second and he closed his eyes to give them a short rest.

"You look like hell."

Leland opened his eyes to see Tully with his hip propped on the desk next to him. "This RFP is a pain in my ass," Leland said.

"I told you to say no. In fact, I said no for you but you're such a stubborn SOB that you had to take it on." Tully angled over to look at the screen. "If I knew how to shut down this program without screwing things up, I'd do it and make you get some sleep."

"Go bother someone else." Leland turned back to the monitor. "I've got work to do."

"You were here most of last night. Driving yourself to exhaustion will not help KRG. And it won't bring your mother back."

"Fuck off." Leland was too tired to put any heat into it even though the mention of his mother twisted a blade in his chest.

"What are you trying to prove? That you work harder than anyone else here? We already know that."

"*You're* here on a Saturday."

Tully didn't give an inch. "I went home and slept in my own bed last night."

"I'm leaving at five o'clock, so get out of my way and let me finish what I need to do before then." That had the virtue of being true.

"I'll be back here at 5:01." Tully stood up. "You'd better be gone."

Leland waited until Tully was out of sight before he slumped back in his chair and closed his eyes again.

What was he trying to prove?

That his mother could be proud of him because nothing came before his job. Not a dark web node. Not sleep. Most especially not a fascinating, sexy woman who made it harder and harder to put her out of his mind and focus on work.

He'd learned from his mother how a reckless relationship could derail your life. He wasn't going to let her hard-won lesson go to waste by falling prey to that.

Opening his eyes, he sat forward in the chair and checked the numbers on the spreadsheet again. He'd transposed two digits in one entry, which was why the total had looked off.

Cursing, he retyped the numbers with ferocious concentration.

Chapter 10

Dawn frowned down at her phone as she walked toward her apartment. She'd texted Leland before she headed out the gym's front door but had received no response. Had he gotten hung up at work or just decided not to come?

When she reached the block her building was on, she saw no tall, lean figure loitering on the sidewalk. Maybe he thought they shouldn't be seen together even away from the gym. After all, her place was pretty close to Work It Out.

She went through her usual ritual of checking that no one lurked inside the foyer and started up the stairs when her phone pinged.

Sorry for the delay. Be there in five.

Relief and anticipation sent her running up the stairs so she could unlock and turn off all her security. She'd seen Leland eyeing the overkill the first time he'd come in with her. She'd just stowed her gym bag in the coat closet when the front-door buzzer sounded.

"Dawn, it's Leland."

The slow southern honey of his voice made it unnecessary to check the video feed. She hit the enter button and opened her apartment door.

In under a minute, he had his arms wrapped around her and his mouth locked on hers. She wound her fingers into his hair and held on as a wave of heat swamped her, spiraling down to pool between her thighs.

He groaned against her lips and ran his hands down to palm her butt and pull her hips against his. She tucked her fingers into the back pockets of his jeans and upped the pressure, while she rocked into him.

He lifted his head. "I've been thinking about this ever since I left you. It did not help my concentration."

She tilted her head back to look up at him and frowned. Despite the hunger lighting his face, he looked exhausted. Shadows were smudged under his eyes, his cheeks were drawn, and his usually clean-shaven chin was rough with at least a day's growth of whiskers. Not that she minded the feel of it, but it meant he wasn't taking care of himself.

"What?" He scanned her face.

She moved her hands to push against his chest. "You're going to bed."

A lustful smile twisted his lips. "I have no problem with bypassing the sofa."

"Sorry, let me rephrase. You're going to *sleep*." She pressed harder until he released her.

"The hell I am," he said. "The only thing that's kept me going is the thought of making love to you."

She took his hand and started toward the bedroom. "That's my point. You don't have to keep going any longer and you shouldn't."

He let her lead him to the bed. "Now I have you exactly where I want you," he said with an exaggerated leer as he sat down and tried to pull her onto his lap.

She used his own momentum to push him back on the bed while she remained standing. "And that's where I want you. With your eyes closed. Snoring."

"I don't snore."

"That was a metaphor. Or something like that." She picked up his legs and swung them up on the bed.

He grabbed her wrist and held on, his blue eyes glinting. "I'll sleep but only with you beside me. Naked."

"That's not a good plan."

"Fine. Bra and panties."

She parked her hands on her hips. "And what will you be wearing?"

"Boxer briefs. It's only fair."

The thought of snuggling up to Leland's mostly bare skin in the cozy nest of her comforter was too tempting to resist. "No fooling around, though. Just sleep." Not that she was anywhere near being tired.

"For an hour."

"We are not negotiating some business contract here," she said.

He gave her a slow, lazy smile. "This is much more important than business." Then he sat up and yanked his T-shirt over his head, leaving her breathless at the sight of the flexing muscles of his bare chest.

They both shucked off the rest of their clothes—except for undergarments—and crawled into her bed together. Leland spooned her up against him so that she could feel the warm satin of his skin pressed to her back and the shape of his semihard cock nestled into her bottom. She snuggled into him and surreptitiously set the alarm on her fitness watch for two hours later. She had no intention of waking him up in a mere hour, even though she knew she wouldn't be able to sleep herself.

He nuzzled a kiss into her hair. "Sweet dreams, my favorite tyrant."

It took only a couple of minutes before his arm went slack over her waist and his breath slowed into the rhythm of sleep. She lay reveling in the heat and solidity of him against her back, wanting to imprint this on her memory in case it never happened again.

An hour later, she started awake as an unfamiliar alarm chimed from the bedside table. Leland stirred, and she realized he must have set it on his phone. She stretched to scoop up the phone and dismissed the alarm. "Go back to sleep," she murmured, dropping the phone on the mattress.

His grip on her tightened. "Want you," he muttered in a groggy voice.

"Later," she said. "You need to rest first."

He said something that sounded like "mmmpf" and subsided.

A strangely tender feeling flowed through her. For all his power and wealth, he still needed someone to care about his well-being. For another hour that someone would be her.

His grip on her tightened. "Want you," he muttered in a groggy voice.

Leland crawled out of a deep sleep as someone shook his arm, a relentless yet soft female voice telling him it was time to wake up. As his senses began to register, he realized a warm female body was snuggled against him and his cock was already interested.

His mind snapped to attention as he remembered that he was in Dawn's bed with an almost naked Dawn in his arms. "Life is good."

"You might not think that when I tell you that it's after eight o'clock," she said over her shoulder.

"But I set an alarm."

"You barely moved when it went off. I killed it and you happily went back to sleep."

He groaned. Not only had he not gotten enough work done, he hadn't even had the pleasure of sex with the delectable woman in his arms. "I thought we had a deal."

She turned within his embrace so she faced him on the pillow, her dark eyes liquid with concern. "I'm not going to be the cause of you collapsing from sleep deprivation. Furthermore, we both need to be sharp tonight."

He hated to admit it but the sleep had helped. He felt far more clearheaded than he had when he arrived. Now a new worry jabbed at him. "You let me in the office and you leave. That's nonnegotiable."

"I came up with a good cover story. You think you left your phone at the gym. You came back to look for it as soon as you could. We're checking to see if it's in the office for safekeeping."

"Will we need a cover story? I thought Vicky and Ramón would be gone." Now he regretted allowing her to be involved.

She shrugged her slender, bare shoulder. He wanted to kiss it. "I think there might be a security camera in the hallway outside their office. I meant to look earlier but you, um, distracted me."

"I would label it mutual distraction." He gave in to his impulse and pushed up onto his elbow so he could taste the silky skin on her shoulder.

"Mmm," she purred before she braced one hand against his chest and pushed. "We don't have time for that now."

"We got it done in under five minutes the last time." He kept his arm banded around her waist so the lower halves of their bodies were locked together.

Her gaze went hot and soft at the same time. "We have all night after we do our job," she pointed out.

He couldn't believe that Dawn was more focused on getting to the router than he was. He felt like he'd become a sex addict, his brain addled by lust.

Still, the only reason he eased his grip on her was the thought of taking his time with her when they got back to her apartment.

Dawn walked into the gym while Leland waited around the corner. Strolling up to the front desk, she said, "Hey, Tiffany, I've got a member coming in who thinks he left his phone here. Do you have anything in the lost and found?"

Tiffany pulled open the drawer where small unclaimed items were stowed. "Nope, just some keys and earrings. Give me the name and number . . . oh, I guess that won't help." She giggled. "Maybe the email address?"

"He's coming in shortly, so we'll see if we can find it before we get all that info."

"Is it that good-looking new guy who swims afterward? I don't know how you focus on training him. I'd be thinking about *other* things." She gave Dawn a smirky smile.

If only she knew . . .

"He's just another body to whip into shape." In whatever way she chose to do it.

"Yeah, but what a body!"

Fortunately, Leland strode through the door at that moment, his body not appearing to need further assistance in the fitness department. Tiffany blushed and Dawn grinned.

"Dawn, thanks for meeting me here," he said. "Any luck?"

"Not at the front desk, but let's retrace your steps and see if we can locate it. Or maybe it's in Ramón's office. Sometimes people hand him things and he forgets to bring them up front." *How was that for casually providing a reasonable excuse to break into the bosses' office?*

Tiffany nodded, her gaze glued to Leland. The only issue with her fascination was that Tiffany was so engrossed in admiring him that she might not remember any of this carefully crafted conversation.

"Are Ramón or Vicky still here?" Dawn asked to snag the receptionist's attention.

"What?" Tiffany turned to look at her with a slightly dazed expression. "No, they left a while ago. Something about date night."

"Okay, no problem. We'll try the locker room first," Dawn said. "That's the most likely place anyway."

"I can't believe I was so careless with my phone," Leland said as they walked away from the desk. "I'm sorry for all the trouble I'm putting you through."

"I get it," Dawn said. "I can't function without my cell."

"Exactly," he said, holding the door to the hallway for her.

"Okay, we can cut the crap now," Dawn said when the door swung closed behind them. "But you have to go ransack the locker room and I'll pretend to search the weight room. Meet you back here in ten minutes."

She was getting a kick out of creating a false front for their real mission. It was fun to outsmart whoever their opponent was.

He gave her a polite smile as a late customer passed them. "See you then."

When she got to the weight room, only one woman was using a machine. But Dawn gave a convincing performance of looking for Leland's phone, even asking the lone customer if she'd seen a stray cell.

She was back in the hallway in eleven minutes. Leland stood outside the locker room already. "Did you find it?" he asked.

She shook her head. "Let's check Ramón's office. Luckily, I have a key."

"He must trust you." Leland fell into step beside her as they headed toward the front desk again.

"We trust each other." Ramón had given her the key when he'd taken Vicky on vacation to Costa Rica, saying that someone might need something from the office while they were gone. No one had, and Dawn had tried to return it to him when he came back. He'd told her to keep it. "I'm only using it now because Ramón wouldn't want the gym to be involved in anything illegal."

No matter what Natalie said, Dawn was sure of that.

"I hope you're right."

"I know I am." As they approached the door, Dawn took a quick glance around the hallway without being obvious. She bent her head as though looking at the keys in her hand. "There's a security camera in the corner diagonally to my right."

"I was afraid we wouldn't find it in the locker room," Leland said in acknowledgment.

Dawn slid the key into the lock and twisted. Opening the door, she flicked on the lights. Leland had warned her to keep to their cover story while in the office until he made sure none of the computers had cameras activated.

"I'll check Ramón's desk," Dawn said. "He's always stuffing things in drawers and forgetting that they're there." Which was true.

She began riffling through his junk drawer while she watched Leland wander around the office as though he were just occupying himself while she searched for the phone.

"We're clear," he said, placing his laptop bag on the credenza behind Vicky's desk where the router was positioned. He had his laptop out and plugged into the router faster than Dawn could sort through the miscellaneous crap she'd pulled out of Ramón's drawer.

Leland didn't bother with a chair—he just bent down and started typing, his fingers flying over the keyboard with the fluidity of a pianist, except the music was a rapid-fire clicking. His gaze was fixed on the screen, the glow of it lighting his face and reflecting in his glasses.

Watching him at work intimidated her. He radiated focus and brilliance, while she had no idea what the crazy stuff scrolling across his screen meant. Yet something about his intensity sent a sexual thrill through her. However, she was pretty sure that she could have stripped naked and he wouldn't have noticed.

She turned back to Ramón's desk to finish straightening the drawer she'd opened. As she shifted the plastic office-supply tray to replace a package of pencils she'd pulled out, the corner of a black metal box caught her eye. She removed the tray to see a gun safe, something she recognized because one of her brothers owned a handgun, much to his wife's disapproval. The safe in the drawer was high-end—it had biometric security. In addition, Ramón's full name was engraved into the lid in a florid gold font.

Shock vibrated through her as she stared down at the ominous box. Ramón claimed to abhor violence of any kind after all the terrible injuries he'd seen—and inflicted—in the boxing ring. How could he say that and own a gun?

Unless Natalie was right, and her beloved boss was involved in whatever illegal activity was pouring through the router.

Bile roiled in her stomach and tears burned behind her eyes. She couldn't—wouldn't—believe that of him. There had to be another explanation.

She blinked hard to stop the tears and debated whether to tell Leland. He would assume the worst, and she didn't know how to defend Ramón when evidence to the contrary was staring her in the face.

She carefully placed the tray back on top of the safe, closing the drawer without a sound. In fact, the room had gone silent, and she glanced over at Leland. His fingers had stilled but code continued to march across the screen. He stared at it for a few more seconds, then nodded. "Got it."

After typing in a few more strings of commands, he closed the laptop and disconnected the cable to the router. Straightening, he shoved his computer back in its case. "I'll analyze this data when I get back to the office."

"You're not going back there tonight," Dawn said, following him to the door and hitting the light switch. She pulled the door closed behind them and tested the knob to make sure it had locked.

The look he gave her nearly collapsed her knees. "Tomorrow morning," he said. "Tonight I have to make up for all that time I wasted sleeping."

"You needed it. I'd remind you that tomorrow is Sunday, but I know that's irrelevant to you."

"The work has to get done." But he sounded more tired than convinced.

They walked in silence until reaching the lobby. Tiffany looked up from her phone. "Did you find it?"

"Despite Dawn's heroic efforts, no, we did not," Leland said, giving her the full treatment with his drawl and a slow smile. "I must have lost it somewhere else. I just wish I could figure out where."

"I don't know what I'd do without my phone," Tiffany said with a sympathetic grimace. "Good luck finding it!"

"I appreciate that, darlin'." Leland started toward the door.

"How much later do you have to stay tonight?" Dawn asked the receptionist, giving Leland time to get to his limo around the corner.

"Another fifteen minutes unless someone comes in—which they never do this late on a Saturday."

"Sorry you get stuck with this every weekend."

"Oh, I don't mind. My friends never go out until after ten anyway." She held up her phone. "We're going to meet at Go Karaoke tonight. Want to come?"

"Me, sing? You don't want that—trust me. But thanks." Dawn pushed away from the desk. "See you Monday."

She walked out of the gym and around the corner, ducking through the limo door that Leland shoved open.

Exhilaration sparkled through her and she planted a hard kiss on Leland's mouth as the limo pulled away from the curb. "We did it! Tiffany didn't suspect a thing and if someone asks her, she'll be all about how hard it is to lose your phone."

Leland snaked his arm around her shoulders and pulled her against him. "Don't get any ideas about doing more of this. People on the dark web don't respect the law. That's why they're there."

That reminded her of the discovery in Ramón's drawer, and her excitement died. "There's something I have to tell you, even though there has to be a good explanation for it."

He eased his grip and shifted back so he could see her face. "You sound upset."

"I found a gun safe in Ramón's desk drawer, under his office supplies." She couldn't bring herself to reveal that it had her boss's name proudly emblazoned on it.

Leland muttered a curse. "Double what I said about your further involvement."

"But he hates any kind of violence. He's very clear on that." She felt the tears well up again. "It doesn't make sense."

He stroked her arm. "I know you respect him but—"

"It's more than respect. He gave me back my life." She hadn't meant to say that, but without the purpose and sense of security Ramón had granted her, she'd still be holed up in her apartment behind her security system and expensive dead bolt. How could the man who made her feel it was safe to go out in the world own a gun?

"Dawn, I won't ask you but when you feel you can tell me, I want to know what happened to make you have an alarm system fit for Fort Knox." He kissed her softly. "But not until you're ready."

She thought about the horrendous day that had ended her college career. Only Natalie, Alice, and one of her sisters knew what had happened. Of course, the college administration did too, but they had pressured her not to report it to the police. She'd refused their offer of counseling out of pride and the sense that they didn't have her best interests at heart. The latter was true, but the counseling would have helped.

She tried to form the words to tell Leland but found them clogging her throat. It was too ugly, too sordid, too raw. Still. "Not tonight," she choked out. "I don't want to ruin tonight." Because she didn't know how many more nights she would have with him, she couldn't afford to waste any of them.

"How could it ruin our night if I understand you better?" His stroking continued, soothing her into resting against him to draw on his strength. "I feel you stiffen in my arms sometimes and I hate that

I've caused it. But I don't know how to avoid it." His voice vibrated with concern.

The tears that had started because of Ramón overflowed down her cheeks. She twisted and reached up to cup his face. "You feel it and you always let me do what I need to get past the problem. That makes all the difference."

He wiped the tears away with his thumb. "I'm an ass for making you cry. Forget I said anything."

"I just don't want to believe that Ramón could be mixed up in this. He seems so decent, so solid . . . so *good*." The tears flowed again and she swiped them away with the back of her hand. "But I felt I had to tell you about the gun safe. Just in case."

She heard and felt him take a deep breath, but he had turned his face away from her so she didn't know what he was thinking.

"You did the right thing," he said. "Even though you don't want to implicate your boss. That takes integrity."

No, it took the realization that she cared more about Leland's safety than Ramón's reputation.

"I don't want you to get hurt. My conscience would kill me."

"Now you know how I feel," he said. "We can go up to your apartment now. The limo's been parked for a while."

She hadn't noticed the cessation of motion, and the driver hadn't announced their arrival. He was either very discreet or he felt it was unnecessary to state the obvious.

Her blood fizzed as Leland pushed open the door and helped her out of the limo, his grip strong and warm. She wanted to wrap herself in him to keep the ugliness of her suspicions at bay.

As they climbed the stairs, she noticed that Leland had his laptop case in his hand. "Are you going to look at the data here?" she asked.

He glanced down at the case and winced. "No. I picked it up out of habit."

"It's like my gym bag. I get the feeling that a part of me is missing when I don't have it."

"Proving that we're both too tied up in our work." He shook off the serious mood and reached out to give her butt a playful squeeze. "But the next few hours will be devoted entirely to pleasure."

Chapter 11

The next morning a shiny black limousine glided to a stop in front of Dawn's apartment building. But it wasn't Leland's. This limo had been sent by Alice to bring Dawn and Natalie to Derek's penthouse apartment in Manhattan, where Alice now lived. A wedding dress designer was coming to discuss Alice's gown, so she'd invited her two maids of honor to help her with her aesthetic decisions. It was a project Dawn felt she had no business being involved with since she spent her life in either workout clothes or jeans.

Dawn quickly locked up her apartment and jogged down the steps, feeling a few twinges from Leland's promised pleasure of last night. He'd certainly kept his part of the bargain—twice—before they both fell into exhausted slumber. He'd awakened early, initiated another round of pure sensual delight, and then had gone to the office, where he said he needed to stay all day.

Maybe the wedding dress would be a good distraction from missing his hot, sexy presence like crazy. Except she knew she would have to confess her relationship with Leland to Alice and Natalie. Friends shared things like that, even when they weren't entirely sure they wanted to.

"Hey, Nat," Dawn said as she ducked through the car door that the driver held open.

Natalie looked as perfectly put together as always, her short blonde hair styled in smooth curves against her cheeks and an array of fine gold chains draped around her neck. A cream linen blouse, slim black trousers, and maroon suede stiletto-heeled booties completed her ensemble.

Dawn sighed as she looked down at her jeans and long-sleeved red T-shirt. "How do you always look so good?"

Natalie raised her elegant eyebrows. "It's my job. Your job is to be in top physical condition. If I attempted to do a single pull-up, I would fail miserably while you would make it look easy."

"Good point." Dawn hugged her friend. Natalie gave the impression of being cool and self-contained, yet she always made Dawn feel better about herself.

"Would you like a mimosa?" Natalie asked, pointing to the bottles of champagne and orange juice sitting in coolers in the limousine's console. "I know how you feel about fashion so you might need something to relax you."

"Are you having one?"

"Now that you're here, I will. I try never to drink alone." Natalie plucked a champagne flute from the rack, waited for the limo to round a corner, and poured some bubbly in the glass. "In fact, I may skip the juice."

"Same for me. You shouldn't ruin good champagne."

They touched their glasses together with a gentle clink. "To Alice's wedding dress. May she wear it in happiness," Natalie said before they drank in unison. "By the way, what's going on at the gym?" she asked. "Have you found your mysterious tech expert?"

Dawn choked on her champagne, even though Natalie wasn't asking about Leland directly. "Not yet," Dawn gasped. "But we're getting close, I think."

"'We'?"

"Leland Rockwell and I."

"You're blushing."

"I might as well tell you because you'll get it out of me anyway. I'm having sex with him. Great sex." *Incredible sex.*

Natalie smiled and squeezed Dawn's hand. "I'm so happy for you, sweetie. It hasn't triggered any problems for you?"

"Every now and then he does something that feels too aggressive, but the moment I start to shift away, he eases up."

"So he knows?"

Dawn shook her head, remembering her cowardice in the face of Leland's concern. "He pays attention so I don't need to tell him. Besides, I want to keep this uncomplicated."

Natalie gave a snort that somehow sounded ladylike when she did it. "Sex is rarely uncomplicated."

"Right now, it's perfect." Because it had been going on for a grand total of thirty-six hours. "Except that he works all the time."

"Pot and kettle there." Natalie took a sip of champagne.

"I get eight hours of sleep every night. Leland is lucky to get four, and we're talking about on the weekend."

"Alice says all those KRG partners are workaholics. Derek less so now, thanks to her good influence."

"You think that Leland has something to prove but it's more like he feels responsible to everyone in his life. He can't disappoint them by not taking on a project. I've tried to get him to let go of the gym issue but he won't."

"Because that would mean letting go of you."

An annoying spark of hope flared to life. "Do you really think that's the reason? He says it's because he can't walk away when something illegal is going on."

Natalie gave her a look. "Were you expecting him to admit—even to himself—that it's a personal, not a professional, commitment? You give the man too much credit this early in the game. He's having sex with you, so trust me, that's why he wants to stay involved." She took a sip of her champagne. "So what is happening with the whole gym problem?"

"Leland plugged into the gym's router last night and collected whatever data a tech genius needs to collect. He's going to analyze it on his high-powered computer at the office."

"And how did he get to this router?"

"I let him into Ramón's office." Natalie was giving her a narrow-eyed stare so she had to defend herself. "I have a key so it wasn't a break-in or anything. We told Tiffany—she's the night receptionist—that we were looking for Leland's lost phone. People give Ramón stuff they find and he often sticks it in his desk drawer and forgets about it."

Natalie drummed her fingernails on the leather seat. "I don't like you doing things that might get you in trouble with bad people."

"I'm not worried." Dawn shrugged. "If anyone asks, Tiffany will spout our cover story. She swallowed it whole." She decided not to mention the security camera in the hallway. "Besides, Leland feels the same way you do so I don't think I'll be involved in any more espionage."

"You listen to him?"

"When he's right." Dawn smiled as she remembered their early email exchange. "Which he claims he always is."

"If you're smiling at that bit of arrogance, you must love the man."

"Love?" The word startled Dawn even though Natalie was using it ironically. "No, just lust after."

Yet there was more to how she felt about Leland than amazing sex. She liked dueling with him verbally because it made her feel smart. She liked training him because he worked hard. She liked the way he listened to her opinions as though they mattered. She even liked his protectiveness. Maybe she loved the fact that he was perceptive enough to know that she had a problem but didn't insist on an explanation.

"Besides, he was just trying to get a rise out of me."

"Instead you got a rise out of him." Natalie's delivery was deadpan.

"Natalie!" Dawn giggled. Yup, hanging out with girlfriends was a good thing.

Once they were settled around the antique refectory table in Alice and Derek's spectacular kitchen, Alice served them eggs benedict topped with caviar before she poured them more champagne. "I'm so excited to have you help me with my gown," she said. "I know I want it to evoke my favorite Regency romances but I also want it to have a modern edge. You're going to figure out how to do that." She beamed.

"Well, some stretchy yoga pants would say 'twenty-first century,'" Dawn said. "And you'd be comfortable at the reception."

Alice laughed. "Okay, so maybe Natalie will help more than you will. Now eat."

The conversation devolved into ridiculous suggestions about how to give a wedding dress a contemporary feel until Natalie announced into a lull, "Dawn is sleeping with Leland."

Alice choked on her eggs and had to grab a glass of water to wash them down.

"Jeez, Nat, could you maybe wait for a natural lead-in?" Dawn said. "Or let me tell her myself?"

"Why?" Natalie showed no remorse. "It's significant news."

"When? How?" Alice croaked. "Wait, is this about the gym Wi-Fi problem? Oh my God!" She fell back in her chair, laughing. "History repeats itself."

"Just because you and Derek fell in love when you were working on that accounting fraud doesn't mean the same thing is happening with me and Leland. It's just sex."

Alice took a swig of her champagne and shook her head. "Wow! I don't think Derek knows or he would have told me."

"It's pretty recent . . . like Friday night," Dawn admitted. "Which is why Nat shouldn't make such a big deal about it."

"I didn't make a big deal of it," Natalie said. "I just told Alice what was going on between you and her fiancé's partner."

"Has it been okay?" Alice's voice was soft with concern. "I mean, despite being a computer nerd, Leland's a tall, well-muscled guy from all that swimming he does. He hasn't triggered any panic attacks?"

"He's figured out that sometimes I get uncomfortable and he lets me shift positions when that happens."

"So he doesn't know?" Alice asked.

"We aren't close like that." With a pang, Dawn realized how true that was.

Alice reached across the table to touch the back of Dawn's hand. "I'm so glad. It means you're healing."

"Or maybe the sex is just good enough to overcome all obstacles," Natalie theorized.

Dawn laughed. "Maybe." She sobered. "It's so strange. I trust him without knowing him."

"What do you mean?" Alice asked.

"Well, I know what's in his bio on the KRG website. Schools, degrees, awards, stuff like that. I know he was an only child and hated his school uniform. And that's about it."

It was a strange kind of trust. She trusted him not to set off a panic attack but she didn't trust him to want a relationship with her. She pulled herself up short. There *was* no relationship after a mere four days. Working so closely together on the gym's issue just made it feel that way.

A melodious but mechanical woman's voice interrupted them to say, "An authorized visitor is arriving on the elevator."

"Darn!" Alice dropped her napkin on the table and stood up. "That's the dress designer." She pointed at Dawn. "We'll get back to you and Leland later."

As she hustled out of the room, Natalie looked at Dawn. "Brace yourself. There's going to be a lot of lace and satin and tulle."

Dawn dropped her head into her hands with a groan. "Why does Alice want me here? I know nothing about this crap."

"Because you're her maid of honor and her friend."

She lifted her head. "So are you and this is more your kind of thing."

Natalie rose from her chair with fluid grace. "She wants to share her joy with us."

"When you put it that way . . ." Dawn pushed up from the table and squared her shoulders. "Although I'm not a hundred percent sure how debating puff sleeves versus cap sleeves shows how happy she is."

Natalie laughed as they followed Alice's voice to the dining room. An older woman propped up poster boards with drawings attached, while a young man draped swatches of fabric over the glossy wood table.

Alice's face glowed with pleasure, so Dawn pasted on a smile before she marched through the door.

Two hours later, the designer and her assistant had packed up their materials and departed, leaving three exhausted friends sprawled in the dining room chairs. They'd brought more champagne from the kitchen to relax after the intense decision-making.

"That is going to be one beautiful and unique gown," Natalie said, waving at the on-the-spot sketch the designer had presented Alice with.

"You'll look stunning in it," Dawn agreed.

Alice threw back the last gulp of champagne in her glass. "Only because you all chimed in when my brain started to fry." She tilted her empty glass at Dawn. "You're going to make sure my arms look slender and shapely in those puff sleeves."

"I love a challenge," Dawn said with a grin.

"Ouch!" Alice held out one of her arms to examine it. "Are they that bad?"

"No, but I figure it will make you work harder," Dawn said.

"You're so evil," Alice said, pouring herself more bubbly and pinning her gaze on Dawn. "Now we're going to get back to you and Leland."

Dawn sighed. Just when she'd thought the worst was over.

Instead of grilling her friend, Alice stared at her fizzing glass for a long moment before she said, "You mentioned that you didn't know much about him, so I've been thinking about what I know that I can share with you." She swallowed a sip of champagne. "Leland was raised by his mother—who died recently. He took it pretty hard because they were close. No father in the picture. I'm pretty sure they were never married to begin with."

Dawn felt a pang of sorrow for Leland's loss. She couldn't imagine losing her own mama, who was the sun around which their family orbited, even though Dawn's siblings were grown and scattered geographically. It would leave a black hole in her heart.

"His mother was from Puerto Rico and she worked more than one job to support them. She's where he learned his work ethic."

"I knew he had something to prove." Natalie looked very pleased with herself.

"So I guess the father is where he got the preppy looks? He always seems like he's slumming in his jeans and T-shirts," Dawn said, trying to reconcile the seemingly aristocratic southern gentleman with his surprising history.

"Evidently. He never talks about his father, so no one knows who he was." Alice shook her head. "Leland is so smart that he got full scholarships at every school he went to but there are always extra things a kid needs. His mom gave him whatever she could but I gather he always felt out of place. You know, he didn't have the latest cell phone or the high-end gaming computer or the right clothes."

"So that's why he never wears a suit." Dawn understood the statement Leland was making. "He's thumbing his nose at the people who made him feel inferior when he was young, showing them that he doesn't have to dress like them to be successful."

"You know him better than you think," Natalie observed.

She wasn't so sure about that. The truth was that his origins didn't change anything about their relationship. If anything, his past life made his present status all the more impressive. He was still a genius who'd risen to the top of his field through his own hard work. She was still a trainer at a local gym in Jersey.

She longed to know more about Leland, but asking Alice about him felt too much like stalking him on the internet. She also had the forlorn hope that Leland would come to care enough to share his story himself. So she redirected the conversation.

"Anyway, I kind of seduced him because the dark web problem at the gym is about to go away and I needed to satisfy my lust before he went back to his life in Manhattan."

Alice looked stunned. "So he's been to Cofferwood? And what is this about the dark web?"

"He came to Cofferwood because he had to in order to figure out what's going on at the gym," Dawn said. "Our cover story is that I'm training him. He signed up for the gym as Lee Wellmont, just so you don't blow his secret identity. Oh yeah, I forgot to mention that you recommended me to him as a personal trainer because you were friends with him in high school."

"It's amazing how many people I knew in high school that I didn't actually know in high school," Alice said, referring to a subterfuge from her work with Derek on the accounting fraud. "You are a miracle worker, though, Dawn. Derek and Tully worry about Leland because he virtually never leaves the office except to go up to the top floor of the office building to use the swimming pool. It's gotten worse since his mom died. They've even been discussing some kind of forced vacation except they figure he'll just work remotely."

"Hormones have a way of shutting down the brain," Natalie said. "Sounds like Dawn is exactly what the doctor ordered for your workaholic computer genius."

"Hey, I'm not some kind of cure," Dawn objected. But inside she preened because she had been able to tempt Leland away from work when no one else could. Well, she and a puzzle he wanted to solve.

"Whatever you are, Leland needs you." Alice held up her hand for a high five. "You go, girl! I'll bet he's a good client. All those muscles and stamina from swimming." She waggled her eyebrows.

"He knows how to go the distance," Dawn said without cracking a smile.

Alice giggled before her grin faded. "Now what about this dark web thing? It sounds sinister."

"We don't know anything for sure yet but we should soon. Leland took data off the gym's router last night to analyze at the office today."

"Dawn snuck him into Ramón's office to do it," Natalie said, disapproval clear in her tone.

"You need to be careful." Alice looked worried. "Bad things can happen even in little old Cofferwood. I learned that the hard way."

"Bad things can happen anywhere and at any time," Dawn said in a flat tone. She'd learned that walking across a picturesque college campus on a sunny fall afternoon.

Natalie gave her shoulder a comforting squeeze. "True, but you don't need to go looking for them."

"What exactly is a dark web?" Alice asked.

Dawn explained to the best of her ability. "So Leland is trying to figure out why someone would use the gym's router and the customers' cell phones as a node. It's really weird."

"If anyone can find the answer, it's Leland," Alice said.

"To ease both of your minds, he's planning to turn the information over to the FBI as soon as he knows what's going on," Dawn said. Then he would have no reason to come to Cofferwood any longer. Except to see her, and how long would that last?

Now that she knew about Leland's past, she tried to decide if it changed anything between them, but she didn't see how. He still lived in the rarefied world that his wealth and power created around him. Alice sometimes talked about how different her life was now that she had moved in with Derek. Dawn couldn't wrap her mind around the level of money required just to maintain the two-floor Manhattan penthouse her friend lived in with its private security and staff. Fashion designers would even make house calls on a Sunday because Derek paid them to as a convenience for Alice's working friends. Leland's life would be similar . . . except for the dress designer.

Then there was Leland's crazy idea that she should come into the city to train him. She was pretty sure that had been a spur-of-the-moment request on his part. He'd looked surprised as he said it, and he hadn't worked out all the logistics, which was not like Leland. It had probably just been his way of seeing if they would act on the attraction flaring between them. Since they had, he didn't need that ploy anymore.

In fact, she wasn't sure she would be able to train him in a professional way. Touching him without sexual intent had been hard enough before they'd had sex. Now she figured they'd both get so aroused after five minutes, they'd end up in a broom closet at whatever gym Leland patronized in Manhattan. No, he undoubtedly had a home gym. Her imagination took flight as she considered possible alternative uses for exercise equipment.

"Hey, Dawn! You still here?" Alice snapped her fingers in the air.

"Sorry! I was thinking about the dark web."

"You look more like you were thinking about Leland naked," Natalie said.

"Busted." Dawn grinned as her cheeks flushed.

"I have an idea," Alice said. "I'm going to arrange for you to go see Leland at his office. Maybe you can drag him away from his computer screens early."

"I don't think that's such a good plan." Dawn had no confidence in the reception she would get if she interrupted Leland at work. "He'd have a right to be pissed off."

"It's for his own good. Seriously, he needs to take one day a week off from work."

Dawn thought of how drawn he had looked yesterday before she'd insisted that he sleep a couple of hours. He was working himself into collapse. "Would you go with me?"

"Heck, no!" Alice said. "I want you to use whatever wiles it takes to tempt him and I don't want to be there to see what those wiles are. They will have to be extreme to distract Leland from his computers."

Dawn turned to Natalie, their older, wiser friend. "Is this a bad idea?"

Nat took a sip of champagne before saying, "The worst he can do is ask you to leave. It seems like he's too much of a southern gentleman to behave rudely toward you even if he's angry."

"I'd rather know if he's angry." Dawn twisted her champagne flute between her fingers. *Would he be?* "Will there be other people there?"

Alice shrugged. "Probably a few. When a project has to be finished on time, everyone makes sure that happens. That's why KRG's reputation is so impressive. But Leland has his own office and his own computer room. They call it Mission Control because there are so many screens in it."

Dawn remembered how sexy it had been to watch Leland concentrating on the code whipping across the screen, and she made her decision. "Okay, but I need to borrow a nice blouse from you. I'm not going to Leland's office in this T-shirt." She waved at her casual top.

"Yes!" Alice slapped the top of the table in approval. "We'll go raid my closet." She looked at Natalie. "This begins to look like a pattern, which means you're next."

"Next?" Natalie raised an eyebrow.

"There are three partners at KRG. Two of them are spoken for." She pointed at Dawn and herself. "That leaves you and Tully."

Natalie laughed. "I don't think real life works that way."

Chapter 12

Leland stared at the computer monitor. "Got you! Now what are you?" He clicked on the dark web address he'd spent the past hour carefully tracking within the torrents of traffic in the deep web node. He believed it was what they were looking for, because more traffic went there than to any other destination.

When the website came up, he rocked back in his chair as shock vibrated through him. He didn't know what he'd expected, but it wasn't a professional-quality photograph of a man dressed in quasi-military camouflage pointing a handgun directly at the viewer.

"Tactical Arms," the header read.

> A vast selection of military-grade guns available now. Handguns, rifles, shotguns, semiautomatics, automatics, and multi-role weapons. Other weapons upon request. All untraceable.

Leland clicked on the button that said "Enter Site Here."

A menu of destruction popped up before his eyes—the website had not exaggerated in its claim to having a vast array of guns. The photos were clear and the guns gleamed with deadly craftsmanship. He clicked on a few categories and was stunned by the quantities the seller was offering. A small army could be outfitted from this one website.

When he navigated to the payment page, he was not surprised to find that prices were calculated in cryptocurrency. There was also a cash-on-delivery option, which he suspected was popular with drug dealers. He just wouldn't want to be the deliveryman.

The whole presentation was impressive and appeared to be well established. The question was whether the website was a scam. The fact that it seemed to be accessed through the gym's router made him wonder. Because it was a stretch to think someone at the gym was involved in arms dealing.

He could maybe wrap his mind around Ramón fixing fights or Vicky selling stolen credit card information or even Chad running an illegal sports-betting service, but this disturbing arsenal seemed out of their league. It was not meant for collectors or hobbyists. It was aimed at buyers who had a desire or need to kill people. Many people.

He needed to get Tully involved with this. He was in over his head and, even worse, Dawn was right there with him. Why the hell had he allowed her to come with him to Ramón's office? Because he'd expected this to be some minor fraud.

You'd think he would have learned a lesson after Derek and Alice's dangerous encounter with a crazy hacker. Even white-collar crime could turn deadly. He should have kept Dawn far, far away from this project.

Shoving his chair back, he stalked out of the room and down the hallway toward Tully's office. His partner probably wasn't there, but Leland needed to channel his tension into movement. Sure enough, the big corner room was empty and showed no signs of its owner just strolling away from his desk momentarily.

Leland ran his fingers through his hair in frustration. He didn't want to tell Dawn anything until he figured out how to proceed. Time for a swim to straighten out his thinking.

He had just hit the perfect rhythm in his stroke, freeing his mind to focus on the Tactical Arms problem, when he caught a glimpse of someone standing beside the pool as he turned his head to breathe. Surprise and irritation jerked him out of his hard-won zone.

On Sundays no one else ever used the pool so he hadn't bothered to lock the elevator door in privacy mode. Since KRG had paid for installation of the pool, the partners had the right to control access to it. Leland didn't often take advantage of that perk because his powers of concentration were substantial. He just hadn't been prepared for the possibility of company today.

Ignoring the intruder, he hit the wall and executed a flip turn, staying underwater as long as his breath held out before surfacing to start his stroke again. He'd already decided that the first thing he'd do when he finished his swim was to call Tully, even though it was a Sunday. Criminals didn't respect weekends, and it was likely that the website would change its address in the near future. That was how the dark web worked to ensure anonymity and to avoid law enforcement. The only way he'd be able to find Tactical Arms again would be to pose as a major gun buyer and try to find it through boards where the dark website links were listed in plain text through anonymous postings. That would be a bear of a search.

He was deep in thought as he approached the pool wall, so he didn't see the bare feet dangling in the water until he was about to touch them.

He slammed his hand against the wall beside the feet and jerked his head up out of the water. "What the h—?" It was a woman with her jeans rolled up to the knees. "Dawn?!"

"Yup. Natalie and I were helping Alice design her wedding gown at her apartment." She looked a little uncertain before she smiled. "I figured I was in the neighborhood so I'd stop by." She flicked a small splash of water with her toe, hitting him in the face and making him sputter.

The mischief in her smile made him react in a way that proved he had lost his mind. He reached up to where she had her hands braced on the side of the pool, grabbed her wrists, and tipped her into the pool, catching her against his chest as she fell.

She shrieked and slammed her hands against the surface of the water to send a deluge into his face this time. He didn't care because his arms were filled with her sweet, tempting body. Her hard nipples were pressed against his bare chest with nothing but wet silk and lace between them.

"You are going to pay for this, buster." But she wound her arms around his neck and pulled herself closer. "In fact, you may have to pay for this blouse because I borrowed it from Alice and I'm pretty sure it's one of those dry-clean-only garments."

"It was worth every penny to see the expression on your face when you started to fall."

She gave him a sideways smile. "I didn't think a proper southern gentleman would do such a thing. Although it's better than throwing me out."

Something twisted in his chest. "Is that what you thought I would do?"

"Honestly, I wasn't sure. You told me you had a lot of work to get through." She stroked her palm over his shoulder, sending a thrill of sensation across his skin. "I'm glad you don't mind that I'm here."

He was still stunned by the idea that she'd thought he wouldn't want her to be there. What did that say about him? Had he really become that kind of person? He tightened his arms around her. "Your appearance here is the best thing that's happened to me all day. Well, except for this morning before I left your bed."

He skimmed down to grab the inviting curves of her denim-covered butt. When she made a delicious little mewing noise and rocked her pelvis, he shifted his hands lower to grip her legs, opening them and lifting her so that his erection pushed at the juncture of her thighs. All he could think of was how it would feel to ease himself inside her as the water lapped around them.

"Leland, what if someone else comes to swim?" she said, but she wrapped her legs around his waist.

"They won't, but if you're worried, I can lock the elevator door so no one else has access. However, you have to promise me you'll stay here while I do it."

"I was thinking I might take off these wet clothes."

He hesitated, half wanting to peel them off her himself. Then he imagined her floating naked in the water with her hair swirling around her like a mermaid when he returned. "That's an offer I can agree to."

He vaulted out of the pool, water streaming off him as he strode to the elevator door. He punched in the lockout code at lightning speed before turning to head back to the pool, anticipation hardening his cock so it tented his swim trunks. Without thinking, he stopped and shucked the trunks off, tossing them aside to land with a wet splat before he continued.

"You read my mind. That's exactly how I wanted to see you," he said as he got to the edge of the pool. Dawn floated on her back, her bare body wet and glistening, her hair swirling around her head and shoulders.

Her gaze drifted down his torso to stop at his groin and she smiled. "And you read mine. We're psychic."

"No, we're horny." He did a shallow racing dive and came up beside her.

"That too."

She started to stand but he slid his hands under her back and butt to keep her floating. "Wait. I want to look at you."

"You're doing more than looking so I won't complain." She wiggled her bottom against his hand. He curled his fingers into the cushion of her flesh to hold her still.

"You're the world's sexiest mermaid," he said, letting his eyes rove over the tight buds of her nipples, the sweep of wet satin skin across her taut belly, and the beckoning triangle of dark hair between her thighs. He wanted to touch her everywhere, to suck at her breasts, to plunge his tongue into her mouth and then between her legs, to bury himself deep inside her.

"Okay, enough with the looking," she said, squirming again. "You're making me feel weird."

"I can't decide what to touch first."

"Let me help you with that." She flipped in his arms and wrapped her hand around his cock, sending a jolt of sensation through his body. At the same time, he realized that her shift in position put his hand under one of her breasts, so he found the nipple and squeezed lightly.

"Yes-s-s-s!" Dawn arched into his hand while she gave his cock a slow stroke, the water allowing her fingers to glide smoothly. "Decision made."

His cock jerked as she hit the base, pleasure spreading upward to the tip.

A realization banged into his brain. His jeans were in the locker room. "I need to get a condom."

Her lips curved into a seductive smile. "If you don't have one, we can do other things to make each other happy."

"I want to move with you in the water," he said, dropping his voice to a purr. "It's very . . . erotic."

"Well, I didn't expect to see you this afternoon, so I didn't bring one." She released his cock and twisted away so she could flip herself upright. She locked her dark eyes with his. "I'm on the pill and I have a clean bill of health."

His lungs stopped functioning for a moment as he absorbed her message. The generosity of it walloped him in the gut, but he never had unprotected sex. His mother had drummed that into him from before he'd even considered girls as something other than alien beings. Because his mother had gotten pregnant from just one bout of careless-ness, born of infatuation—not love, she insisted—for a man who told her she could trust him.

She never called it a mistake, because it had given her Leland and he knew she loved him fiercely. But he also knew that his arrival had sent her life into a downward spiral, making her a single parent at age eighteen, repudiated by her own rigid parents and by Leland's father and his family. Not that he would ever do that to a child he fathered, but wearing a condom seemed a small precaution to take to avoid such life-changing consequences. So he carried one with him always.

Still her breathtaking offer deserved an acknowledgment.

"I'm honored that you would trust me that way," he said, pulling her back against him and brushing his lips against hers. "But I just have to get to my jeans in the locker room. Can you wait that long?"

She had lost her mind. She never had sex without a condom. It was a hard-and-fast rule for her for all kinds of reasons. But Leland, with his lean, muscled body and his brilliant perceptiveness, had destroyed her common sense.

It was the ticking clock of their relationship that drove her to desperation. She might never have another chance to make love with Leland in a private pool contained in a glass box perched high above the streets of Manhattan. Who turned down that opportunity for lack of a latex sheath?

So why didn't she feel relieved when he told her he had a condom close by? Because it felt like her trust had been thrown back in her face. He didn't reciprocate it.

"Sure," she croaked. "I'll be here."

He searched her face before he said, "I'll be back in two minutes flat."

He leaped out of the pool as though gravity didn't exist, rivulets of water glistening in the sun as they rolled down his muscles.

His beauty struck her like a dagger because she wanted him so badly. The hunger for him twisted in her gut.

She should be glad he had a condom. Glad that he wanted to protect her. That was what good, responsible men did.

Yet once she'd made the decision to trust him, she'd wanted him to be as irresponsible as she was. As though it would prove how much he desired her.

When he strode out of the locker room, she shoved away her irrational feelings and let the sight of his sculpted shoulders, ripped abs, long, powerful legs, and erect cock fan her arousal to full flame again.

He arced into the pool, swimming to her underwater. He wrapped his hands around her thighs and kissed her right at the juncture of her legs, the unexpected touch sending a sparkle of sensation fountaining up through her.

He surfaced, blowing a spout of water into the air. "I wish I had gills so I could do more than just kiss you there."

"A merman? I like you better as a human."

"Right now I feel human in the finest of ways, darlin'," he said with a hot smile.

Then he locked her against his body so his skin warmed her front with the water around her back cool by contrast. Her nipples were so tight that the pressure against his chest sent arousal streaking down between her legs. His mouth was hot against hers as he gave her a devouring kiss, turning the ache between her legs into a raving need.

She slid her hand down between them to stroke the hard, smooth length of his cock, and he tore his mouth away from hers, his head falling back as he groaned, the sound loud enough to echo off the glass walls.

Another stroke and he groaned again, louder, while his fingers dug into her waist. And then he tilted his head down to look at her, his eyes blazing with hunger. "I want you now. Is it too soon?"

Her answer was to hold out her hand. He tore the envelope open with his teeth and handed her the condom. "I've never tried to do this in water," she said. "Maybe you could float on your back?"

"You're a problem solver," he said, tipping back to let the water lift his hips.

She took her time rolling the tight latex over his erection, savoring his moans. As soon as she hit the base of his cock, he flipped upright and hooked his hand under one of her thighs, lifting her leg to rest against his hip.

"Lean back and use the water's buoyancy. I've got you," he said, bringing her other leg to his waist as she allowed herself to tilt backward. His cock rubbed against her clit and she arched as pleasure shot through her. "Yes," he said. "Like that. I'll support you."

His arms were around her, easing her down until she floated in the water. He shifted so he gripped her upper arms, and she reached down again to position the head of his cock.

He drove inside her in one long, fluid thrust.

The feel of him stretching and filling and moving within her ripped a spasm of pleasure from her body so that she arched again without thought of being in the water. But he kept her head above the wavelets they'd created, grinding his hips against her so that he hit her clit.

"Leland! More!" She fought off the orgasm.

He pulled back and then plunged into her again. The water stroked her sensitized skin, adding gentler sensation to the intensity of Leland's cock impaling her. He towered over her, his face a mask of pure lust, yet she felt no fear because only the water and his hands cradled her body.

"This is perfect," she whispered.

"You are perfect." He withdrew and thrust again.

This time she couldn't stop it. Her orgasm crashed through her entire body in a wave, her muscles contracting all the way down to her toes so that they curled into his butt. "Leland!" she shouted at the ceiling, her voice bouncing off the glass. Pleasure flooded her and she added to it by rolling her hips against him.

"Oh, Dawn, yes!" he yelled as his climax hit.

They convulsed together, their groans intertwined and echoing, the motion of one setting off an answering, amplifying response in the other. Until finally the last tiny ripple shivered through Dawn's body, leaving her limp and drifting on the water. Leland softened inside her, his hands still cupping her shoulders while his head was bowed. She could see the rise and fall of his chest as he sucked in breath to replenish the oxygen he'd expended.

"I've never . . ." He shook his head. "That was . . ."

She gave a ghost of a laugh at his inability to describe the experience. "Yup. I agree."

He lifted his head enough to meet her eyes. "That was beyond the reach of mere words."

His grip tightened on her shoulders as he pulled her up and against him. His cock slipped out of her, sending one more tiny shudder of sensation through her. He cocooned her in his arms, resting his cheek on top of her head. His heart beat against her breast, still rapid from his exertions.

She wanted to stay there in his embrace, despite the goose bumps rising on her skin as it cooled in the water.

But he ran his hands down to twine his fingers with hers and stepped back, pressing a quick kiss on her lips. "You're getting cold. Let's find you a towel."

She was grateful for the buoyancy of the water because her knees were wobbly. Leland sent her up the ladder first, his hands cupping her butt to give her a boost out of the pool. He demonstrated the upper-body strength he'd developed from his years of swimming by bracing his hands on the side of the pool and rocketing upward to land on his feet without any need for a ladder.

"Show-off," she said. But he looked like a sea god with water sluicing down the ridges and indentations of his muscles as he straightened.

"I'm sure you could do the same." He grinned. "But I'm glad you didn't because I enjoyed copping a feel."

"Truth be told, my muscles are feeling a bit depleted after that orgasm."

He bent to kiss her shoulder and spoke against her skin so his lips grazed it with each word. "That's music to my ears."

Leading her to a chaise longue, he said, "Sit and I'll grab the towels."

"I like the view," she called as he walked away, his butt cheeks shifting with each stride.

"Are you ogling me?"

"Oh, yeah."

He chuckled—a warm, rich sound of amusement. Even more, it sounded relaxed, almost carefree. That wasn't a mood she associated with Leland.

He returned with a thick white towel wrapped around his waist and an armful of extras. Dropping the pile on the adjacent chaise longue, he shook out the oversize terry cloth and wrapped it snugly around Dawn's upper body. "Lean back," he commanded before he tucked another towel around her legs as she lay on the lounge.

"May I dry your hair?" he asked, a third towel already in his hands.

"Aren't you cold?"

"Not with you around." He lifted the towel in a questioning gesture.

She wasn't sure how she felt about the hair-drying thing. She wasn't used to being touched that way by a man. But this was Leland. "Sure," she said.

He walked behind her and gently peeled her hair away from where it clung wetly to her shoulders and neck so he could drape it over the back of the lounge. Then he began to wrap the towel around a small section at a time, soaking up the water before moving to the next tress.

The gentle tug and shift of his movements sent tingles of delight dancing over her scalp. She gave a little moan of pleasure.

The tugging stopped. "Did I pull too hard?"

"No, it feels so good. Almost as good as pool sex."

The chuckle sounded again, sending a different kind of tingle through her. *She* had made him sound this way. "I might be insulted," he said. "Except I feel too good myself."

He continued with his drying and she hummed her approval. "I may have to dive back in just to get my hair wet again."

"Go ahead. I like doing this for you."

It was a strange thing for a man to offer, and she wondered what had made him think of it. But she wasn't going to risk stopping him by asking.

When he finished, he stretched out on the lounge chair beside her, reaching across the space between them to take her hand, resting it on his bare chest and idly playing with her fingers.

The golden autumn sunlight poured down through the glass roof. It bathed Leland's skin and hair in a soft glow so that she felt as though he radiated warmth. He closed his eyes, his face without his glasses looking vulnerable and at peace. A slight smile curled his lips so that he looked like a cat who had just lapped up a bowl of cream.

His touch on her fingers sent little zings of heat through her so she had to kick off the towel tucked over her shins and feet.

For long, blissful minutes, they lay side by side in silence, although she could swear that their bodies exuded a low hum of satisfaction that was nearly audible.

"I want to tell you what happened to me," she said, surprising herself. But she needed him to know the gift he had given her.

His fingers tightened around hers and he sat up, swinging his legs off the chaise longue to set them on the cement floor so he was at right angles to her. "You don't need to do that."

She rolled her head to look at him. The angles of his face were taut, as though he was bracing himself, but his eyes were soft with concern. "Yes, I do. You've changed something in me in a good way. You should understand how important that is."

He sandwiched her hand between his palms and took a deep breath. "Okay. I'm ready."

"I was a sophomore at Glenn State University. First semester." She used her free hand to clutch the towel tighter around her shoulders. "It was late on a Saturday afternoon in the fall but I'd been in the library all day because I had a paper due on Monday." She tossed a wry grimace at him. "I was a real nerd. Studied all the time. Had to make dean's list every semester."

"That doesn't surprise me. You give every job your best."

Her heart began to pound as she pushed herself to describe what occurred next. "I had left my cell phone in my room and decided to go get it before I met some friends for dinner. So I packed up my stuff and left the library to walk across campus to my dorm." She closed her eyes, remembering how blue the sky was; how the trees were scarlet, gold, and russet; how crisp and clear the air smelled as she drew it into her lungs after being shut up in the stuffy library. She even remembered thinking how lucky she was to be in this beautiful place. Which made everything worse. "There'd been a football game. I think we won but it doesn't matter. As I was walking past a building that was under construction, three guys were walking toward me, laughing loudly, yelling cheers for the football team, and chugging from water bottles that it turned out held straight vodka. They asked me if I wanted a drink but I said, 'No, thank you.' For some reason, that made them angry. I tried to keep walking but they surrounded me and started yelling insults at me. I pushed by one of them and kept going."

Terror seeped into her gut, twisting her stomach, as she relived the moment when one of the men had shouted, "Get that stuck-up bitch. We'll teach her a lesson." Then the rough seizure, an arm snaked around

161

her waist and lifting her nearly off her feet while a hand slammed over her nose and mouth, making her lips bleed where her teeth cut into them.

"But one of them grabbed me. He put his hand over my mouth so I couldn't scream. I bit him." She'd sunk her teeth into the fleshy pad at the base of his thumb, kicked at him with her sneakers, and tried to twist out of his grasp. But back then she didn't know how to use leverage against a man so much bigger than herself. Now she did. "He was too drunk to care. He just squeezed harder against my nose and mouth."

She'd thought she was going to suffocate. Now she dragged in a ragged breath.

"Dawn, you don't have to tell me any more," Leland said. She felt him ease his hold on her hand. She'd just noticed how tight it was.

"You should know this about me. It's made me who I am now," she said. If anything was going to move forward between them, it was important for him to understand fully the event that had damaged her.

"Nothing will change how I feel about you."

"We'll see." She locked her gaze on the sparkling wavelets in the pool. "Anyway, they dragged me behind a dumpster at the construction site. I tried to fight them but there were three of them." Her vision started to gray out as she remembered the feeling of being utterly helpless. She had vowed never to feel that way again.

"Shit!" Leland hissed. His grasp had gone tight again. It anchored her and somehow pulled her out of the threatening panic attack.

"They decided that they wanted me naked. Since they were drunk, it took them a while to get all my clothes off. Jeans don't rip easily." She coughed as the smell of their vodka-laden breath seemed to fill her nostrils again. "That's what saved me, because a campus security guard heard all the noise they were making as they yelled directions at each other. So the first one had just gotten on top of me when the guard found us."

She panted a couple of times to stave off the wave of nausea. She'd fought them with everything she had in her, but one had held her arms while the other wrenched her ankles apart so that his buddy could settle between her open thighs. The nurse who'd treated her afterward had picked pieces of gravel and even a small nail out of her back from where she'd been pushed into the ground by his stifling weight. Thank God, he'd decided to grope her breasts before he raped her. The guard had pulled him off her just in time.

"Dawn!" Leland dropped his forehead onto their clasped hands. "I can't imagine . . ." His voice held so much anguish that she almost wished she hadn't started this.

"It's okay." She forced her fingers open from her convulsive grip on the towel to reach over and stroke his hair. "You've helped me heal."

He lifted his head enough to look at her. "I hate that I made you . . . feel that way again when we were together."

"Do *not* take that on yourself. I didn't tell you. I *couldn't* tell you. Not right away."

"I understand that one hundred percent, but I . . ." She could hear the pain she was causing him.

"No guilt! You've been good for me." She waved toward the pool. "That was good for me."

He nodded although she could see that he was still beating himself up. "I hope to God they went to jail."

This part was almost as hard as the attack. "No. They got suspended for the rest of the semester."

"What the hell?! They attacked you! They tried to . . ." He looked away, as though he couldn't finish the thought.

"For obvious reasons, the university administration didn't want it made public. They pressured me not to file charges. They had the nerve to say that since I wasn't actually raped, it wasn't that bad." Tears burned in her eyes. Angry tears because the administrators should have protected her, not her scumbag attackers. Sad tears because she had been so young and naive. "I didn't want to tell my parents because I knew they'd go ballistic. I thought I wanted to stay at the university so I figured I should go along with the plan. I kept my mouth shut and tried to pretend it hadn't happened."

Leland let out a string of curses.

"Yeah, that was stupid on my part. They offered me counseling but I believed them when they said without the actual rape, it wasn't so terrible. So I didn't go."

Leland groaned. "And I'm guessing that you didn't tell your parents."

"I didn't want to upset them. My father would have . . ." She shrugged. "I thought I was okay."

"But you weren't."

"Not even close. I couldn't walk anywhere unless I had someone with me. My roommates got pretty sick of me always tagging along with them. So I missed classes. I couldn't go to the library. My grades began to deteriorate. Finally, I gave up and withdrew. I think the administrators heaved a sigh of relief." She shook her head to stop the memories. "I moved back here and got a job at the gym."

"And you became an expert at self-defense because that's how strong you are. If I'd known . . ." He shook his head before he lifted her hand to his lips and brushed on a kiss so light and tender it made her want to cry. "Thank you for your courage in sharing this with me. I'm humbled."

"You deserved to know."

"May I hug you?"

Her gut twisted that he would feel he had to ask her permission. She scrambled off the lounge, her towel falling away, and curled herself onto his lap.

He kissed the top of her head and said her name over and over again as he held her ever so gently. Then he reached down to snag her towel and drape it over her shoulders and back. That broke her and she felt hot, salty tears roll down her cheeks.

"I'd tell you not to cry but I think you deserve the privilege," he said, his arms cocooning her. "Cry as long as you need to."

"I hate it. It makes me feel weak."

His splayed fingers pressed against her back. "A weak woman wouldn't have turned a terrible experience into a mission to help other women be strong."

She lifted her head and swiped at the tear streaks. "It was Ramón who got me into self-defense. He gave me the gym space to teach my classes for free. Then he sponsored me for certification as a personal trainer." She locked her gaze with Leland's. "He pulled me out of my paranoia and allowed me to feel safe enough to go out in the world again. That's why I can't believe he's doing something illegal at the gym. I can't reconcile the compassion with the criminal."

He let out a long breath. "I'm afraid I have bad news about that. But maybe now is not the time to discuss it."

"I can handle it. Tell me." She sat up straight on his lap.

"You can handle anything but you might not want to hear this." He tightened his arms around her the tiniest bit before he said, "I found what I think is the reason for the dark web traffic at the gym."

Chapter 13

Dawn pulled her towel tighter around her shoulders. She could tell by his expression that she needed to brace herself. "What is it?"

"A large, professional-looking website selling weapons of various descriptions, mostly guns. All untraceable, as they boast." His lips were a grim line.

"Guns?! Who at the gym would do that?" She shook her head but the sight of Ramón's gun case flashed through her mind. "I can't imagine anyone there being an arms dealer at that level."

"Then why would they route traffic through the gym's deep web node? There must be a connection." His face was tight with resolution. "You have to step away from this. It's too damned dangerous. Especially after what you've been through."

She wasn't sure if she liked being told what to do. However, she drummed into her self-defense classes that a gun changed the whole equation. "Are *you* stepping away?"

"I'm getting Tully involved. He's former FBI. He knows how to deal with this kind of situation and he can bring in the right people."

"You didn't answer the question." She laid her palm against his cheek. "I don't want your body that I've worked so hard on training to end up riddled with bullets." She'd been trying to joke but an image of him bleeding as he lay on the gym floor seared itself into her brain.

"I have a bulletproof vest. Tully insists." His expression gentled. "I have training in self-defense, kidnap avoidance, and a bunch of other things that people don't realize I need." He made a wry face. "Hell, I didn't realize I needed them until Tully pointed out that founding partners in a highly visible international firm are targets, especially when they're traveling. So I'm used to some level of threat."

Natalie's warning about Leland's success making him different from a normal person echoed through Dawn's mind. No one else she knew—except Leland's other partners—needed to be adept at kidnap avoidance. Certainly, no one owned their own personal bulletproof vest. That was the dark side of rising to the top of a prominent profession, something she hadn't had even the faintest clue about. His revelation underlined the vast gulf between their lifestyles in a way that made any hope she'd had of a real relationship seem distant. The incredible sense of intimacy she'd felt when she'd told him her story began to waver.

"I like Tully more and more all the time." She wiggled off his lap and onto her lounge, as though that would help distance her feelings for him too. "I think arms dealers are even worse than kidnappers. Kidnappers want to keep you alive. Arms dealers not so much. Not to mention that they probably know how to use what they sell. And they have a lot of inventory to choose from."

"I don't intend to get shot," he said. "It would prevent me from making love to you in the pool again. And that would be a terrible thing."

A strange nostalgia jabbed at her chest. She hoped they would return to the pool but she wasn't convinced it would happen. "I assume there's no harm in me looking at the website. I might spot something that ties it to the gym," she said.

"I was going to suggest that, but only if you feel up to it." Leland scanned her face, his jaw tight with concern.

"Do you really think I'm going to have a problem looking at a website, even one with guns?" But his hesitation touched her.

It took him a moment but he shook his head. "I'm the one who's still processing your experience."

She smoothed a lock of his hair back from his forehead. "It was a lot to have dumped on you. I'm sorry."

"I'm glad you told me but I just want to . . ." He made a slashing gesture of frustration. "Those men should have been punished far more severely."

"That can't be changed. My goal is to forget them so completely that they don't exist for me."

He nodded somberly before he stood up, drawing her with him. "Let's get dressed and catch some present-day bad guys."

"One problem," she said. "My clothes are soaking wet, thanks to you yanking me into the pool."

Guilt threw a shadow over his face. "I don't know what got into me. I apologize for that."

"Hey, I'm kidding. It's no big deal. I just don't know what I'm going to wear."

"How about a bathrobe while I call my concierge service to pick you up some dry clothes? They have robes in the locker room here."

"Your concierge service? What does that mean?"

"When I need something, they get it. Simple as that."

Dawn shook her head in wonder. "You truly don't live in the real world."

"I am very familiar with the real world." His face and tone were rough-edged.

"Sorry!" She held up her hand, remembering Alice's revelations about his upbringing and his mother's recent death. "I don't know you well enough to say that."

"I forget that it sounds impressive to have a concierge when really it just allows me to work without interruption." He started toward the hallway where the elevator had delivered her. "Let's get you into the bathrobe while I make the call."

In an astonishingly short time, the concierge service had delivered three pairs of designer jeans, three blouses in various styles, and three pairs of shoes, all far more stylish and expensive than anything she owned. Leland stood outside the locker room, talking on his cell phone about something incomprehensibly techie, while she pulled on a pair of jeans and chose a rose-colored blouse that made her sigh at the drape of the exquisite silk. She'd balked at having Leland order her lingerie and used the time before the delivery to blow-dry her bra and panties. Since Leland had already dried her hair, she just used one of the locker room combs to smooth it out.

Then she picked up one of the shoeboxes and gasped at the label. Christian Louboutin. She opened it to find a pair of block-heeled black ankle boots accented with a red sole. She ran a finger over the butter-soft leather with a longing that she hadn't known she could feel about a pair of shoes. She closed the box and checked out the next one. Saint Laurent. Inside were black-and-silver-striped ankle boots with narrow tapered heels. Utterly gorgeous. The third box claimed to be sneakers but the label said Balenciaga. She didn't know they even *made* sneakers. She opened the top to find what looked like normal running shoes, albeit in an ultra-stylish combination of taupe, gray, and white with the designer's name embroidered along the sides.

She tried to gauge which of the shoes was the least expensive because once she wore them, there was no taking them back. She had tried on her own boots, but they squished out water with every step she took, so she had to pick one of these exorbitantly expensive offerings.

She shrugged and chose the ones she would most like to wear again: the Louboutins. They didn't shout their origin like the others. Besides, the leather was delicious.

"Did you find something that fits?" Leland called through the door.

"Yes, I'm coming." She packed all the extra clothing back into the bags and carried them out with her. "What do you want to do with these?"

"They're for you," he said. "Keep them."

"Look, you may not realize it but this stuff is all designer. It's bad enough that I have to keep this one outfit because I'm wearing it. You can return the rest of it." She held up the bags.

He hesitated a moment before he took them out of her hands. "We won't argue about the clothes. It's more important for you to take a look at the website."

The elevator whisked them downward to stop at a floor that required Leland to key in a code before the doors would open.

"This is the executive level of KRG," he explained. "If you don't have the code, you have to go through multiple guardians of the gates to be escorted up here. Unless you're staff, of course. They always have full access."

The doors opened onto a sleek, contemporary seating area done in shades of blue and taupe. The wood-and-chrome reception desk was unmanned whereas the one on the floor she had originally been sent to by Alice's arrangements was attended by a security guard. He had directed her up to the pool enclosure on the roof.

Leland led her across the thick blue carpeting and down a hallway lined with glass-walled offices until he turned into a windowless interior space. What it lacked in windows, it made up for in computer equipment, all clearly cutting edge, with slim, curved monitors set on utilitarian gray built-in desktops. Giant screens hung on all the walls while high-end gray-and-chrome ergonomic chairs stood scattered in front of the various workstations.

"Is this your office?"

He set the shopping bags down on the floor and gave a short laugh. "Define 'office.' This is where I spend most of my working time. I have an official and fairly useless office in one of the building's corners because partners' offices are required to look impressive."

"This is a lot more impressive than a view of some skyscrapers. It looks like something out of that old movie *WarGames*."

Leland's eyes lit up. "You know *WarGames*? It was one of my favorites as a kid. I bought a used DVD of it and watched it until the disc wore out."

She was fascinated by this unexpected glimpse into the young Leland. "So you were into computers from a young age?"

The excitement drained from his face. "You might say that a computer was my best friend."

She wanted to bring the light back. "My oldest brother loved that movie. Every time he'd see me doing my homework, he'd say, 'Learn, goddamn it!' And then Mama would yell at him for cursing."

She winced. The mention of her mother had just slipped out. She would have given anything to take it back.

Leland did smile, but with such an effort that she ached for him. "Of course, I completely missed the overarching message of the movie. I was only interested in the computer teaching itself. I tried to write programs that would do that, which is what eventually brought me here." He swept his hand around the room, clearly wanting to move on. "My partners call it Mission Control."

"Yeah, I can see why. Does anyone else work in here during the week?"

"Any staff member assigned to a project under my supervision is welcome. Some like it here. Some prefer to work alone because they can concentrate better." He rolled an extra chair over to what was clearly the central workstation since it had the biggest monitors arrayed around it. "Let's take a look at Tactical Arms."

Dawn sat in the chair he held. Leland slid onto the chair beside her in a way that showed he'd done it so many times it had become second nature to him, requiring no conscious thought. He woke up the screens in front of them with a sweep of his finger over a large, freestanding touch pad. She watched in fascination as his long fingers seemed to dance over the touch pad's surface, reminding her of how skillfully he touched her body. As a frisson of heat surged through her, she considered how much demand there might be for a cross-training course that used a computer to train men's hands for other, more intimate purposes. She figured wives would be a good source of funding.

"There," he said, wrenching her attention away from her inappropriate but entrepreneurial thoughts. He sat back as three monitors displayed the image of a man pointing a gun straight at the viewer.

"They sure did a good job of making the product they're offering obvious." She scanned the copy beneath the website's name. "Wow! They have quite a selection."

"It gets better . . . or worse, depending on your perspective." His fingers did a jig on the touch pad and a menu with photos of various types of guns flashed up.

"'Handguns, rifles, shotguns, submachine guns, machine guns, grenade-based weapons, portable antimateriel weapons,'" she read. "I don't even know what that last one means."

"Those are used to shoot at tanks, airplanes, and buildings."

"Jesus H. Christ! Are they outfitting an army?"

"Someone could, if they had the money to spend." Leland clicked on the first menu heading, and a listing of handguns with accompanying photos popped up.

Most of the pictures were just a gun against a white background, but a few showed someone's hands wrapped around the grip as though they were shooting it.

"It's a long shot—pardon the pun." Leland gave her a tight smile. "But I thought you might take a look at the ones with actual backgrounds. Maybe you'll recognize a location in or near Cofferwood."

When Dawn examined the screen more closely, she realized the photos with hands had more than blank walls behind them. Some seemed to have trees or grass or even an occasional bit of building. "They're cropped so tightly around the gun that I can't see much."

"Keep looking because even a single location will help us." He nudged the touch pad toward her so she could scroll through and enlarge the photos. Then he shifted his hand to her back, idly stroking up and down in a way that sent tingly shivers waltzing along her spine.

She glanced sideways to confirm that his gaze was still focused on the screen. After savoring his caresses for several seconds, she said, "I love it, but I can't concentrate when you're doing that."

"What?" He swiveled to look at her in surprise, his hand still on her back.

She gave a little shrug under his palm.

"Oh, didn't mean to distract you." He lifted his hand away. Losing its warmth made her feel chilled, but the sweet seduction of his smile counteracted it when he said, "You generate a magnetic field so I'm drawn to you without being conscious of it."

A delicious bliss filled her chest but she couldn't let that show. "Aren't magnets bad for computers?"

"That's an old fear left over from the days of floppy disks. Nowadays computers actually use magnets internally, so my tech is safe around you." His smile went a little crooked. "Although I'm not sure I am."

The bliss swelled until she thought her rib cage might burst. "I like being dangerous to you." She shifted to place a kiss on his smiling lips, the feel of them sending a happy little zing through her. "Now let me work."

He rolled his chair a few inches away from her, which gave her some smug satisfaction. But she focused on the screen, examining the photos with care. She flipped to the second page and found a submenu that read: "Concealed Carry Compacts." She clicked on that to find a few small pictures of short-barreled revolvers. One showed hands so she enlarged it.

And gasped.

"What is it?" Leland rolled his chair in close and peered at the screen.

"This is going to sound crazy but I think I recognize those fingernails."

"Fingernails?"

"How often do you see leopard spots and rhinestones together in a manicure?" She scrutinized the picture closely. There were none of the rings Vicky usually wore, but maybe rings and shooting didn't go together. "I think those are Vicky's hands."

Leland followed her gaze. "Granted, I know very little about manicures, but isn't it possible for two women to have the same style?"

"Yes, but have you ever seen another human being with that combination of decorations on their nails? Besides, the shape of her hands is familiar too." The copy under the photo touted how perfect the gun was for a woman's small hands. "I guess they decided to make it very obvious the shooter is female. So the nails are a statement."

The scary part was how expert Vicky's hold seemed on the weapon, right hand around the grip, left hand around the right, thumbs stacked along the side. Of course, she might have been coached, but the image still sent a chill through Dawn's brain, especially when she remembered that there was video of Leland and her going into Vicky and Ramón's office.

Leland muttered a curse. "How did a gym owner get mixed up with arms dealers in Cofferwood, New Jersey?"

"The Mafia? They're still around in Jersey, I hear. Vicky could be related for all I know." She certainly looked like a mob moll.

"My understanding is that these days the Mafia is more about drugs, prostitution, and extortion. Arms dealing isn't really their bailiwick."

"'Bailiwick'? Has the mob gone British?" Dawn teased. "They have territories."

"You're an authority on organized crime?"

"More of an authority than someone from Georgia."

Leland smiled but it was brief. "What about Ramón? He was a professional boxer. That's a sport the mob is often involved in."

She had been trying not to think about the possibility. But Ramón adored his wife. If she was involved in arms dealing, it was hard to imagine that he wouldn't know. There was also the engraved gun safe in his desk, a direct contradiction to his claim that he no longer believed in violence of any kind.

"I just can't see Ramón doing this." She rubbed her temples.

"Although I don't believe in guilt by association, it's his gym the data traffic is flowing through, and his wife's fingernails are on the website." Leland's tone was gentle and he laid his hand over hers where it rested by the touch pad. "That's a lot of connections."

She turned her hand to clutch at his. "So what do we do now?"

"You do nothing. You stay far, far away from this. I call Tully." His grip tightened and the set of his jaw was hard. "I wish like hell you hadn't gone to Ramón's office with me. That was stupid and reckless on my part."

"It made the most sense and we weren't expecting guns." But she felt as though he meant *she* was stupid and reckless as well.

"It involves the dark web. I should have expected the worst." He raised her hand to kiss the back of it. "Tully will want to talk with you. Is that all right?"

"Why wouldn't it be?"

"Because I don't want anything to drag you back into your past."

Strange, but nothing about this had triggered her fear in that way. Maybe because she trusted Leland so completely. "No, I'm fine."

He searched her face for a long moment before he reached for his cell phone.

"Tully, it's Leland," he said almost immediately. "I need your help."

In less than half an hour, Tully strode into Mission Control. Dawn had met him at a couple of the parties thrown by Alice and Derek. He'd seemed like a big easygoing cowboy with his tooled leather boots, plaid shirts, and booming laugh. But the man who entered the computer room didn't look at all easygoing. His gray eyes were pure steel, his mouth was set in a grim line, and he looked like laughter was an alien concept to him.

Now she understood why Leland and Derek had been intimidated by him when they first met in business school.

"Did you find any other indications of a connection to the gym in the photos?" he asked after greeting them with efficient brevity.

At Tully's request, Dawn and Leland had combed through the rest of the photos on the Tactical Arms website, looking for any other clue that pointed to Work It Out, Vicky, or Ramón. But there had been no sparkly, leopard-spotted nails highlighted against the grips of the submachine guns or grenade launchers.

Dawn shook her head. "Just that one photo."

Tully seized a chair and wheeled it over to the computer station where Dawn and Leland sat. "Let's see what you've got."

Fortunately, the desk and screens were so large that all three of them could sit side by side and view the website. An unaccustomed sense of safety enveloped her as she sat between the two powerful men. Right here and now, no one and nothing could hurt her. She sat very still, savoring a feeling she hadn't experienced since that hideous, life-destroying Saturday afternoon. If she could sit here long enough, maybe the feeling of safety would become her normal once again.

Leland was talking about how he'd found the website, using technical language she found incomprehensible. Tully seemed a little more advanced in his dark web knowledge, but even he finally held up his hand to stop Leland's spate of acronyms.

"The website is well hidden and encrypted," Tully said. "I get that. Someone who knows what they're doing set it up. But that leaves us with a hell of a lot of questions. Like why would they suddenly start directing data traffic through the gym's router? Can't they get it there through some other node in the deep web?"

"Illegal websites tend to have to relocate frequently," Leland said. "The authorities like your FBI buddies are getting better and better at finding them, so they move to stay ahead of the game. In this case, someone may have gotten too close so they had to move unexpectedly.

They wouldn't want to shut down so they rerouted traffic from the old website address to the new one through a router they already controlled. That's a simplified explanation, of course. My guess is that the website will move again soon."

"Yeah, because you had to go and poke the hornet's nest." Tully was clearly not happy about that.

Dawn refused to let Tully shred her newfound comfort. "We didn't know the hornets had bullets. And we had a perfectly believable reason for being in the office."

"Arms dealers don't survive without being paranoid." Tully dragged his finger over the touch pad to scan the website's menu. "Holy shit, this is a serious operation. They've got some military-only weapons on here. Where the fu—sorry—hell did they get it?"

After rapidly but thoroughly examining every page of the website, he sat back, his expression downright chilling. He swung his gaze around to Leland. "You screwed up, buddy."

Leland's lips tightened.

Tully rolled his chair back from the desk so that both Dawn and Leland had to swivel theirs to look at him. He pinned first Dawn, then Leland, with that gimlet-hard stare. "You all are done with this situation. Totally, completely, and absolutely done. You will forget all about it. This is for your own safety and well-being. And to keep the sightlines clear of civilians so my colleagues at the FBI can take these bastards down. Do you hear me?"

Dawn nodded. Leland said, "Loud and clear."

Tully's tense jaw relaxed infinitesimally at their instant capitulation. "You will also stay totally, completely, and absolutely away from each other. Hopefully, that will allay any suspicion these bastards might have that you are working together."

She had not expected that and she didn't like the lurch of dismay that vibrated through her suddenly hollowed-out rib cage. "But Leland just bought a gym membership. Won't it look even more suspicious if he suddenly cancels it?"

Tully looked at Leland. "You find a really good reason to try to get a refund. Make it convincing."

Leland nodded, his face impassive. "I can do that."

The dismay turned to something much more upsetting. Abandonment. No, rejection. He didn't care enough about her or about their relationship to try to argue with Tully. Even after she'd spilled her guts to him.

All the stupid, misguided hope she'd allowed to grow shattered under his indifference.

She blinked back the pathetic tears that burned behind her eyelids. It was her own fault. Natalie had warned her. Hell, she'd warned herself. This should have been just a casual sex thing. She'd been an idiot to believe it could mean more.

She braced her spine. She'd survived far worse.

"And I'll bitch about clients who fill up my schedule and then bail after a few sessions. That should reassure them that we're not in cahoots." She was proud of the fact that her voice didn't waver.

She snuck a glance at Leland. His expression was unreadable.

"Do you need anything else from me?" she asked Tully. She had to get out of there before she crumbled.

"Yeah. Let's go through all the possible suspects, one by one. Even people you think couldn't possibly be involved."

She squeezed her eyes shut for a moment, trying to collect her thoughts in the face of Leland's coolness. Opening them, she kept her gaze on Tully as she listed the people she'd discussed with Leland and Natalie. Tully probed deeper with his questions, making her examine her colleagues in ways she didn't enjoy. She'd spent a lot of time and effort creating this little world where she felt unthreatened. Now Tully forced her to turn that on its head and search for evil in the one place where she had almost convinced herself it didn't exist.

"What about the gym's layout?" Tully asked. "Can you give me a rough description?"

"I'll do that," Leland interrupted. "I think it's time Dawn went home."

His words were clipped but when she turned toward him without thinking, his gaze held a tender concern that made her swallow hard. "But you don't know about the basement."

"Tully can look it up. He has ways to get construction drawings." Leland stood and made a chopping motion with his hand when Tully opened his mouth. "I'll get you an anonymous town car to keep Tully happy."

So they wouldn't even get to share the limo one last time.

"Good idea," she said, pushing up out of her chair. "Might as well begin as we mean to go on." Platitudes were useful when your heart was ripping itself in two. Really, how had her heart gotten involved in this anyway?

Leland had his phone out and frowned at the screen as he typed.

"My apologies, ma'am," Tully said, his cowboy persona reappearing as he stood. "I can get a little intense when I'm on a case."

"It's a pretty intense case," Dawn said. "Will you at least let me know what's going on when you can? Work It Out is, well, more than just the place I work."

Tully nodded. "I could tell by the way you spoke about it. And about Ramón Vazquez. I assure you that I'll do my best to keep the takedown as quiet as possible."

"I guess if Ramón and Vicky are involved, the gym will have to close." The tears welled in earnest. She pinched the bridge of her nose to fight them back.

"You won't have any problem finding another job," Leland said, looking up from his phone. "You're an excellent trainer."

He knew that wasn't the issue. Did he think he had to make it so crystal clear even here that they were no longer together?

He nodded and held up his phone. "Your ride will be here soon. I'll go with you down to the lobby to make sure it's the right car."

"Just give me the license number. I can take it from there." She couldn't bear to be alone with him in the elevator, knowing that he could let her go so easily.

⸺

Leland walked beside Dawn down the hall toward the elevator. She seemed so small and vulnerable and feminine with her hair swirling loose around her shoulders. Not the warrior-athlete he had trained with or the wildly passionate lover he'd brought to orgasm in the pool. Now he understood that she had good reason to be fearful. He'd felt her stiffen and struggle to shift positions at times when they made love. Although he'd swear she felt less that way the longer they were together.

Now his reckless, thoughtless actions had brought her terror roaring back to life. A dagger thrust of guilt slashed through his gut.

"As long as I stay away from you and the gym, you'll be safe," he said, trying to convince himself as much as her. He hated that he had brought danger back into her life, but even more, he hated feeling helpless to protect her.

He wanted to wrap her in his arms and shield her from the criminals with his own body. Or at least to whisk her away to his Manhattan townhouse with its sophisticated alarm system and full-time security guard. But they'd all learned a lesson about supposedly unbreachable security from Alice and Derek's run-in with another cybercriminal. Being in Leland's home might put Dawn in the crosshairs instead of safeguarding her.

Tully was undoubtedly correct in his assertion that keeping them separate was the best possible defense. And Leland would make sure that his partner sent undercover bodyguards to shadow Dawn, just in case.

He keyed in the unlock code and pressed the button to summon the elevator. He had no intention of letting her get in the town car without checking to make sure it was the one he had ordered. But he'd learned that arguing with Dawn wasn't always the best way to get things done. So he stood beside her as they waited.

He was surprised by her silence but not by the tension that showed in the clench of her jaw. She usually covered up her anxiety with smart remarks. This time it must have closed up her throat in the way letting her go tightened his. He started to slip an arm around her shoulders but then considered that his uninvited touch might trigger her. So he shoved his hands into the pockets of his jeans.

"I won't let anyone hurt you," he said as the doors opened. He flattened his palm against the doorjamb to hold it so she could enter first. Then he followed.

"I told you not to come down with me." There was an edge to her voice that bothered him.

"You're not getting in any car until I know it's safe."

As the elevator descended, she looked at him, her eyes bleak in a way that made his heart twist. "Safety is an illusion."

He wanted to punch the wall. "There will be a bodyguard with you at all times, I promise."

She shook her head. "If the gym suddenly has a bunch of new members who have that intimidating look in their eyes like Tully, that will just make it worse."

"Tully's people are better than that. Someone will be there, but you'll never see them."

The elevator glided to a stop. As soon as the doors opened the smallest crack, Dawn slid through them and headed across the lobby.

"Dawn!" He lengthened his stride to catch up with her before she reached the front exit. He stepped between her and the doors, trying to read her face. But it was set in a blank mask. "I want to kiss you."

Some unreadable emotion flashed through her eyes and was gone. "A goodbye kiss. Sure. Why not?" She tilted her chin up, closed her eyes, and stood like a statue, a carved goddess with golden skin and dark, satin hair.

"Don't worry, darlin'." He ran his hands up and down her arms as though to warm her. "We'll keep you safe."

"Just kiss me," she said, her eyes still shuttered. "We need to go our separate ways."

He didn't know what else to do, so he stepped forward to bring their bodies together in the lightest of contacts. Bending, he brushed her lips with his. A shudder ran through her, and then her arms were around his neck and she was pressed against him the way he wanted. Her mouth was hot and inviting as she opened to him. A tiny whimper broke from her throat as their tongues met, the sound sending a jolt of desire into his belly.

As he skimmed his hands around to pull her harder against him, his phone chimed with a message. She threaded her fingers into his hair while she devoured his mouth for a brief moment. Then she twisted out of his embrace in one swift movement. He wanted to hurl his state-of-the-art phone on the floor and grind it into the marble.

"That must mean the car is here," she said, but she stood looking at him as though she'd never seen him before. He could almost feel her gaze traveling over his body, burning wherever it touched.

Her hair was rumpled from where he'd plunged his hands into it, her lips were wet and red from their kiss, and her eyes were huge and lit with the same arousal he felt.

"The hell with the car," he said, reaching for her.

She took a step back and shook her head. "A goodbye kiss. That was it."

She pivoted and yanked open the door. He grabbed the heavy steel frame to hold it for her and followed her onto the city sidewalk. A black sedan waited by the curb.

"Don't get in until I check the plates," he said, walking to the front of the car and comparing the license number to the confirmation on his phone. It matched. "Wait," he said as Dawn reached for the car door. He came back to tap on the front passenger window to indicate the driver should roll it down. "What's your full name?" he asked the young man behind the wheel.

"Tigran Ohanian, sir. I'm here for KRG Consulting."

"You need to forget that last part," Leland said. "No one but me and your boss needs to know that."

"Yes, sir."

Leland nodded and held open the sedan's back door while Dawn slipped onto the leather seat.

"Thanks." She looked down to fiddle with the seat belt.

He wanted to slide onto the seat beside her and break through this strange distance between them. But he knew Tully was right. "Goodbye, darlin'. I'll miss you."

That got her to look up. "Right back at you," she said in that smart-mouth Jersey girl way he found so beguiling. But there was a sadness in her eyes.

She reached for the handle and tugged at it so he had to close the door.

When the sedan pulled onto the half-empty avenue, a strange panic squeezed the air from his lungs. He tried to tell himself that it was his apprehension about entrusting her safety to other people when it should be his job.

But as the car swerved around a taxi, his body swayed with it. Because when Dawn had climbed into the back of that sedan, she'd taken some part of him with her.

Chapter 14

Dawn stared at the ceiling of her bedroom, waiting for her alarm to go off so she could stop trying to sleep. The sheets and blankets were a mess, tangled by her wrestling match with the churning nausea that Leland's easy relinquishment of their relationship had left in her gut.

She knew their separation made sense from a security standpoint, but couldn't Leland have raised at least one objection? All he'd talked about was her safety. There was no sign of the desolation that had swept through her when Tully decreed they couldn't see each other any longer.

At the rooftop pool, she'd felt so close to him. The sense of intimacy had lured her into telling him the sordid truth about why she was the way she was. Maybe it had been too much for him to cope with. Too messy and too emotionally demanding.

Maybe he couldn't deal with that on top of mourning for his mother. She should cut him some slack for that.

Natalie had warned her about what kind of man Leland was. Dawn had stupidly thought she'd gotten past the workaholic and found the lonely person inside, the one who longed for a connection.

She let out a bitter laugh. At least Leland's desertion kept her mind off the danger she might be facing from Vicky and Ramón.

As soon as she thought of her boss as a bad guy, her stomach roiled with another wave of nausea. That betrayal went nearly as deep as Leland's. How could the man who had coaxed her into believing she could have a normal life turn around and sell implements of death on the black market? It just didn't compute.

That last word reminded her of Leland, hollowing out her chest with loneliness. She groaned and slammed her fist into the pillow next to her. It was time to drive away the heebie-jeebies with the one thing she had learned could save her: intense, strenuous, violent exercise. So what if she wasn't due at the gym for another two hours? She needed to sweat.

An hour later, she was propped up against a weight bench, her gray workout shirt plastered to her body by sweat, her rubbery legs stretched out on the floor, while she chugged the second bottle of water since she'd arrived. She nearly choked as she tried to swallow and catch her breath at the same time.

She wasn't sure sprints on the treadmill, pounding the heavy bag, and practicing tae kwon do moves had done anything to fill the void Leland's absence had opened up, but they'd sure worked the tension out of her body. Mostly because her muscles were too exhausted to tense up.

"You're here early."

Dawn started as Vicky's slightly nasal voice came from behind her. The other woman walked around the bench and stood close enough that Dawn had to tilt back her head to look her in the eyes. "I couldn't sleep."

Vicky scanned down Dawn's perspiring body with a look of distaste. "I hope you're going to clean up before your first client arrives."

Dawn knew she shouldn't poke a rattlesnake with a sharp stick but Vicky pissed her off. Dawn had never been anything other than professional at the gym. "Actually, I thought it might inspire my clients to work harder if they saw how much their trainer sweats."

"At least don't get in the pool without showering."

Dawn had considered a relaxing float in the pool, but when she'd looked at the glassy expanse of blue, all she could see was the powerful ripple of Leland's shoulder muscles as he stretched out his arms to pull himself swiftly through the water. "No worries. Swimming wasn't on my agenda this morning."

"So did your client find his cell phone?"

It turned out her muscles weren't too exhausted to tense up after all. She pushed up from the floor to stand, deciding that Vicky had too much of a psychological advantage towering over her like that. "Yeah. It was in his car. It had fallen down between the seat and the center console. He had the darned thing on mute so he couldn't call it."

"You'd think he would have looked in his car first."

"You'd think." Dawn shrugged and swiped her sweat towel over her face. "I'm going to shower so I can look good for my first client."

Vicky didn't acknowledge the dig. "I hear you got pretty chummy with him."

"Who? You mean Lee Wellmont?" All her stress-busting exercise had been for nothing. Now every nerve in her body was on screaming red alert. She had no idea where Vicky was going with this. "There's no rule against hanging out with clients."

"No, but I hear you were pretty hot and heavy at Carmella's."

"Hot and heavy?" They'd barely spent any time there. "We just had dinner." Actually, only antipasto.

"Hey, I don't blame you. He's a long, tall drink of water." Vicky was trying the girlfriends-exchanging-confidences-about-men tack now. Except they weren't girlfriends. "I'd be interested in getting hot and heavy with him too, if I wasn't in love with Ray."

A sense of unease nagged at the back of Dawn's mind. "It didn't work out any way."

"Yeah? Men are shits. Except Ray." Vicky flicked at the air with her fingers and Dawn couldn't stop herself from staring at the glittering leopard-spotted manicure. A tremor of fear ran through her.

"So are you still going to train him?" Vicky asked. "Or should I assign him someone new? Chad has some openings."

"It, um, wasn't exactly amicable, so I don't think he's coming back to the gym."

"Shit! That's why I don't like trainers and clients socializing."

Dawn gave Vicky an apologetic grimace. "Yeah, I'm really sorry about that." She decided to go with Vicky's pretense that they were friends and gave her a knife-edged smile. "Do me a favor . . . don't give him a refund if he asks. He doesn't deserve it."

"Sure thing, hon." Of course that would suit Vicky's profit-driven little soul. "It sucks that you got burned."

More than she had any idea of. "You said it. Men are shits."

The other woman turned and swayed away on her silver heels. Vicky would have reprimanded anyone else who dared walk on the gym's pristine wood floor in stilettos, but the owner's wife had special privileges.

Dawn slumped onto the cushioned weight bench, elbows braced on her knees. She mentally reviewed her date with Leland at Carmella's. There'd been a hell of a lot of sexual tension and she'd fed him one bite of antipasto from her fingers, but no one could call that hot and heavy.

Cold shivers walked down her spine as she realized that there must be a security camera somewhere in the gym's basement. That's how Vicky knew they'd been sexually involved. She'd seen them down there.

A hot flush of embarrassment rose in her cheeks. God, she hoped the camera was in the hallway and not in the storage room itself. She sure didn't want that video posted on Twitter.

However, there was nothing suspicious about having sex with your client in the basement storeroom. In fact, it might have worked in their favor, since it gave them a valid reason to be spending extra time together.

But why would there be security cameras in the basement hallway? There hadn't been in the past. That's why the trainers used it for the occasional tryst. The two basement exit doors were alarmed, but those were the only security measures known to the staff.

There was no reason for subterranean cameras because there was nothing of value down there. Just some basic storage for cleaning supplies, cases of water, and worthless old athletic fixtures. Plus all the systems that ran the gym: HVAC, the pool's filtering equipment, electric panels, and plumbing. Given the dimensions of the gym above it, Dawn figured the basement encompassed a lot of space that she'd had no desire to explore, since it seemed exactly the kind of creepy place that might trigger her.

All that space that no one ever went into.

The perfect place to store lots and lots of guns.

She stared down at the wood floor between her feet, as though she would be able to see what lay underneath it. Had Tully, with his FBI training, already thought of this possibility? Is that why he had wanted a layout of the gym?

Another chill shuddered through her as she pictured crates filled with pistols, rifles, and submachine guns piled below the soles of her sneakers, waiting to be sold into the hands of drug dealers and other bad guys who wouldn't hesitate to use them.

Whether Tully had thought of it or not, she should tell him about the security camera. Although explaining why she knew about it would be embarrassing.

Except he'd told her not to contact KRG, Leland, or him unless it was an emergency. She had a suspicion that he'd said that to keep her from trying to participate in the investigation. For her own safety. She got that.

She stood up and paced across the weight room to see if the fridge was fully loaded with water bottles. It was and she muttered a curse word. No excuse to go down to the basement to bring up a case to restock it. She just wanted to see if she could find the security camera that had caught Leland's and her visit belowground. Nothing more.

She was definitely *not* going to look for clues that would show recent illegal activity. That would be stupid.

But she would check back on the fridge later in the day.

At two o'clock, Dawn shrugged into a sweatshirt and headed for the front door. She needed to get away from the cloud of malevolence that now seemed to permeate the gym, at least in her imagination. As she passed the front desk, she said to the daytime receptionist, "I'm going to grab a salad at Eat Healthy. You want anything?"

"No, I'm good, but I've got a package for you." The young woman disappeared below the desk and came up with a medium-size cardboard carton, which she set on the glass top.

"For me?" Dawn frowned in perplexity. Sure enough, the carton had her name and the gym's address on it but no return address and no visible postage. "How did it get here?"

"Some guy from a delivery service brought it in. Said to make sure you got it as soon as possible." The receptionist shrugged apologetically. "You were with clients all morning and I know I'm not supposed to interrupt."

"That's fine. You did the right thing." Dawn decided to take the box back to her apartment to open it since she didn't know what it contained. A crazy thought struck her. *It couldn't be a bomb, could it?*

She shook her head at her paranoia and applied logic. Ramón and/or Vicky couldn't assume that she would take the carton out of the gym to open it. They wouldn't want to blow up their own building and the weapons that might possibly be stored in it.

When had life become a James Bond movie?

"I guess I'll run it back to my apartment and then get lunch." She should have just enough time if she got a smoothie instead of a salad.

Dawn hefted the box off the desk. It wasn't particularly heavy and she couldn't resist shaking it a bit. Something shifted inside it but only slightly. She was pretty sure it was from KRG but what on earth were they sending her so mysteriously? No one had said a word about a package yesterday.

Back at her apartment, she sliced the tape with a box cutter and flipped open the flaps. Nestled inside the carton were the two extra pairs of shoes and the designer clothing she'd given back to Leland at the pool, wrapped in tissue paper.

She pulled a Balenciaga sneaker out of its box and sat on the sofa with it cradled in her hands. Was this a farewell gift? Something expensive to say *Thanks for the sex?*

Or maybe it was just too much trouble for the concierge to return the clothes to the stores where they'd come from.

No, she was being mean because she was so hurt. He'd wanted her to have these, but he knew her well enough not to argue with her when she handed them back. So he'd found another way to give them to her. It made it all the worse that Leland understood her well enough to slip in his gift with such subtlety.

She put the shoe down on the coffee table and rummaged around in the carton in the hope that there was a note of some kind. She hadn't seen one but maybe it had fallen between the shoeboxes. Instead of an envelope, her questing fingers found a small box hidden among the folds of one pair of jeans.

Prying open the lid, she tipped a cell phone onto her palm. The square black device wasn't any brand she recognized. A yellow sticky note covered the screen and read: "Use private cell number to unlock."

She frowned, wondering what the heck that meant. Then understanding hit her. Leland had a private cell number that he'd given to her. She turned the phone on and keyed in the number.

The screen lit up with a text message.

I knew you would figure out the unlock code.

A blip of pleasure pinged in her chest that he thought she was smart enough to catch on to his cryptic note.

This phone is encrypted so we can communicate without security concerns. It locks down after 5 seconds of inactivity so keep touching the screen. Text me as soon as you can.

The pleasure was no longer a blip. It was a full-on tidal wave of joy that she would be in contact with Leland once again. That was bad.

He hadn't exactly written her a love note, had he? She searched for some clue as to whether he wanted her to communicate about the arms dealing or on a more personal level, but there was no subtext in his message that she could find. Only his request to contact him soon, which could mean anything or nothing.

The package arrived, obviously. Thanks for the clothes, even though you were supposed to return them.

Now *he* could try to discern the subtext. A new message pinged in almost immediately. Evidently he wasn't sweating over hidden meanings.

The clothes will look better on you than me. Are you all right?

She chuckled without being able to stop herself. That disarming humor of his got her every time. But how was she supposed to respond to his question? She didn't know the answer.

Back to skimming the surface.

No one has pulled a gun on me yet. One note of interest . . . there must be a new security camera somewhere in the basement. Vicky sort of alluded to our visit down there. Which is weird because the reason the trainers go down there was the previous lack of security cameras.

This time there was a substantial pause before he responded.

Not good. I've told Tully. Can you talk now? I want to know what else Vicky said.

She glanced at her watch. If she skipped the smoothie she could hear Leland's voice pouring into her ear. She tapped in his private cell number.

"Dawn! Thank God! I hate not being there with you. Talk to me." He sounded more worried than distraught but maybe she was just being sensitive.

"I'm at my apartment now, which I assume means that Tully's guard dog is somewhere around." She had tried to spot her shadow this morning without success, and the package had distracted her from the bodyguard on her way home.

"Her report says no suspicious activity but that makes me feel only marginally better. Why was Vicky discussing our tryst with you?"

She tried to remember how Vicky had introduced the topic of Leland. It had shocked her so much that she hadn't really focused on the reason for it. "Um, the cell phone. She wanted to know if you'd found it."

"Which means that she knows we were in her office. Shit! Then what did she say?"

"She was doing her gym-owner thing, checking up on how much I was fraternizing with my client. She mentioned us being hot and heavy at dinner at Carmella's. But we weren't. In fact, we barely spent any time there, so she must have seen us in the basement. That's the only explanation. Anyway I told her it didn't work out and not to give you a refund."

He gave a ghost of a laugh. "Damn, that's a hundred and fifty dollars down the tube. But the rest of it is no laughing matter. She's suspicious enough to keep tabs on you."

"Yeah, but the fact that we really *were* hot and heavy works in our favor." She put an emphasis on the past tense to see if he reacted.

"Granted, but it's still a problem."

Maybe he hadn't noticed the past tense. The edge in his voice was growing sharper and sharper, which meant he wasn't thinking about their relationship. He was thinking about the arms dealers.

"I had a thought about the basement," she said, following his lead. "It's huge and no one goes down there, except in the part where we were. Wouldn't it be the perfect place to store guns?"

"Not only perfect, but all the gym members coming and going provide an excellent cover for any customers. Tully got hold of blueprints of the building. Luckily, the college had them archived. There's a hell of a lot of potential storage down there."

"But how did they get all the guns in there without anyone noticing? That's a big delivery."

"In multiple small shipments. Or one truck late at night. There are several ways it could happen without creating a scene. That's assuming the weapons are really there, which we can't be sure of until we see them. It's useful to know that there are security cameras down there now."

She decided not to mention her plan of grabbing a case of water from the basement to scope out the camera location. Leland wouldn't approve.

"Are you really all right?" His voice changed from clipped consultant to southern charmer, his honeyed drawl whispering through her body. "It sucks that I'm not there with you. This can't be easy."

Hope fluttered its wings. "Seriously, I'm fine." She decided to go out on a limb. "I miss you, though."

She heard a voice in the background and realized someone, probably Tully, was there with him. "Ditto," he said. "In a big way."

The wings fluttered a little faster, just like her heartbeat. "I guess you can't talk freely."

"Not about that. What time do you finish at the gym?"

"Seven. My late appointment canceled at the last minute, the inconsiderate jerk." Leland had been on her schedule for seven thirty that evening.

"Yeah, I hear you on that." He did not sound like he was smiling. "I'll call you later."

He disconnected before she could tell him to stop worrying about her.

However, she did a little jig at the prospect of talking with him when she got off work.

$\rightsquigarrow$

Leland set his own encrypted phone carefully on the desk. He'd had to browbeat Tully into allowing him to ship its counterpart to Dawn. His partner hadn't wanted to chance spooking the arms dealers and thereby putting Dawn in danger. But after Leland asked him for the tenth time if the bodyguard had reported anyone following Dawn, Tully had relented, mostly to get Leland off his back.

"I'm not blind," Tully said. "I know you wanted to whisper sweet nothings into that phone. You didn't have to hold back on my account."

Leland scowled at him. "I wanted to tell her not to go anywhere near that damned basement but that's like waving a red flag in front of a bull."

Tully raised his eyebrows. "Takes one to know one." He turned serious. "I like Dawn. She's a strong woman."

"More than you know," Leland said. "But that won't stop a bullet."

"I meant that I'm glad you and she are together."

Leland held up a hand to stop him. "Not here. Not now."

"Where the hell else am I supposed to talk to you about it? You never leave this office except to swim or—thank God for Dawn!—to go to the gym in New Jersey." Tully bent forward, his forearms on his thighs. "She's good for you. You should try to hold on to her."

"Right now, I just want to make sure she stays alive and unhurt," Leland said, irritated at Tully's interference in his personal life. He had enough concerns about Dawn without adding the future of their relationship to the mix.

"Fine. I've said my piece. You just think about it." Tully straightened up. "I've gotta get in there tonight before they move the goods."

Leland jumped on the change of subject. "The data traffic is still going through the gym node, so why do you think they're going to relocate the guns?"

"Gut instinct. Dawn said customers have been complaining for a little over two weeks." Tully smacked his forehead. "I forgot to ask her . . . Did she mention whether any tech guys had come in? She said Vicky had told her she would call them today."

Leland didn't want to ask Dawn anything about the situation because he knew she would try to help. He shook his head. "I'll ask her tonight." That way she couldn't do anything about it until tomorrow. By then Tully should know if the weapons were at Work It Out. "I'll go with you to the gym tonight. I've been there several times so I know the lay of the land."

Tully squeezed Leland's shoulder. "Thanks, buddy, but no. Ex-FBI agents are a dime a dozen. Computer geniuses are hard to come by. I've got a couple of good guys lined up to go with me."

Guys who were better trained for a situation like this than Leland was. Tully would be safer with them than with him. Like Dawn was safer with her professional bodyguard. Which made Leland feel like a useless piece of crap. He slumped in his chair.

"You've been whining about not being involved in any SBI projects," Leland said. "Looks like you finally got your wish."

"I reckon I did." Tully's expression was sober. "I wasn't expecting an illegal arsenal, though."

Guilt jabbed at Leland. Because of Dawn's devotion to Ramón, Leland had been the one who wanted to keep the authorities out of the situation until they had confirmation the gym was involved.

"I've changed my mind," he said. "We should turn this over to your former colleagues at the FBI. They've got the right equipment and the staff to handle it."

"Hell, no, partner!" Now Tully was smiling, albeit with a feral edge. "I'm not letting them have all the fun. This is just a recon mission. No big deal."

"Don't decide to ride in and capture the bad guys," Leland said. "I don't want to have both you and Dawn on my conscience."

"No way am I getting myself killed." Tully stood up and grinned. "I want to see Derek's face when he sees those Class V rapids we're gonna shoot."

Leland groaned as Tully exited Mission Control. He'd put that whole bachelor-rafting-trip-catastrophe-waiting-to-happen out of his mind.

What he couldn't seem to get out of his head were Tully's words about holding on to Dawn. He hadn't thought beyond the resolution of the dark web mystery at first. Not until he realized that once it was solved, he would have no compelling reason to trek out to New Jersey. That's when he had come up with his half-baked idea to have Dawn travel to the city to train him. He smiled. She hadn't been fooled by his pretense. She knew he wanted her for reasons other than her expertise as a personal trainer.

But did he want her for the right reasons? Or was he using her the way he used his job, to push away the guilt and gut-wrenching sorrow over his mother's death? Hell if he knew.

So he plunged back into what he always did when he needed to avoid feeling—the controlled, logical world of his computers.

Chapter 15

"It's Josh's birthday," Tiffany said as Dawn walked by the reception desk on her way home at the end of her day. "We're all meeting at Arthur's to celebrate with him after the gym closes at nine. You have to come!"

"Darn! I wish I could"—total lie!—"but I've got plans." Yup, a phone call with Leland counted as plans. Dawn waved a hand vaguely and kept going.

"Bring your plans," Tiffany said, giving her a sly wink.

A heavy hand landed on Dawn's shoulder, making her jump and twist away to tense in a defensive stance. "What the——?" she said, finding herself glaring at Chad.

"Sorry!" He held up both hands, fingers spread and palms out, but his gaze on her was sharp. "I just wanted to encourage you to join us. Be friendly for a change."

"I'm friendly at the gym," Dawn said, trying to hide the fact that her heart was beating at twice its normal rate. "I just don't like to mix my professional life and my personal life."

"We know that's not true," Chad said with a slight leer.

Now how the hell did he know about Leland? She decided not to deny it. "That was a bad idea. Proved by the fact that it didn't work out." She forced her body to relax by taking a deep breath. "I've learned my lesson."

"Show some solidarity with your fellow trainers," Chad insisted.

He was being more annoying than usual tonight. "Okay, I'll meet you there at nine." She didn't have to show up.

"Josh has a crush on you," Tiffany said, clapping her hands together. "It will make him so happy to see you."

Dawn stopped herself from rolling her eyes. She'd been nice to Josh when he started at the gym, showing him the ropes. No good deed went unpunished. "That's sweet but he's a little young for me."

"It doesn't matter. He just wants you to be there." Tiffany giggled. "Maybe you could give him a birthday kiss."

It was harder not to roll her eyes this time.

"We'll see you at Arthur's. First beer's on me." Chad smiled, but something in the tightness of his jaw was not friendly.

"That certainly sweetened the pot. I'll be sure to join the fun now." There might have been a wee bit of sarcasm in her tone. "I have to get home to change for the celebration."

In four strides she was through the door. As she walked home in the gathering dusk, she groaned at the thought of treading the fine line of being kind to Josh while making it clear that he had no chance with her. She wished Tiffany hadn't shared that particular bit of gym gossip with her. Ignorance was bliss, in this case.

Her step quickened as she realized she needed to shower and change before she called Leland. She didn't want to have to rush their conversation since all they could do tonight was talk.

Damn Chad and Tiffany! She started to jog.

⌒

The encrypted phone began to dance across Leland's desk. A blip of something that might be happiness dinged in his chest as he seized the cell. "Dawn! I was going to call you soon." He'd forced himself not to dial her the moment he thought she might get home.

"I hope you can talk now. I got roped into going to a birthday party for one of the trainers at nine." Her voice dropped into a flirtatious purr. "I'm told he has a crush on me, so I have to give him a birthday kiss."

"I am extremely envious of him." He could hear the rasp in his own voice as he pictured her soft lips pressed against another man's mouth. "Don't make it too good."

Her laugh was light and delicious. "I wouldn't have gone but Chad was being unusually persistent tonight. That man is beyond irritating."

"Chad was worse than normal?" Leland lost all desire to flirt. "That worries me."

"He's just a harmless jerk. I know his type. Besides, I have Tully's bodyguard to keep me safe, right?"

"You have two shadows now. Tully has some gut instinct that makes him think something will happen tonight, so he doubled up." In fact it was Leland who had insisted on that.

"Wow! Really?"

Chad's refusal to take no for an answer combined with Tully's forecast of activity sent a chill down Leland's spine. "Where's the party?"

"At a bar called Arthur's. Why?"

"How are you getting there?"

"Walking. It's not far from my building."

Leland put the phone on speaker and did a fast search on his computer. It would take her about eleven minutes to walk there. "Dawn, be very careful. Stay with people you trust at all times. And stay away from the gym!"

"You're making me nervous." There was a tension in her voice that made his chest ache.

"As much as I hate worrying you, that's a good thing because you'll be alert." Uneasiness hollowed out his chest. "I don't like this at all. I need to tell Tully and then I'll call you back."

"I only have another twenty minutes before I have to leave." He could hear the disappointment in her voice.

"I'll get back to you before then. And if you're awake, we can talk after the party." He deliberately slowed the cadence of his speech. "Maybe while you're in bed?"

He heard the catch in her breath and congratulated himself on giving her something else to focus on. Although now he couldn't stop himself from picturing her spread naked across that green comforter of hers, her skin glowing, her eyes heavy lidded, her hand cupping . . . He pulled himself up short.

"I'll be sure to get home by ten," she said, the purr back in her voice.

"I'll be waiting for your call." He put all kinds of undertones into the sentence and then disconnected and headed for Tully's office.

His partner was talking into a phone headset but waved Leland into a chair in front of his desk.

"I want someone on the roof across Park Street with a camera." Tully stared at his computer monitor, his eyes narrowed. "Use the fire escape on the north side. Remember this is a DNA operation. Do not approach, surveillance only. We don't want to spook them. Let me know when we're set up." He pulled off the headset. "What's up?"

"You've got two people watching Dawn now, right?"

"They just reported in. She's at her apartment. No signs of unwelcome interest."

"She's going to be leaving soon and going to a bar called Arthur's on Haddonfield Road. Tell them to be extra vigilant."

Tully frowned. "Want to tell me why?"

"Call them now. Then I'll explain."

Tully put his headset back on and tapped his computer screen. It was good to have partners who trusted you enough to do what you asked before requiring an explanation.

As soon as Tully had contacted both of Dawn's guards, he gave Leland a sharp look. "Okay, partner, what's got your knickers in a twist?"

Leland explained about Dawn being pressured into attending a party she didn't have any interest in. "Chad has been persistent in the past but this took it to a new level. Combined with your bad feeling, I'm concerned."

"Chad's the new trainer," Tully said, swiping at his screen and taking a moment to read what he'd brought up. "We did a background check on him and nothing popped. But we didn't dig that deep because he didn't seem worth it."

"I see a pattern that says whoever is involved in the arms dealing has gotten suspicious of Dawn and wants to make sure they know where she is. Which means if anything goes wrong with your surveillance operation, she could be in danger."

"Nothing will go wrong." Tully's expression and tone were hard.

"I know you're good at your job but I also know you can't control all the variables in this situation." Leland realized he'd already made a decision and he stood up. "I'm going to Cofferwood."

"You know that's a bad idea."

"*You* know I can't leave Dawn alone to face whatever it is we've stirred up." Leland locked eyes with his partner for a long moment.

Tully shook his head in resignation. "Yeah, I understand that. Let me get one of my people to take you. I'll put you in contact with Dawn's shadows. You do what they tell you. Agreed?"

"Depends on what they tell me." Leland grinned. He felt better now than he had all day. He'd hated being separated from Dawn when she needed protecting.

"Shit, you are a pain in the ass." Tully stood up and offered his hand across the desk. "Stay safe, buddy."

Leland shook it. "You too, cowboy."

"Hap-py birth-day to you!" The ragged singing ended in cheers as Josh blew out the candles on the ice cream cake, his long, curly bangs flopping into his eyes.

"Hey, what'd you wish for?" someone called out.

The young man blushed and smiled as he slid a sideways glance toward Dawn. She gave an inward sigh. She supposed she'd have to give him a kiss on her way out. Damn Tiffany anyway! Dawn would never have noticed the longing looks Josh had thrown her all evening if the receptionist hadn't shared his secret with her. When Dawn had bought him a beer, he'd spilled it on his shirt in his haste to give her a kiss on the cheek in thanks.

Her encrypted phone vibrated against her butt where she'd stowed it in the back pocket of her jeans. She had her regular phone in her other back pocket. Since a few of the guys in the bar were more than a little inebriated, the phones made excellent armor against unwanted groping.

Actually, Chad had been a pretty good deterrent too but not one she welcomed. He had hovered nearby ever since she arrived, giving her the heebie-jeebies after what Leland had said. Maybe it was just the dim light of the bar and her imagination, but he looked different. The jovial jock had developed a hard, watchful edge that made her nervous.

A casual glance around placed him about four feet to her right, which meant she couldn't pull out the phone to check the message. It was too obviously not a normal device. Time to go to the ladies' room.

She took the last swallow of beer from the bottle she'd been nursing for a half an hour, held it up, and said to the people standing nearest her, "Too bad you just rent this stuff." Someone laughed and she threaded her way through the crowd to the corridor leading to the restrooms.

And nearly freaked out when she pivoted to open the door to the bathroom and saw Chad coming down the hallway toward her.

He winked. "In heaven, there is no beer. That's why I drink it here. A hell of a lot of it."

She forced a laugh as he passed her to get to the men's room.

Yanking open the door, she bolted into an empty stall, her heart racing, and locked the latch. Was Chad following her, even to the bathroom? She pressed her back against the cold metal wall, counting as she breathed in, held it for a count of ten, and breathed out again, trying to calm down enough to think clearly.

Then she remembered the text and jerked the phone out of her pocket.

Equal parts of relief and anxiety vibrated through her as she saw Leland's message.

> On my way to you. Make it easy for your bodyguards to follow you home. Go up to your apartment and I'll text you when I'm on my way up. Don't open the door to anyone but me.

She sagged against the stall door for a moment, letting the confusion of emotions swirl through her. The joy of knowing she would see him tonight overshadowed all the others. But she needed to keep her mind sharp until she got home.

She typed back: I thought Tully was against that. Has something new happened?

His response surprised a choked laugh out of her. No, I just told Tully to go to hell and take his stupid idea with him.

Someone walked into the bathroom, so Dawn flushed the toilet to make her visit sound authentic. Who knew if Chad had enlisted a female associate to spy on her?

Did it count as paranoia if there really were bad guys around, but you didn't know who they were? Or was it just smart to assume everyone was out to get you?

All she knew was that she felt a lot less afraid now that Leland was coming. And what did that say about her feelings for him?

She pushed that thought aside as she washed her hands and strode out the door without bothering to scan for Chad's presence.

That was the power of Leland's message.

Half an hour later, she had given Josh the expected kiss, which he had prolonged a little more than she wanted—but, hey, it was his birthday. Now she was strolling along the well-lit sidewalk toward her building, taking it slow to make sure her unseen guardians could easily keep up with her.

Her heart lilted in her chest because Leland had told off his partner in order to be with her. That had to mean something. Even if it didn't, she could enjoy his company for another night and that was almost enough.

"Good party, right?"

Dawn shrieked and leaped sideways as Chad jogged up to her. "Jesus Christ, don't scare me like that!" She wanted to smack him for sending a crash of adrenaline through her so that every nerve was screaming, *Run!*

"Sorry," he said without sounding at all sincere. "You were just kind of sauntering along so I thought you might like some company."

"Maybe if the company hadn't snuck up on me."

"I'll walk you home." He matched his stride to hers.

Even knowing that she had two guardians somewhere nearby couldn't quell the alarm bells ringing in her brain. She decided not to antagonize him since she was now convinced that he was shadowing her. "I live three blocks from here," she said, picking up her pace, "but thanks."

She couldn't figure out what his game was. The gym was closed. She didn't have a key to get in, so how was she a threat to whatever Tully thought was happening?

"It was good to see you out with the staff tonight." Chad gave her a gentle fist bump on her upper arm. "I know it's not so easy for you with what you've been through."

How the hell did Chad know what she'd been through? At the gym, only Ramón knew the most barebones version of her story.

Undoubtedly, he'd shared it with Vicky, since he thought his wife walked on water. The alarm bells in Dawn's mind turned into a wailing fire siren.

"They look up to you, you know," Chad continued when she couldn't think how to respond. "You're the best trainer at Work It Out. You're a role model for others."

She needed to just skate on the surface of this conversation, not let her brain go into a tailspin as she delved into the subtext. "Wow! Thanks for the nice compliment. The trick is that I care about my clients."

"Hey, sorry I made a crack about that guy Lee. That was unprofessional on my part." Again, he didn't sound sincere. It was like he was reciting from a script.

"It's okay. I might be a little sensitive on the subject because it ended badly." She hoped her guards had told Leland she had company so he would make sure to be well concealed. "Honestly, I don't usually get involved with clients. It was a dumb idea. And unprofessional, to use your word."

"The heart doesn't listen to logic, does it?" Chad gave a sigh.

Dawn nearly snickered at the absurdity of Chad talking about the heart. "I guess not."

Three blocks had never seemed so long.

"So where did you work before Ramón hired you?" she asked to steer the conversation away from her.

"A gym in California. It was a nice place but I'm an East Coast kind of guy. So I loaded up my car and drove across the country. I figured I'd settle wherever I got the first job offer. And here I am."

"Did you grow up around here?" She just wanted to keep him talking until they reached her building.

"Nope, in Florida. That's where I played ball too." He seemed to be enjoying himself now.

"Quarterback, right?"

"Yeah, the buck stopped with me." He winked. "'Pain heals, chicks dig scars, glory lasts forever.'"

"Thank you, Shane Falco." She'd loved that movie once, but she associated football games with drunken attackers now.

"You know *The Replacements*?" He seemed astonished.

"I have brothers." She stifled a sigh of relief and walked even faster as they reached the corner of her block.

"They play football?"

"Only for fun. Not high-level like you." She pulled her keys out of the pocket she'd tucked them into before she left the bar. "Here we are. Thanks for the escort. Good night." She practically jogged to the front door.

"Let me just take a quick look inside the foyer," he said, coming up behind her. "It'll make me feel better to know you're safe."

"It's fine. I can see it through the window. It's all clear." Her hand was shaking, so she had a hard time fitting the key into the lock. He was crowding her back, which was beginning to trigger her panic response. She could use that since he'd brought up her past. "Could you give me some space? You're triggering me."

"Oh, sorry!" To her surprise, he backed off. "Didn't mean to freak you out."

She managed to get the door unlocked and opened it just wide enough so that she could slip through. When it was closed behind her, she lifted a hand to wave through the glass.

Chad waved back with a smile before he turned and left. She sat down hard on the bottom step and fought back the blackness that threatened to overwhelm her vision.

Breathe in-2-3-4-5-6-7-8-9-10. Hold it. Breathe out. Repeat.

Her heartbeat slowed and the blackness receded. She sat a moment longer, hating her weakness. Tully was right to keep her away from the action. She would be a liability.

She needed to text Leland a warning, just in case her minders hadn't.

> Be careful you don't get spotted. Chad insisted on walking me home. I'm pretty sure it wasn't gallantry. He said some slightly creepy things. He may still be lurking around the building. I'm headed to my apartment now.

It wasn't coherent but she sent it anyway. No time to edit. She waited a few seconds to see if Leland would respond. When he didn't, she grabbed the handrail to pull herself to her feet. Her knees were still a little wobbly, so she held on as she trudged up the stairs.

Once she had relocked the dead bolt and reset her alarm, she went to the kitchen and pulled out a bottle of Smirnoff vodka that she kept for special occasions with friends. She poured a generous splash into a juice glass and swallowed it down in one gulp. The burn of the alcohol steadied her.

The next time she saw Chad, she was going to knee him in the balls for making her feel like that scared young girl again.

She recapped the bottle and put it back in the cabinet. Because she wasn't that girl any more. Being afraid around Chad was logical, not weak. He was some kind of criminal who sold guns to even worse criminals. She *should* be wary around him.

When a text pinged into her secure phone, she didn't even start.

Chapter 16

I'm outside your door.

Dawn practically danced to her entryway. However, she still checked the video camera to make sure no one was holding Leland at gunpoint. Instead she saw him laden down with a couple of silver metal briefcases.

Disengaging all her security measures, she opened the door and let him take two steps in before closing the door behind him. "God, am I glad to see you!" Ignoring his burdens, she wrapped her arms around his neck, stood on tiptoe, and poured all her fear and relief into a kiss.

He gave as good as he got, even though he couldn't put his arms around her. By the time they came up for air, her insides had gone liquid with wanting and she could feel his erection pressing against her belly.

He put the briefcases on the floor and drew her into his arms, his blue eyes blazing down at her. "That was one hell of a greeting, darlin'. I'm tempted to go out and come back in the door again." His voice had gone all southern so it warmed her even more.

She leaned back in the circle of his arms, all her fear vanishing like smoke in his presence. "I'm glad you decided Tully was wrong.

I feel so much better having you here. It's been a little nerve-racking today."

His arms tightened around her and a shadow darkened the heat in his eyes. "You shouldn't have to go through this alone." His mouth went grim. "You shouldn't have to go through it at all."

"Don't start blaming yourself." She laid her palm against his cheek. "You keep forgetting that I started this whole thing about the Wi-Fi. I've been fully involved since the beginning."

"Too involved, but you're a hard woman to say no to." His lips curved into a sly smile. "Good thing that most of the time I don't want to."

She relaxed into his chest again, seeking the sense of security he gave her. "Just stand here with me for a minute."

"I'd stand here all night with you if I could." He stroked a hand over her hair with a ghost of a laugh. "Well, maybe I'd talk you into taking it horizontal."

"Talk away. You know I love your accent." She snuggled in closer to him while he began to glide his hands up and down her back.

After a little while, she hummed a sound of contentment and tilted her head back to ask him what was in the metal cases. But there was such sorrow etched on his face that she couldn't get the words out. She started to ask him what was wrong but he smiled with an obvious effort. It had been a private moment he didn't mean to share with her. She wondered if it had to do with his mother's death. So she kept her question generic. "Are you okay?"

"Now that I know you're safe, I am." He kissed her on the forehead. "I need to set up my equipment. Then we'll talk about what Chad said to you."

It hurt that she had shared a devastating event her life, but he didn't trust her with his sadness. Though now was not the time to push for revelations. She stepped out of his embrace. "I figured you didn't have pajamas in those briefcases."

He laughed, picked up the cases, and carried them to her kitchen counter. She realized he was dressed entirely in black from head to toe: jacket, T-shirt, jeans, and sneakers. And he looked really good in it, the width of his shoulders and length of his legs accentuated by the dark hue. "Were you lurking in the shadows while you waited for me?"

"What?" He had shucked off his jacket and was focused on unlocking the cases. He glanced down at his clothes. "Oh, right. Actually, Tully's guy got me into your building through a basement window." He met her gaze. "But don't worry. After I was in, he fixed the lock. In fact, he's going to come back tomorrow to reinforce the security down there. It could be better."

Dawn slid onto a counter stool beside where Leland stood. "Okay, what is all this?"

He pointed to one case, which held something that looked like a laptop with a massively reinforced shell. "Most people who see this have to sign a nondisclosure agreement. It's something I helped develop for the government." He pressed a switch, and the screen came to life, showing the interior of a car from the point of view of the driver. She could see the steering wheel, the dashboard, and windshield, as well as a tree-lined street lit by overhead lights. "Tully's wearing a bulletproof vest with a video cam embedded in it. What you're seeing is his current position in Cofferwood."

"He's wearing a bulletproof vest?" Her nerves tightened again.

"Just as a precaution. Tully always plays it smart." Leland flipped open the second case, which held a more normal-looking laptop. "This is for monitoring the data traffic."

When the display booted up on that one, it was filled with gobbledygook, as far as she could tell. "Any change in the node?" she asked.

"Still going strong. I assume your customers continue to complain about their phones."

"Most of them turn off the data when they're at the gym. Vicky promised to make an announcement when the problem is fixed."

"Which leads me to believe that Tully is right. They're going to move the node soon." Leland began typing, his face and shoulders taut with concentration.

"You're really sexy when you work on the computer," Dawn said.

His fingers stilled on the keyboard and he turned his head to look at her, the light of the screen flashing on his glasses as he gave her a long, slow smile. "I don't believe anyone has ever said that to me before."

"I guess I have a nerd fetish." She grinned. "Don't let it go to your head."

He laughed full out. "My *head* has already felt the effects of your presence." His expression abruptly became serious as his gaze traveled over her face. "In the midst of all this"—he swept his hand through the air over the laptops—"you make me smile. Thank you for that gift."

Delight and something deeper, something she couldn't quite bring herself to find a name for, fizzed through her. She'd given this incredible man a gift. It was a gift she didn't take for granted herself because she'd struggled to learn how to smile again. Maybe that's why she could help Leland do the same thing.

"Sorry, didn't mean to distract you," she said. "Go back to catching the bad guys."

He planted a quick, hard kiss on her mouth. "You inspire me to work harder. The sooner I catch them, the sooner I can concentrate on you."

"As a personal trainer, I use every tool I have to motivate my clients."

"Consider me highly motivated," he said, going back to his keyboarding. "Tully, can you hear me?"

"Ten four, good buddy, you're humming in my ear like a mosquito at a blood bank." Tully's voice issued from the heavy-duty laptop's speaker.

"Could you dispense with the CB radio slang? Dawn won't have a clue what you're talking about. I'm not sure I will either," Leland said, but the corners of his lips twitched. "What's the latest news on Chad's whereabouts?"

"Evening, Dawn," Tully's voice said.

"Hi, Tully." She felt a little reticent with him, given his law enforcement background and extra years of experience, but she decided gratitude was always welcome. "Thanks for sending your guardians. Knowing they were there made me feel better when Chad insisted on walking me home."

"I'm glad to hear that. We'll keep someone with you until this is over." Tully switched back to business mode. "After Chad left Dawn at her building, he went to the gym. He has a key and let himself in through a back door."

"He has a key?!" Dawn exclaimed. "I thought I was the only trainer who has ever been given a key to the gym."

"Useful to know," Tully said. "He's more than a trainer, I'm guessing."

"Yeah, I'm beginning to grasp that," she said.

"So you're not going inside the gym now that we know Chad is there," Leland said sharply to Tully. "Observation only."

"We'll see how it plays out," Tully said. "How's the data traffic?"

Leland glanced at the other screen. "Steady." He bent closer to the laptop. "Tully, swear to me you won't do anything stupid."

"The question is how you define 'stupid,'" Tully said.

"You know what I mean." Leland's posture telegraphed frustration. She almost expected him to leap through that screen and drag Tully away from the gym physically.

"I'm not going to spook them, so you can rest easy, partner. However, I am going to get out of the car so I can get a better view of the door Chad used. Don't panic when you see me move."

Leland straightened up and rolled his shoulders. "Don't get too close."

Dawn nudged a counter stool toward him. "Sit down and be comfortable."

He nodded and turned the stool toward her before he sat. "Tell me what that scumbag Chad said to you."

"Can Tully still hear me?"

"No, our mic is off now. We can hear him but not vice versa." He took both her hands in his, his grasp warm and comforting.

"I don't remember everything because, honestly, I was trying to figure out what to say back to him half the time."

"I can imagine that wasn't easy."

"Two things stood out for me. One, that he decided to walk back to my apartment with me. But not immediately. It was kind of weird that he caught up with me. I think he'd expected me to walk faster and was afraid I might have noticed him behind me." She gave Leland a slanted smile. "I was walking slowly to make sure my bodyguards could keep up with me."

He gave her hands a light squeeze. "I appreciate that you followed my suggestion. Sorry it stuck you with Chad."

"His presence convinced me he's involved somehow, so that's useful." She shrugged. "The second thing was that he referred to my past experience. Which means either Ramón or Vicky told him. No one else at the gym knows about what happened to me. I only told Ramón, although I'm sure he shared it with Vicky."

"That ties them together even more closely."

"I hate that Chad knows." She shivered. And she didn't want Ramón to be the one who had told Chad about her.

Leland's grip tightened around her hands. "I hate it too. I wish I could erase it from his memory the way I can delete a file."

She looked down at his long, supple fingers curled around hers and thought of all the ways he'd touched her. Suddenly, it didn't matter so much that Chad knew because Leland had given her back the joy of being touched without fear.

"I need to tell Tully this." He released her hands and turned back to the computer, keying on the mic and relaying the salient points of the conversation to Tully.

"No surprise," Tully said. "Okay, I'm going to move now. I want to be in position before any shit hits the fan. Pardon my language, ma'am."

"Don't edit your language for my sake. I've heard it all at the gym," Dawn said.

The image on the heavy-duty screen began to change as Tully exited his car and moved swiftly along the street. After a few minutes, he turned, and Dawn recognized the alley that ran behind the gym. The image was clear and bright, even though it was about eleven by now.

"How come we can see everything so well when it's dark?" she asked.

Leland smiled as his fingers danced over the keys. "Some enhancements I made to the camera and software. Video technology is becoming quite advanced, so I simply built on what existed. Now I'm going to pick up all of Tully's watchers on-screen."

Windows began to pop up around the periphery of Tully's image. Each one showed a different view of the gym from various distances and angles. Tully's was the closest, though.

For half an hour, nothing happened other than an occasional car passing.

"The TV scriptwriters never show you this part," Tully murmured into his mic. "A whole lot of waiting."

"And patience isn't your strong suit," Leland murmured back.

"When there's a goal in sight, I can be as patient as an alligator eyeing a nice, fat muskrat on the riverbank."

Dawn choked back a laugh. Tully's imagery was certainly vivid.

Leland hissed in a breath and swiped at the computer screen, enlarging one of the small windows. A procession of six black SUVs cruised down one of Cofferwood's quiet streets. Dawn thought it might be Elm Avenue. "Showtime," Leland murmured. "You've got six SUVs coming in your direction."

"Yeah, my guy on the roof just told me. He says it looks like they're one convoy. But no trucks. If they're moving inventory, they'd need bigger vehicles."

Leland pulled up multiple screens to track the vehicles, occasionally tapping the track pad with one long finger. "I've got screenshots of all the plate numbers," he said to Tully.

"Send 'em to Novak. Tell him to put a rush on it. This is some major honcho coming to inspect the goods."

Dawn watched as Tully started to move again. Leland swore and snapped, "Tully, you're close enough."

But Leland was typing and swiping as he spoke, undoubtedly getting the license plate numbers to Novak, whoever that was.

"Just want to make sure I get a clear view of whoever gets out of those cars. You want to get good screenshots, right?"

"Not at the cost of your life, you asshole. Stay where you are!"

The view on the screen continued to shift and Leland swore again.

"Keep it down, partner," Tully muttered. "I need to be able to hear what's going on."

"You've got a directional mic in that vest. Just face them and I'll pick up the sound," Leland gritted out. He hit the key that she recognized as turning off their mic before saying in a normal tone of voice, "I don't want to have any unexpected sounds from our end getting Tully killed."

Tully himself went silent as the SUVs hulked past him, seemingly almost close enough to touch. Dawn hoped the video camera had a zoom lens. Otherwise she agreed with Leland about Tully being way too close.

The cars halted and the doors seemed to fly open at once, disgorging an assortment of men dressed in black. They fanned out, heads swiveling constantly. She held her breath as one seemed to look straight at Tully for a long moment before he turned his head and moved on.

"That looked close," she said.

"The camera has a long lens, but he's close enough to be spotted," Leland said, his face tight with anxiety.

Some of the men took up what were clearly guard positions around the cars and door.

"Those guys are professionals," Leland said. "And I can see the guns under their jackets."

One of the men walked up to the third SUV and opened the back door, saying something in rapid-fire Spanish so that a phalanx of men formed up around him. Dawn gasped when a woman emerged from the car, wearing high-heeled pumps and a long black raincoat cinched around her waist. Her silver hair was pulled back in a low bun and her earrings flashed in the light. Really big diamond studs, Dawn guessed. She barely glimpsed her before the woman moved into the protection of the phalanx and disappeared through the gym's back door.

"Holy shit!" Tully's voice was so low it barely came through the mic, but she could still hear the excitement vibrating in it. "That's Griselda Rodriguez, one of the most violent drug kingpins in the world. The DEA has been trying to catch her for years. I'm pulling back so I can call in the cavalry."

The camera began to back away from the scary-looking guards very slowly. Dawn glanced at Leland to find his eyes locked on the screen, his jaw tense, his mouth set in a grim line. "Easy, Tully, easy," he whispered as the camera swiveled away and picked up speed. "Don't catch their attention."

Tully's car came into view. Dawn blew out a breath of relief as the image showed the interior of it as Tully got in, started the engine, and drove down the street at a careful speed. As soon as he reached the next block, he turned the corner and roared forward so the streetlights strobed past at high speed.

"Leland, get me the best shot of the woman you can," Tully said, swerving into a municipal parking lot and braking to a stop. "Send it to my cell because I'm going to forward it to my contact at the DEA immediately."

Leland's fingers flew over the keyboard. "Done!"

Tully was already on his cell, clearly waking up whoever he had called. He used some colorful language to get the person's attention but then he relayed the information. There was some waiting and he repeated his story. He slotted his cell phone into the stand on the dashboard and turned on the engine again. "I'm going back to keep an eye on things until the DEA gets here."

"Tully, you've got your guys everywhere. Let them keep an eye on things," Leland said. "You're going to draw attention to yourself if you keep driving by."

"Don't worry. I have very clear instructions not to be seen." He sounded grouchy about that. "They want to follow Rodriguez back to wherever she came from, try to round up more of her top lieutenants. There are a couple of bad dudes they really want to nab."

"What's wrong with that plan?" Leland asked.

"She's slipped through their fingers before. We know where she is right now. I say grab her. A bird in hand and all that. But it's not my call."

"Thank God," Leland said under his breath.

"I heard that," the other man said. "I'd say Rodriguez's presence confirms that the weapons are being stored in the gym. So at least we'll be able to keep those out of the cartel's hands."

He turned onto the street where he'd originally been parked and slid into the same spot. "Don't worry, Rockwell, I'm staying near this car. I don't argue with the DEA. Much." The image shifted as he climbed out and walked into the recessed entrance of an empty storefront. When he turned, Dawn could once again see the alley. However, only the back of one SUV was visible from Tully's vantage point.

Leland muted their mic before he said, "Tully may be worried about losing Griselda Rodriguez, but it's better for everyone at the gym this way."

She thought about that for a moment. "Because Griselda won't know that it was someone at the gym who tipped off the DEA?"

"Drug lords have a long reach, even from prison. I'd hate to have you in the crosshairs." She could see fear in the set of his mouth and the tightness in his jaw. His caring reached deep inside her. "Even Chad and whoever he's working with are better off this way."

"I guess I'm glad about that." Especially if one of Chad's collaborators turned out to be Ramón. Even if he was selling guns, she didn't want her boss to be murdered by drug dealers. "I sure don't want anyone innocent getting hurt because of Griselda's capture."

"I don't want *you* hurt." Leland brushed a finger down her cheek, making her feel a curl of comfort in her chest. He unmuted the mic. "Tully, you need to make sure Work It Out is not mentioned anywhere in any report about Griselda Rodriguez's capture."

"It's not my call. It's the DEA's but I'll do what I can."

"I want to talk to your connection there."

"You don't need to talk to my connection."

"Then I'll trust you to get it done." Dawn had never heard that tone in Leland's voice before. It was like hardened steel sharpened to a point. Not a trace of southern honey in it.

"I heard you, buddy, and I know why you're asking. I'm on it." Tully surprised her by sounding sympathetic and reassuring rather than insulted.

"Good." Leland sat back on the stool and rolled the well-defined muscles of his shoulders. "Thanks."

He sat for a moment, his long legs encased in that sexy black denim and stretched out to brace on the floor despite the height of the stool. The short sleeves of his black T-shirt pulled tight over his biceps but left the chiseled ridges in his forearms exposed. She wanted to run her finger down one. The sculpted planes and angles of his face caught the illumination from the computer screens, painting them with light and shadow.

But the heat that raced through her was fanned as much by his confrontation with Tully as by his lust-inducing body. Leland had pressured his *partner*, a man he considered more than a brother, to protect her. That stirred her in a way she didn't want to analyze because it went far beyond sex.

"Are you and Tully okay?" She preferred not to have a wedge driven between them on her account.

He glanced away from the screens, his expression still hard. "If he keeps his promise."

"Thank you," she said. "For asking him."

"The DEA will owe you as much as Tully, so that's the least they can do. I just hope he can convince them of that."

He still looked tense and unsettled, so she decided to drop the subject and let him work.

For another half hour, Leland monitored all the cameras, but nothing changed until Tully said, "The DEA is here." He turned so the camera was pointed across the street. "There's one of their agents."

Dawn could just barely make out the shape of a man in black clothing working his way toward the alley.

"Guess my job is over," Tully muttered, his voice laced with disappointment.

"Get out of there, partner."

"Don't worry. I was one of them once, and I didn't want civilians around to gum up my operation. I'm pulling my guys out too."

"Don't sound so dejected," Leland said. "You're the one who had the smarts to recognize a drug kingpin. They wouldn't be taking her down without you."

"Don't underestimate Griselda Rodriguez. She's not in custody yet." But the camera headed back to his car.

"What about the guns?" Dawn asked Leland.

"That's the FBI and ATF's area," Leland said. "The DEA should bring them in for that. Interagency cooperation."

"I'll keep you posted about the guns," Tully said. "The DEA may want to leave them in place until they've rounded up the Rodriguez crew. They won't want to tip anyone off that Griselda has been spotted."

"Hell and damnation!" Leland said. "I don't want Dawn having to face Chad again."

"Chad's small potatoes compared to Griselda Rodriguez, as far as the authorities are concerned," Tully said, his visual showing his car on the move again.

"But Chad has a lot of guns," Dawn said.

"Hey, I've got incoming communication from the DEA. I'm gonna sign off," Tully said. His video feed went blank.

Leland shut down all the windows since they were no longer actively surveilling the site. He swiveled toward Dawn. "You can take a sick day or two, if the DEA wants to keep things looking normal." He laughed without humor. "If having an arsenal in the basement could be called normal."

"Chad's already suspicious of me. Wouldn't that make him even more so?" She shook her head. "I'd almost rather be at the gym where there are lots of people around and Chad has to act like he's just a personal trainer."

"Then I'll be there too."

"We broke up and you quit the gym, remember?"

He smiled with an edge. "Ah, but I didn't cancel my membership because you told Vicky not to give me a refund. Maybe I'm trying to win you back." He lifted her hair away from her neck before he brushed a whisper of a kiss just under her earlobe.

A tingle of delight ran over her skin. "I like being won back. Do it again."

He obliged and then moved his lips along her jawline with the same light pressure. The tingle turned into a full-body shiver of delicious sensation. It was probably the heightened tension of the evening, but her nerve endings felt ultrasensitive. She ran her fingertips over the slight scruff of late-night whiskers on Leland's chin, testing the springy bristles and thinking how they would feel on the inside of her thighs. The tingling grew hot and migrated down between her legs.

"Do you still need to monitor the dark node?" she asked, an edge of huskiness in her voice.

His lips curled into a sensual smile of comprehension. "I can set up an alarm to alert me if it changes."

"I'll meet you in the bedroom." She gave his denim-covered thigh a squeeze before she scooted off the stool.

She figured they might not have much time, so she stripped off her clothes, brushed her hair to a high gloss, and slipped under the covers. She'd barely settled back when Leland strode through the door and stopped dead, his smile turning so sexy it practically set her on fire. Without saying a word, he jerked his shirt up over his head so hard that his glasses went flying through the air.

"I think they went—" she started to point.

"I'll find them later." He stripped off his jeans and boxer briefs and stalked around to pull the covers down to her ankles. "How did you know that I had pictured you exactly like this?"

Just the way he gazed at her made her go hot with longing. "Well, being naked isn't a stretch," she said to cover her instant arousal.

He put one knee on the bed, making it sink under his weight before he stretched his hand out to splay it on her stomach. It felt almost like he was branding her as his. "In this room. On this bed. Naked and waiting for me with that hungry look in your eyes."

"Oh. *Oh!*" He skimmed his hand down and slid one finger down between her legs to gently stroke her clit. She arched into his touch as sparks scattered through her belly. Two more strokes and he dipped his finger inside her.

"Oh," he said in imitation of her. "You're so wet already." He slid his finger in deeper and she rocked her hips to welcome him. But he withdrew, bringing his finger to his mouth to suck it, his eyelids half-closed. "You taste like everything I want."

"And I want you," she said. "There's a condom in the drawer right beside you."

"Hey, darlin', we're not in a rush." His accent was thick and smooth as he ran his palm over her thigh.

"I told you that watching you on the computer makes me hot. So I'm in a rush."

"Well, okay, then," he said with a slow-curving smile. "You just had to explain that."

Opening the drawer, he pulled out the foil envelope and tossed it on the pillow before sliding onto the bed beside her, his long, hard body pressed against her side. He cupped a hand over her breast and gave her a lingering kiss. His erection was hard against her thigh, so she reached over to wrap her fingers around it and stroke. The motion pushed her breast harder into his palm, which wound her even tighter. She was ready to explode.

He started to roll onto his back but she braced her hand against his chest. "I want you on top," she said.

"Are you sure?" He brushed her hair away, his gaze questioning as he scanned her face. "I'm happy with you anywhere you choose to be."

"I want to be surrounded by you." She yearned to open herself completely to Leland. She wanted to feel his weight anchoring her while trusting his strength to keep her safe. She craved the sense of being filled to the fullest. She ripped open the envelope and rolled the condom onto his cock. Then she kissed him deeply, tempting his tongue with hers, circling her thumb on his nipple, and hooking her leg over his. As he turned onto his side to meet her halfway, she used the leverage of her leg to roll them both so she was under him, her thighs spread on either side of his hips. She checked for any signs of a panic attack, but all she felt was aroused and aching.

He braced himself with his forearms on either side of her shoulders, once again checking on her reaction. "You tell me the second you feel uncomfortable. No matter what I'm doing."

"I won't need to. This feels very right." She did her best to rock her hips but could barely move under the weight of muscle and bone that held her exactly where she should be. Without any fear.

He shifted so his cock nudged her clit, making her moan as an electric current of pleasure jolted through her. "More," she begged. "More of you."

He straightened his arms so he hovered above her as he eased himself slowly inside her, making her gasp at the exquisite sensation of being filled. "Yes, yes, yes!" she chanted, her insides turning molten with satisfaction and yearning at the same time.

She looked up at him, savoring the tautness of his jaw, the power of his braced arms, and the silk of his hair falling around his face. It was his eyes that nearly undid her, though. They blazed with desire but held a stunning tenderness. He understood what she was asking of him, what she was giving to him.

She planted her feet on the bed and tilted her hips. "Move!"

He laughed, a growling rumble of sheer exultation, and followed her command, sliding out and thrusting back in with a driving rhythm that brought her right to the edge.

For a moment every cell in her body seemed to go still, a suspension before the coming explosion. Then the cataclysm hit her, sending her into a mind-blowing, muscle-wrenching orgasm that seemed to go on forever.

When she finally relaxed into the mattress, she opened her eyes to see Leland staring down at her. "That was the most intense thing I've ever watched," he said.

"You should have felt it," she said.

"Oh, I did. That was incredible."

But he was still fully hard inside her. The heft of him there sent tiny tremors vibrating through her. Tremors of pure pleasure.

"You didn't come," she said.

"Only by calling on every ounce of self-control I possess." He lowered himself to his forearms again so their faces were only inches apart. "I wanted to make sure I could stop if you needed me to."

His words burrowed into her chest, finding her heart and lodging there. His care for her, shown in so many ways this evening, left her breathless with longing for something she feared was out of her reach. She forced a breath into her lungs, but that only intensified her awareness as she caught the scent of clean, aroused man that was so distinctively his.

"Am I crushing you?" He started to straighten his arms.

Unable to push sound past the emotion clogging her throat, she shook her head and tugged him back down, loving the feel of his chest against her breasts. She coughed to clear her throat. "It's your turn."

"I'm in no hurry." He kissed her shoulder. "I'd be happy to stay like this until my arm muscles give out."

"All that swimming pays off." She skimmed her palm over the bulge of muscle in his shoulder and squeezed her internal muscles around his cock.

His eyelids slammed shut and he groaned, his hips rocking slightly. She squeezed again.

"Holy hell! I could come just from you doing that," he rasped. But he started to move, his strokes slow and sensual.

He was being gentle, considerate, still worrying about her demons. But that wasn't what she wanted from him now. She tightened her inner muscles one more time.

The sound that came from his throat was ragged and primitive. He picked up his rhythm, his thrusts powerful and deep. She wrapped her legs around his waist and dug her fingernails into the flexing muscles of his butt, feeling her own arousal coiling tight again.

"Oh my God, Dawn!" he panted, driving into her again and again. And then he plunged in and stopped, head thrown back, arms ramrod straight, hips wedged hard between her thighs. "Yes!" he shouted as she felt him pump inside her. "Yes! Darlin'! Yes!"

The slam of his climax set her off. Her voice joined his as she pulsed around the hard length of him, her insides molten with release.

After the last shudder shimmered through her, he let himself down and rolled them so that she came out on top, sprawling over him as his softening cock slipped out of her. She whimpered as the satisfying sense of fullness disappeared.

"You okay?" he asked between ragged breaths.

"Just missing you." But it felt wonderful to be pressed skin to skin, trading body heat, their hearts pounding against each other.

Knowing that he cared for her. Knowing that she cared for him. She wouldn't use the word "love," but it hovered there.

She sighed and kissed his pectoral muscle because it was under her cheek. "Can we stay like this forever?"

"In a perfect world, we could," he said, one of his hands stroking lazily up and down her back with an occasional detour down to her buttocks. "Unfortunately, we still have some arms dealers to reckon with. But for now, we're golden." His accent caressed like velvet, which meant he was relaxed.

She'd done that for him. For now that was enough.

Chapter 17

Dawn woke up to find the room in darkness and Leland gone. When she ran her hand over the pillow where his head had left an indentation, it was still warm. She pushed the covers off, pulled on a white cotton sleep shirt, and padded out of the bedroom, the wooden floor slightly chilly under her bare feet.

Leland sat at the kitchen counter, the glow of the laptop's screen illuminating his face while his fingers pirouetted over the keyboard. The only lights he had turned on were her kitchen's undercabinet fixtures so his black clothing faded into the dimness. He hadn't bothered with shoes either, and one of his long, bare feet was hooked over the support bar at the bottom of the stool while the other was braced flat on the floor. She wanted to run her finger along his arch to see if he was ticklish.

"Did the data traffic change on the node?" Dawn asked as she came up to lay her body against his solid back while she ran her hands up and over the swell of his shoulders. She allowed herself to briefly bury her nose against the fabric of his T-shirt to inhale the scent of warm skin, clean cotton, and the crisp undertone of his soap. She felt like she would remember that aroma the rest of her life.

"No, it's about the same." He twisted his head to kiss one of her hands, his lips warm and firm.

The video monitoring laptop was dark, which meant nothing was happening with Tully. "So what are you working on"—she glanced at the microwave's display—"at 4:07 in the morning?"

"A report for a client. I didn't get a chance to finish it earlier today." He continued to type as he talked.

She peeked around his shoulder to see words appearing on the screen at high speed. "Is it due tomorrow—er, today?"

"It's due to Derek later today. He needs to incorporate it into his proposal."

She pulled her hands back, edged around the stool, and tilted sideways to get her face between Leland and the computer. "Leland, Derek is your partner. You're involved in a situation involving guns and drug dealers. He's not going to expect you to hand in your report on time."

He stopped typing to run one hand over his face. "I couldn't sleep."

"Why didn't you wake me up? I'm pretty sure we could have found something more interesting to do than write a report." He looked exhausted in the low light, not surprising given that he'd gotten about two hours of sleep so far.

He smiled and swiveled on the stool, pulling her in to stand between his thighs. "You needed to rest." He set his hands on her hips and kissed her forehead.

"So do you."

"Yeah, but I couldn't, which is no excuse for keeping you awake."

She thought of what Natalie had said about the demons driving Leland. Maybe the dead of night was when he could be persuaded to reveal what they were. She brushed her fingertips through his rumpled hair. "Why can't you sleep, sweetheart?" Yup, she'd said "sweetheart." It was just to lull him into confiding in her.

"Too wound up from chasing drug kingpins and arms dealers, I guess." He gave her hips a playful squeeze.

She laid her palms on either side of his face without smiling. "Seriously, what makes you type reports in the middle of the night? I want to know."

He skimmed his hands down to cup her butt and move her in closer as though he would kiss her. She braced her elbows against his shoulders so he had to meet her eyes. "What?" she demanded.

He closed his eyes as though weary. "Obligations."

"To whom?"

He opened his eyes and the lines of his face tightened. "This isn't the time for diving into my psyche. I have tasks to finish before tomorrow morning."

"The middle of the night, when it's quiet and dark and there's no one but me to hear what you say, is the perfect time for diving into your psyche."

He released his grip on her butt and moved his hands to rest on his thighs. "Did Derek and Tully put you up to this?" He gave his head a tiny shake between her palms. "Forget I said that."

"It sounds like all three of us are worried about you." She took one of his hands and tugged at it. He unfolded himself from the stool and stood, towering far enough above her that she couldn't see the expression on his face in the minimal lighting. That wouldn't work.

She interlaced her fingers with his and pulled him toward the sofa. For the briefest moment, he resisted. Then he let her settle him on the cushions. She grabbed the fake-fur throw draped over the back of the couch and wrapped it around herself before she sat sideways and curled her legs under her. She made sure her knees touched his thigh. The contact would provide a literal connection between them.

"Did they tell you?" he asked.

"I haven't discussed your work habits with either of your partners. This is just me, wondering why you're trying to drive yourself to exhaustion."

"Huh." He dropped his head into his hands and rubbed his face again. "They think it's because my mother died three months ago."

He stopped again, so she prompted, "Had she been ill?"

"That's the hell of it. She was perfectly healthy except for the undiagnosed aneurysm in her brain." He shook his head. "Jesus, I have all this money for the best possible medical care, but no doctor caught it. She died alone. Probably in pain."

She laid a hand on his forearm. "No one can know whether she was in pain."

"The doctor said she might have had a severe headache or nausea immediately before the aneurysm ruptured. But he said it was a blessing she died. If she'd survived, there would have been extensive neurological damage. She would have hated being less." He turned away but she caught the glint of tears on his cheek. "She was such a strong woman."

She understood one part of his sorrow. "You didn't get to say goodbye. That must be hard."

He gave her his profile again, after he wiped his cheek on the shoulder of his T-shirt. "Mama raised me single-handedly. We were a team, a unit, allies, as well as mother and son. We had each other's backs. But I wasn't there when she needed me. I didn't have her back at the most important moment."

She picked up his hand from his thigh and sandwiched it between both of hers. "Your love was with your mom. She knew that. I'm sure she felt wrapped in it when she died. Because I can feel it radiating from you."

"I don't believe in any of that woo-woo stuff about projecting energy through the universe."

Stubborn man. "When you think of your mom, what do you feel?"

"Loss. Grief. Absence. Guilt."

"What about love? You don't remember being loved?"

"Of course I do." He was almost angry. "My mother worked three jobs to put me through school. She encouraged me and supported me and told me I could do anything I put my mind to. She loved me deeply."

"When she was dying, I guarantee she thought of you and felt your love in that same way."

"It's not the same as being there to hold her hand so she wasn't alone when she faced death."

His pain ripped at her heart like claws. "I get that, but you said she was a strong woman. I'm sure she faced death with courage."

He was silent for a moment. "She was religious too. A Catholic. She believed in heaven and hell. God knows, she deserved to go to heaven."

"She sounds extraordinary. I wish I could have met her." The woman who had created this man whom Leland was must have been quite a force. She would have loved to see them together to watch the dynamic between them.

Finally, he curled his fingers around one of her hands and tilted his head to look at her. "You have a lot in common with her when it comes to strength. I think you would have gotten along well, the two of you."

"That's a lovely compliment." She brought his hand to her lips for a brush of a kiss.

He turned on the sofa, crooking one knee flat on the cushion so he faced her full-on. "Derek and Tully think I work to bury my grief." He shrugged. "That's partially true. But I also do it to honor Mama. She gave up so much to make sure I had the tools to succeed. I owe it to her to use them."

"Um, I think she knows you succeeded."

He managed a ragged cough of a laugh. "Yeah, maybe." He toyed with her fingers without seeming to be aware of it. "I bought her a house, a car, jewelry, designer clothes. All the things she couldn't have when I was a kid. Honestly, I don't think she really cared about any of it. She just wanted to see me doing well. So I'd fly her up here to stay in my apartment. A penthouse I bought to show her I'd made it." His lips twisted into a wry smile. "I took her to fancy restaurants, to expensive stores. She was happy about that, not for herself, but because *I* could afford all those things."

"So you saw her often?"

"As often as she would come." A silent sob shook him. "I miss seeing her face light up when the maître d' showed us to the best table in a restaurant where reservations were supposedly impossible to get. Or when the manager in a designer store would wave away the minions and serve Mama herself. She'd give me this sly look that said, 'We're really something, aren't we, getting this kind of treatment?'"

His adoration for his mother vibrated in every word he spoke. Tears pooled in her eyes. "I'm so sorry."

"Maybe I'm not handling it well, but I don't know any other means to bear it," he said in a near whisper.

She and Leland really were kindred spirits. They handled pain the same way, pouring themselves into jobs that demanded so much attention they wouldn't have time to feel. Maybe it wasn't healthy but it worked for them . . . eventually.

Something shifted within her, making her heart flip. Beneath all the outward trappings of their different lives, they shared a fundamental way of dealing with what life threw at them. His money could buy all those things Leland had given his mother, but it couldn't save him from the terrible grief of losing her. He was as human and vulnerable as Dawn was.

Which meant she could see past the computer genius and the founding partner with the pool built for him on the roof of a skyscraper. Whatever else might come between them, she could love him simply as a man.

She rose up on her knees and put her arms around him. "I understand."

He didn't move for a long moment. Then he wrapped his arms around her like he was drowning and she was his lifeline. When he buried his face in her shoulder, she stroked his hair and let him hold on to her.

As the minutes passed, she could feel the tension drain out of his shoulders and his grip on her loosen to an embrace. She continued to skim her palm over the silk of his hair, demanding nothing, as she savored the heat and weight of his body enveloping hers.

His ragged breathing evened out and he lifted his head to press a gentle kiss on her mouth. "You mentioned doing something more interesting than writing reports. I might take you up on that, darlin'."

~

When her alarm went off the next morning, she had to squirm out from under the arm and leg that Leland had thrown over her during the night. Once she stopped the beeping, Leland made an inarticulate noise and pulled her back against him again. Exultation fizzed through her as she realized he'd slept through the rest of the night after they'd made slow, tender love. Well, they'd had to negotiate what time to set the alarm for, but she'd convinced him to make it a semicivilized hour.

"Are you awake?" she murmured quietly in case he wasn't.

"About half and only happy about it because I woke up with you beside me." His voice rumbled in her ear, its sound sleepy and relaxed. That sent another twirl of satisfaction through her.

She turned in his arms so she could face him on the pillow. "Before we have to deal with whatever Tully throws at us, I want to ask you to do something."

His eyes opened, their blue especially brilliant so close up. "Go ahead." But his voice was wary.

"When you're missing your mom, tell me. I don't care what time it is. Tell me instead of working."

"Why?" Genuine surprise laced the single word.

"Because I know about using work to avoid the ugly feelings. I learned that it's not healthy. You need to bring them out into the open. It makes them easier to bear." Natalie and Alice had taught her that. She hadn't really begun to heal until she'd shared with them how her past still controlled her life.

"I'm not going to wake you up in the middle of the night," he said. "You need to sleep."

"Yes, you are." She brushed her fingertips over his cheek. "I want you to. I hope I'll be here beside you, but if I'm not, call me."

He frowned. "What am I supposed to say?"

"Just 'I can't sleep' will do. I'll know the reason." She traced his eyebrow and then his cheekbone.

He caught her wrist and kissed her fingers. "I appreciate the thought."

She didn't push any further. Maybe the first time he got hit by grief he wouldn't wake her up, but the second time he might. If he didn't, she'd remind him until he took her up on her offer.

He snaked his arm under the covers and around her waist, sliding her close enough so her breasts were crushed against his chest and she could feel his semihard cock against her thigh. "God, I wish we could just stay here," he said, nipping her earlobe.

How could that tiny pinch make her entire body flash to full arousal? "You have no idea how much I agree with you."

He gave her butt a quick squeeze. "But we have arms dealers to catch." He threw the covers off. "It's your shower so you get to go first."

"I have a better idea. Let's go at the same time."

He groaned and shook his head. "That will lead to distractions we don't have time for. But I'll take a rain check."

She laughed and rolled off the mattress and onto her feet, stretching because her body hummed with a delightful combination of contentment and arousal.

Leland groaned again. "Stop torturing me, woman!"

An hour later, Dawn was dressed in her Work It Out training uniform and Leland wore the black outfit from the night before. They sat at the kitchen counter in front of Leland's laptop, videoconferencing with Tully.

"Dawn, I'm really sorry to ask this of you," Tully said. "The DEA wants you to go to the gym as usual. They're setting up the operation to capture Rodriguez and her honchos today, and they don't want anything out of the ordinary to spook them into running. I told them I wanted to send some of my people into the gym with you but they're against it." He shook his head. "I'm not running this show so I can't butt in."

"Yes, but I can." Leland's hands were balled into fists. "There is no way in hell that Dawn will walk into that gym today."

"I hear you, partner, but the authorities have the chance to take down a major drug cartel's top leaders. It will be a huge victory. So they're being very careful." He shrugged. "Honestly, if I were in their shoes, I'd probably do the same."

"They can't force Dawn to go into work today," Leland said, his tone hard as steel.

She laid her hand on his rigid arm. "Hey, it's okay. I want to help them catch this Griselda and her nasties. What could happen at the gym? There are people around all the time." Chad gave her the creeps, but she couldn't picture him bashing her over the head in the weight room.

"What if Chad jams a gun in your side and forces you to go with him to the basement?" Leland's voice was tight with disapproval.

"I'd scream before I got anywhere near the basement. He wouldn't shoot me in front of witnesses."

"I'll put a wire on you," Tully said from the laptop. "If you scream, the cavalry will charge through the doors. In fact, I'll give you a code word so screaming won't be necessary."

Leland was shaking his head. "I don't like this."

"I have a lot of training in self-defense," Dawn pointed out. Much as she loved Leland for his protectiveness, she could do this. Last night she'd been shaken up by Chad's sudden appearance. Today she was braced and almost eager to face him again—the asshole. "I'm ready."

"I applaud your courage, ma'am," Tully said. They set up a rendez-vous away from both the gym and Dawn's apartment where Tully could install the wire on her. "My people say there's no one but us watching your building, but I'd advise you to leave separately anyway. I'll meet you at our agreed location in fifteen." His image disappeared.

Leland drew in a deep breath before he turned to take her hands. "You don't have to do this. In fact, it would be a hell of a lot easier on me if you didn't."

"Now that's hitting me where it hurts." She slid off her stool to stand between his knees. "I love that you want to keep me safe. However, if I can help take down not just an arms dealer but a major drug dealer, that seems worth a small amount of risk." She tried to beam reassurance into his troubled mind. "Not to be immodest, but I'm really good at protecting myself."

She decided not to remind him how well her training had served Alice when she was being held at gunpoint. That reference wouldn't ease Leland's anxiety.

"Darlin', I know how strong you are but I just found you. If I lose you, who will I wake up when I can't sleep?" His gaze locked with hers and something in his eyes made her heart do strange twisty things.

"That's the best motivation for staying safe you could give me." She poured her feelings into a kiss that left them both panting.

"We'd better go." She'd somehow ended up wedged between Leland's thighs and crushed against his chest. "Tully's on his way."

He held her tighter. "I could refuse to let you go."

"Don't make me hurt you." She smiled against his shoulder.

He released her with obvious reluctance. "You go out the front. I'll use the back exit a few minutes later." He kissed her again. "Make sure you yell the code word if Chad even blinks funny."

Chapter 18

Dawn tugged down the zipper of her lightweight trainer's jacket another inch in an effort to let in some air. After Leland had taped the wire to her chest early that morning, they'd realized that her gym shirt was so snug that the tiny device would be outlined by the stretchy fabric. So she'd been forced to add another layer, which made her sweat in the heated gym.

"You're ready for ten-pound weights for your biceps curls," Dawn told her client as she pulled the dumbbells off the rack. She'd reached her fourth training session for the day without any guns being pointed at her, so she could focus most of her attention on her job.

"Are you sure I can manage these?" The woman accepted the weights with a dubious look.

"Watch your upper arms in the mirror when you curl." She turned her client sideways to her reflection. "See that nice bulge? You've worked hard to build that strength."

When she'd arrived at the gym, Gina, the daytime receptionist, had told her that Ramón had a stomach flu and was taking the day off. Dawn had uttered a mental prayer that he wasn't secretly in the basement packing up guns for Griselda.

Vicky always did paperwork on Tuesdays, so she was holed up in her office.

Chad was the bigger problem because he had clients to train, so he moved around the gym. Every time Dawn saw him, cold fingers of fear walked down her spine. So it seemed smart to head in the opposite direction the moment she spotted him. She'd been avoiding him for weeks anyway.

When her nerves started to jitter, she reminded herself that all she had to do was say the word "Zulu" to bring Leland, Tully, and their reinforcements racing into the gym. The image of Leland sprinting to her rescue across the wood floor in his black undercover outfit evoked equal parts of comfort and heat.

So far no rescue was necessary so she turned her mind to counting reps. As soon as the session was over, she jogged to her locker to check her encrypted phone. She didn't dare keep the strange-looking cell on the floor, even in her jacket pocket.

A text from Leland had come in ten minutes before.

The DEA bust is headline news. Your sound check is loud and clear but be VERY careful. This is going to piss people off.

She wished he had added something personal, an endearment, a sign-off, a little word of affection. It was hard not knowing what their relationship was, especially when she felt so anxious. Were they lovers or just working together but with benefits? Would they continue on after the case was closed or had this been a short, intense fling?

They'd had that moment at her kitchen counter when Leland had said he didn't want to lose her. The look in his eyes had made her believe him. But it wasn't exactly a commitment.

She tucked the phone back into her locker and headed for the treadmills, finding an empty one and turning on the screen to an all-news channel. As Leland's text had promised, the news footage showed a rather mundane-looking house surrounded by an array of official vehicles, among which walked people in police uniforms or dark jackets with DEA printed across the back. The caption read: NOTORIOUS DRUG KINGPIN GRISELDA RODRIGUEZ CAPTURED IN SUCCESSFUL DEA RAID.

Dawn did a mental fist pump and flicked off the screen. Score one for the good guys in the war on drugs. Now they needed to take down her local arms dealers and she would be done for the day.

The question was *when*. Griselda was in custody so that cleared the way for a raid on the gym. Dawn's heart started to race in an unpleasant way as she pictured the vehicles and agents from the television footage, only clustered around Work It Out. They would wait for night, wouldn't they? To minimize civilian involvement?

She glanced around at the cheery, well-lit equipment room, filled with nothing more sinister than treadmills and ellipticals. About half were in use, mostly by women of all shapes, sizes, and ages. Some chatted with each other. Some stared at their screens. Some listened to music on their headphones. All worked out in serene ignorance of the illegal arsenal under their feet.

Dawn had found refuge here when she could find it nowhere else. She was pissed off that Chad, Vicky, and maybe Ramón had ruined that for her. She wanted to be like the women on the treadmills, not even questioning that they were safe.

A glance at the clock reminded her that she should meet her next client in the gym lobby. As she walked in that direction, Chad fell into step beside her, making her jerk sideways as apprehension spiked through her. "Jeez, where did you come from?" she exclaimed before she could stop herself.

"Sorry, I forget you have a reason to be jumpy." His tone was syrupy with unwanted sympathy. "I finished restocking the water fridge and saw you walking the same way I was headed."

"Right. Okay." She made herself breathe normally despite her heart going double time. *What would be an ordinary thing to say next?* "Thank you for walking me home last night." Even though she'd hated every minute of his company.

"I don't like to see ladies walking alone at night."

Because they might see you selling guns to drug dealers. Nope, not good to think those thoughts when Chad was a foot away from her. "Did Josh enjoy his party?"

"I'm pretty sure he did since he called in sick this morning." Chad gave her a conspiratorial wink. "He's still young and doesn't know how to hold his liquor yet."

As they walked into the lobby, Vicky emerged from the hallway to her office and stalked toward them, high heels tapping, gum snapping, and rhinestones on her nails flashing. "Chad, I need to talk to you." She jerked her head back toward the hallway. "In my office."

Chad raised his eyebrows at Dawn in exaggerated dismay.

"Sorry, Dawn," Vicky said without sincerity.

"No problem." Relief flooded Dawn. No further conversation with Chad would be necessary.

~

"That's it," Leland said as soon as he heard Chad's voice. "I'm getting Dawn out of there." He ripped off the headset, glad to be able to take some action. Sitting in the monitoring van, listening to Dawn go about her day without being there to protect her, made him want to punch someone. Possibly Tully, who was squashed into the back of the less-than-spacious van beside him.

Another van with five of Tully's best bodyguards was parked around the corner, ready to leap out the moment Dawn spoke the word "Zulu." Leland had insisted on being closer to the front door, overruling Tully's request for less visibility.

"Hold on there, partner." Tully clasped a hand on Leland's forearm while he continued to listen to Dawn's wire. "Let's see how this plays out."

Leland remained standing but he picked up his headset and held the earpiece to his ear. A slight wash of relief flowed through him when Vicky dragged Chad away. However, he now wanted to strangle Chad, slowly and with great relish, for bringing up Dawn's past.

"Damn," Tully muttered. "I wish we could ask Dawn to follow them to see what they say."

"Are you kidding me?! She's not going anywhere near those scumbags." He was back to considering how good it would feel to have his fist connect with Tully's nose. If Tully would let him, of course.

Tully's cell phone rang and he glanced down. "It's Alex from the FBI." He brought it to his ear. "Tully here. Yeah. Yeah. Got it." He put his phone down and tipped back to meet Leland's eyes. "They've decided there are too many civilians at the gym, so they're waiting until tonight after it closes to pick up the guns. They've got the names of the dealers from Rodriguez's people."

Finally, an answer. "Who are they?"

Tully shook his head. "The FBI is confirming independently so Alex wouldn't share that with me."

"Shit!" Leland combed his fingers through his hair in frustration. "I don't want Dawn there when the raid happens."

"Calm down. She'll be long gone home by then."

"No, she leaves now." Leland was done with this waiting.

Tully grabbed his arm again. "Hey, the FBI has asked her to keep it normal for one more day. Your lady agreed to that because she wants to help. You have to let her make her own decisions."

"You don't know what she's been through. She doesn't need this too." Leland stared down at his partner, his jaw clenched.

Tully shook his head. "She's a strong person and she can handle herself. You have to trust her." He stared back at Leland. "And me."

Leland tamped down his anger but then the fear it was repressing rose up. He slumped into his chair again. "It's making me crazy to sit in this goddamn van with nothing to do except worry about her."

"Don't you have a computer program you could work on? That might take your mind off things."

Tully knew him well, but he was talking about the old Leland. The one who buried himself in work so he wouldn't have to feel the emotions he didn't like. "No, I'm going to suffer through this with her."

Tully gave him a long, considering look. "Not that I want you to suffer, but it's good that you're getting your head out of the cyberworld. I'm liking Dawn more and more all the time."

"Glad to hear it because you're going to be seeing her more and more."

"Oho, so that's the way the wind blows." Tully smacked him on the shoulder. "I was hoping you'd wake up and smell the coffee."

"Jesus, Tully, could you mix any more metaphors?" But Leland grinned as elation rushed through him like a clear mountain stream. Sitting in a truck with nothing to do but feel profound anxiety breathing down his neck had forced him to consider some serious matters. Like his grief and how he had buried it. And how Dawn had shown him a way to face it.

"All I know is she's gotten you away from the office when no one else could," Tully said. "That argues for some strong feelings on your part."

Leland thought about claiming it was the Wi-Fi issue that had drawn him out of the office. He'd told himself that often enough. But he was done with avoiding his emotions. "I'd say my feelings are getting stronger every minute. Which explains why I don't want her hanging around arms dealers who might be pissed off that their buyer is in custody." He glared at Tully as the image of an unarmed Dawn facing down a machine-gun-toting Chad seared through his brain.

"We've been through this before."

"Okay, but I go in to get her just before the gym closes. I don't want her to be there without customers to protect her."

Tully shook his head. "They'll recognize you."

"Of course they will. As Lee Wellmont, looking for a refund of his membership dues since things didn't work out with his personal trainer. Or maybe Lee realizes he made a big mistake letting Dawn go and he wants to make amends." Leland smiled at the idea of playacting a reunion with Dawn and leaned back in the chair, bumping his head against a monitor. "Jesus, couldn't you get a bigger van?"

Tully snorted. "You're just cranky because I won't let you see your girlfriend."

Chapter 19

"And breathe out," Dawn instructed her client, completing the final portion of her last training session for the day. Or rather for the night, since she'd had appointments all evening. She offered her hand to the middle-aged insurance salesman stretched out on the mat. "You worked hard. Make sure to keep hydrating when you get home."

He allowed her to pull him to his feet. "I work hard every time with you. But it's always worth it. I feel so much better after I'm done. And I look better too." He smiled a happy smile before he took a long swallow of water.

Sometimes she loved her clients. Tonight, though, she wanted nothing more than to get the hell out of the gym with its stench of danger. She'd been so tense all day that she could count the knots in her neck and shoulder muscles. It infuriated her that the place where she usually felt secure had become a prison she needed to escape from.

But she understood why the FBI—or whoever was running this show now—needed her to stay. She realized that she hadn't seen Chad around since Vicky had yanked him into her office. That was weird because he definitely had evening clients.

She shrugged to counteract the clench of anxiety his unusual behavior induced.

"See you tomorrow," her client said as he started toward the locker rooms.

"Try to stretch before we begin," she reminded him.

He held up a hand in acknowledgment and kept walking. Dawn wiped down the mat and hung it on the rack before a bad feeling made her stomach spasm again. Chad couldn't have slipped through the FBI's fingers, could he? At least she didn't need to feel guilty if he had. She'd done what they asked her.

Fifteen minutes till closing time and then she could bolt out of there to find out what was going on.

As she walked toward the locker rooms, she noticed that the towel shelves in the treadmill room were nearly empty. She'd check her secret phone for messages and restock the shelves. Better to keep busy than to worry fruitlessly about Chad's whereabouts.

"Dawn, wait!"

She stopped and turned at the same time to see Leland striding toward her, wearing an odd, apologetic smile. Her heart did a somersault as she took in his long legs, wide shoulders, and nerdy glasses over those vivid blue eyes. He managed to look both hot and comforting at the same time. She had to resist the overwhelming urge to throw herself into his arms.

"Leland, what are you doing here?" Shit, he was supposed to be Lee here. She glanced around to see if anyone was nearby to hear her slip, but the room was deserted.

He didn't look worried so her tension ratcheted down a notch.

However, when he got close, he threw her a warning glance before setting that strange fake smile back in place. "Dawn, I came to ask for a refund, but then I realized I had made a terrible mistake. Will you give me a second chance?" He spoke loudly and she realized he was putting on a show. But for whom?

"A second chance?" Then she remembered their silly cover story. She exaggerated a wary glance. "Maybe. Take me out for dinner and we'll see if we can talk things through. You really hurt me, you know."

He let his head drop forward as though ashamed. "I know. I was a jerk. Can you forgive me?"

It seemed like they were going through this whole charade for no one since the room was empty.

"Dawn, you still here?" Chad's voice made her twitch and comprehend Leland's act.

"Yeah, I was just going to refill the towel shelves when my, um, client showed up."

"No need. I'll take care of it." Chad walked into the equipment room. He was dressed in jeans and a black T-shirt rather than his training clothes.

Leland pivoted around to face him. "Chad, good to—"

"You!" Chad shouted, his face contorting with anger. "I know who you really are, you fucking asshole!"

"Chad!" Dawn cried. "He's a client!"

"No, he's a fucking rat and the reason I just lost my best customer." Chad's face was bright red. "That deal was going to put me in the big time but you screwed it up."

"I have no idea what you're talking about," Leland said in a voice of utter disdain. "I came to ask Dawn for a second chance and you start calling me names. You're the asshole."

He must have learned that tone at his fancy private school.

Chad smiled in a horrible way, his mouth curving but his eyes flat and hard. "You're some kind of computer genius, so you traced the dark web traffic to my website." He shifted his creepy gaze to Dawn. "You brought him in. All that whining to Ramón about how unhappy the customers were. Jesus, you couldn't keep your nose out of it for the few weeks I needed to close this deal."

He reached behind his back in a gesture that sent a wave of panic through Dawn. But panic was an old nemesis, and she'd learned to deal with it. She fought back the blackness fogging her vision, refusing to freak out.

Before Dawn could see what Chad had in his hand, Leland shouted, "Zulu, Zulu!" and shoved her behind him, his body shielding her from Chad.

A piece of information popped into her head from one of the self-defense classes she'd taken, something she'd thought was useless at the time. She grabbed Leland's wrist and yanked him backward, yelling, "Pool!" Then she turned and bolted for the big glass doors, praying that the thud of footsteps following her was Leland and not Chad.

"What the fuck?!" Chad bellowed.

Dawn slammed open the door and ducked as a gunshot cracked from behind her and glass shattered around her shoulders.

"Leland?" She looked back to see him upright and running, his body still between her and Chad. Another gunshot rang out and she heard Leland curse.

Then they were at the edge of the pool. Dawn screamed, "Zulu," just in case Tully hadn't heard Leland, and dove in, Leland arcing into the water beside her.

She struggled to swim underwater, her clothes and sneakers creating enough drag to make it like moving through molasses. How many feet of water had the self-defense instructor said would slow a bullet to nonlethal speed? She was pretty sure it was five, and the pool was six-and-a-half feet deep, so she stayed as close to the bottom as she could. Of course, they'd have to come up for air soon, but she hoped Tully and his team would have ridden to their rescue by then.

She glanced sideways to check on Leland. He swam beside her but with an awkward, lopsided stroke. When she looked more closely, she saw a ribbon of blood trailing through the water behind him.

Rage and terror boiled up inside her. She fought back the terror with the fact that he was keeping up with her in the water, so he couldn't be dying. She embraced the rage for the strength it gave her.

When they got to what she estimated was the middle of the pool, she slowed the pace, her lungs beginning to crave fresh oxygen. Being an experienced swimmer, Leland could probably hold his breath longer than she could, except he was injured. She paddled just enough to keep herself flat against the tiled bottom of the pool and turned her head to check on him.

He was doing the same, his face toward her. His glasses were gone and the ribbon of blood spiraled upward now, seeming to come from his left arm. She wanted to put her hand against it to stanch the flow but knew the pressure would just push his body away from her.

She heard more gunshots but they were muffled by the water. She prayed her memory of the depth was correct, although she supposed it didn't really matter. She couldn't make the pool any deeper.

Her lungs began to burn and her vision began to blur, but she stayed down. She knew that Leland wouldn't let her surface alone, and she wasn't going to expose him to another bullet. They just needed to give Tully enough time to find them. It was hard, though, when the water pressed against her chest like it wanted to squeeze the air out of her. She let out a slow stream of bubbles to ease her bursting lungs.

Suddenly, Leland took off away from her, his long legs kicking powerfully. What the hell was he doing? When she saw him rotate and plant his feet on the bottom of the pool, she realized he knew she needed to breathe and was planning to surface first to draw Chad's attention away from her.

No way was she going to let him be the only target. She twisted to get her sneakers down and pushed hard so she would shoot to the surface. Now Chad would have to figure out who he wanted to shoot more. Maybe making that decision would slow him down enough for them both to dive again.

As her head broke through the surface of the water, she braced herself, wondering how much being shot would hurt. While she sucked in a deep breath, she did a swift scan of the pool's edge and nearly gulped water when she saw Chad, using a two-handed grip to aim his gun toward the spot where she knew Leland had come up.

"Hey, Chad, you asshole, I'm the one who screwed you!" she yelled before sucking in a fast breath and diving hard.

She struck off the bottom to launch herself in Leland's direction, relieved to see that he was underwater again. Her lungs were already complaining because she'd used up precious air shouting and hadn't had time to fully replenish it. As long as her distraction had kept Leland from getting shot again, she didn't care.

And then she heard voices—commanding voices, the kind you heard on TV shows when the cavalry showed up and told the bad guys to drop their weapons. The water muffled the words so she couldn't be sure, but it sounded like Tully had arrived.

She kept swimming toward Leland, just in case it wasn't Tully or he needed more time to disarm Chad. She realized Leland was moving toward her too, his hair billowing around his head with each surge forward, that terrifying red ribbon still streaming from his arm.

He gave a final kick to reach her, grabbing one of her hands to pull her in against him before rocketing them both to the surface.

She gasped in air at the same time she saw Tully standing by the edge of the pool wearing a bulletproof vest and gripping a big black handgun. Two men were holding on to Chad, whose arms were wrenched behind his back. "Oh, thank God!" She pressed her face into Leland's neck, his skin wet but warm against her cheek.

His arm tightened around her as the scissoring of his powerful legs kept them afloat. "Are you all right?" his voice rasped beside her ear.

She nodded against him, relief and the need for air making it hard to speak. Then she remembered that *he* wasn't all right. "Tully," she shouted. "Leland got shot. He needs a doctor."

The curses that came out of Tully's mouth were impressive before he yelled to his guys to call an ambulance. Then he placed his gun on the cement, shrugged out of his vest, and did a racing dive into the pool. He came up on Leland's opposite side, his gaze already searching his partner's body. "Where are you hit, buddy?"

"It's just my arm," Leland said, sounding irritated. "I don't need an ambulance and you didn't have to dive into the pool like some kind of superhero."

Tully raised his eyebrows at Dawn. "He can't be hurt too badly if he's grousing at me. Which arm?"

"The left one," Dawn said to forestall Leland's refusal of attention.

"Okay, let's get you out of the water so I can see what's going on." He looked at Dawn. "Will you be okay if I take his right arm?"

Leland still held her against his side with his good arm. It felt so wonderful that she hadn't thought how hard it must be for him to keep them both up.

"I'm capable of swimming on my own," Leland panted when Dawn tried to twist out of his grasp.

"Well, you can't swim while you're holding on to me," she pointed out.

"If you don't put your arm over my shoulders, I'll put you in a headlock and tow you to the side," Tully threatened his partner.

"Traitor," Leland muttered at Dawn, but he let Tully sling his right arm over his shoulders and guide him to the ladder at the edge of the pool.

Dawn paddled along behind, hating the swirl of red in the water. At least it was only coming from Leland's arm. Or so she kept repeating to herself to stave off the fear that squeezed her heart.

Leland hauled himself up the ladder one-handed, water cascading from his clothing. As Tully's men grabbed Leland to help him, a loud screech sounded from behind them.

"What the fuck is going on in my pool?" Vicky's voice was shrill. "Who the hell are you? This is private property. I'm calling the cops."

"Vicky, shut up!" Chad snapped.

Tully vaulted out of the pool despite his soaking-wet clothes and positioned himself in front of Vicky, where she stood glaring in the glass-strewn doorway. "Ma'am, I'm Tully Gibson, here on behalf of

250

the FBI. One of your employees"—he gestured toward Chad, who still stood between Tully's two men—"attempted to shoot one of your clients as well as a trainer."

Vicky spun to face Chad and shrieked, "You fucking moron, why'd you have to shoot at them? Now there's blood in my beautiful pool and the health department's probably going to make me drain it. Do you know how much it costs to fill this pool? Why didn't you just take your goddamn guns and go, like we agreed?"

"Because your nosy little bitch of a trainer brought down whoever the hell these guys are on top of us," Chad yelled back. "The blood in the pool is the least of your worries, you stupid cunt."

"That's enough," Tully snapped.

Vicky spun again and pointed a glittering talon at Tully. "What the fuck do you mean 'on behalf of the FBI'? Are you the FBI or aren't you? Because if you aren't, get the hell out of my gym!" She began to advance toward him.

"Ma'am, stop or I'll have to handcuff you," Tully said. "The FBI will be here soon."

Dawn scrambled up the ladder behind Leland. Taking his right wrist, she tugged him away from Chad and Vicky toward a chair on the opposite side of the pool. "Sit and I'll get a towel."

He obeyed, sinking onto the chair before he caught her hand. His blue eyes blazed up at her from under the wet hair plastered to his face. "You're sure you're okay?"

She squeezed his hand. "I'm fine." At least physically. Emotionally was a whole different ball game. "You're the one leaving a dramatic trail of blood in the water."

"It's just a graze, I swear. More annoying than painful."

She didn't believe him because she'd seen how awkwardly he swam. "We'll let the medics give us their expert opinion on that. In the meantime, I want to stop the bleeding." She gave him a soft kiss and rested her forehead against his for a moment before she slipped her hand out of his grasp. "Maybe press your hand against the wound until I get back?"

He dutifully put his palm against his upper arm and winced. She made no comment before she headed toward the towel cabinet, her sneakers squishing with every step.

Two of Tully's men now stood on either side of Vicky, but she continued to spew vitriol at Chad. He ignored her, gazing straight ahead as she berated him about the pool, the guns, the Wi-Fi, and his stupidity. Dawn gave them a wide berth.

She yanked clean towels off the shelf and heaved a sigh of relief when a group of people wearing jackets with FBI stenciled on them strode through the door to the pool, their shoes crunching on the broken glass. One shouted, "Hey, Gibson! What have you got for us?"

Tully stepped forward and gestured toward Chad and Vicky. "The arms dealer and his co-conspirator."

Not wanting to draw attention to herself, Dawn scurried back to Leland and the quiet side of the pool.

"Reinforcements have arrived," she said. "Maybe they can shut Vicky up."

"Or take her away."

When Leland lifted his hand from the wound, Dawn grimaced at the bright red blood staining his palm before he scrubbed it off on his soggy jeans. Folding one of the towels, she handed it to him. "I'm going to let you hold it because I don't want to hurt you by applying too much pressure."

"Sit by me," he said, his tone pleading. "I need to have you where I can see you."

She understood because she felt the same way. "Let me just give you this to keep you warm." She draped a towel around his shoulders while she worried about how much blood he had lost.

She forced back the tears that held all her fear before sliding onto the chair next to him, her wet clothes squelching against the cushions.

Her body was beginning to tremble in reaction to the adrenaline over-load, so she wrapped a towel around her own shoulders.

Glancing across the pool, she saw FBI agents swarming around Chad and Vicky. Tully stood to the side having an intense conversation with one of the agents. She couldn't hear what they were saying, but when they both swiveled their heads to look across the pool toward where she and Leland sat, a shiver of nerves ran through her. She buried her face in the crook of Leland's neck to block out everything but the feel of him alive and well beside her.

"You're shaking," he said, his voice a concerned rumble.

"I'm soggy and relieved to have the good guys in control of the situation." She felt him shifting on the chair and lifted her head. "What are you doing? Do not take your hand off that towel!"

He gazed down at her with worry in his eyes. "I want to hold you."

"Nope." Although the temptation of having his strong arm wrapped around her was powerful. "I'm good. I just want to go home and change out of these wet clothes." And burrow under the quilt on her bed snuggled up against Leland's big, comforting body.

Instead, Tully and the FBI agent he'd been talking with walked up to them. "Dawn and Leland, meet Senior Special Agent Chris Wertz." Tully held out Leland's glasses. "I thought you might want these. We found them in the pool."

Agent Wertz, a man with short iron-gray hair and a beak of a nose, nodded to them. "We appreciate your assistance with this case. You were instrumental in taking down the entire command structure of a major drug cartel." He cut his gaze to the towel Leland held against his arm. "We regret your injury."

Leland seated his glasses firmly on his nose before he stood up. "It's just a scratch. I'd like to get Dawn home so she can change out of her wet clothes. She's shivering."

Tully shook his head. "Not yet. The EMTs are on their way in to treat your wound. You got shot, buddy."

"As soon as they're done, we're leaving," Leland said.

"Only if you don't need to go to the hospital," Dawn said, coming to her feet as well.

Leland scowled at her but his expression quickly shifted to dismay. "There's blood all over your shirt."

She glanced down to see a splotch of red on the turquoise fabric over her chest and shoulder. "Don't worry. It's all yours."

Her Work It Out shirt reminded her of something she needed to know. She turned to Tully. "Is Ramón involved in the arms dealing?"

Tully shrugged. "It's hard to get any sense out of Vicky right now, so I don't know. She's batshit crazy. Pardon my language."

"We'll find out when we question her," Agent Wertz said, his voice hard and confident. "I'll make sure to pass the information along to Mr. Gibson."

"May I talk to her about Ramón before you take her away?" Dawn was afraid she would regret it but she couldn't bear thinking the worst of her mentor.

The agent hesitated a moment before he nodded. "I think we owe you that."

"No!" Leland snapped. "I don't want you anywhere near those two."

"They're in handcuffs." She laid her palm against his good arm. "I need to know for sure about Ramón." Even if it broke her heart.

He held her gaze for a long moment before he pivoted toward Tully. "You go with her."

"You got it, partner," Tully agreed. "But I'll be checking in with the EMTs before they leave. So you won't be able to feed me any bullshit that you're all right if you're not."

There was a flurry of movement by the door and two paramedics came striding into the pool area. Tully waved them over.

Dawn stretched up on her toes to kiss Leland on the cheek. "Don't be stubborn. Let them do whatever they need to." She pulled her soggy shirt away from her skin and tugged it down over her hips, like she was putting on armor for her encounter with Vicky. "Okay, let's do this."

"Mr. Gibson and I will be right beside you, ma'am," the agent said, walking on one side of her while Tully took the other. "Just don't expect a rational answer."

"She might not tell me the truth but I need to ask." With everything Ramón had done for her, maybe she could do something for him in return. If he was innocent.

If he wasn't, then she would seriously question her judgment of people.

"What do you want, bitch?" Vicky snarled as Dawn walked up to where the woman stood handcuffed between two agents—one male, one female.

Dawn took a deep breath and gestured toward Chad. "Does Ramón know about any of this?"

"Ray? Oh, right, you're his little pet," Vicky sneered. "You don't want your sugar daddy to be a bad guy."

"He's not my sugar daddy and you know it." Dawn kept her voice steady even as fury roared through her.

Vicky flicked her glittering talons at Dawn dismissively. "You know how Ray feels about guns. What do you think?"

Hope flickered in Dawn's belly. "He says he hates violence of all kinds, but he has a monogrammed gun safe in his desk drawer. And he stayed home sick today." She needed a definitive answer.

"The gun safe was a joke between him and me. He uses it to keep excess cash," Vicky said before a shadow crossed her face. "I feel bad about him being sick. I put some nasty stuff in his dinner last night to make sure he didn't come to the gym today. I didn't want him to catch Chad moving the merchandise. Kept poor Ray up all night vomiting." Her face crumpled. "I love him. This is gonna kill him."

"Why would you do this to him?" Dawn asked, her heart hurting for her boss over the truth of Vicky's statement.

Vicky's face went hard as nails. "It takes a shitload of money to keep this place going. We weren't exactly getting rich. That Griselda woman forced Chad to bring his product to the New York metro area so she could inspect it. He offered me a cut of the sale if I'd let him store his inventory in the basement for a couple of weeks. It was a lot of money." She shrugged. "I have nothing to do with Chad's shit. First time I've seen him since high school." She rounded on Chad, making the agents grab her arms. "You hear that, you asshole? I got nothing to do with you anymore."

"Good luck convincing the cartel of that when they come looking for revenge," Chad sneered, but he looked pale himself.

"I'll just tell them it was this bitch and her fancy consultant boyfriend."

"They're not going to have a nice chat before they kill you, you moron," Chad said, clearly goaded beyond all self-control.

"Okay, it's time to get them to headquarters," Agent Wertz snapped. "Take them out of here."

Tully held up his index finger to signal he needed a minute before he said to Dawn, "Do you want to ask her anything else?"

Dawn shook her head. "I'll go see how Leland's doing. You do what you need to do."

Tully gave the okay to Agent Wertz, who hustled off to organize the prisoners' exit.

She thought of what Chad had said and turned to Tully. "Should Leland and I be concerned about the cartel coming after us?"

Tully grimaced. "Wertz has promised to do everything in his power to keep your names out of this. He's solid so I believe him. The FBI will be more than happy to claim credit for finding Griselda through their own work. It's in the best interest of both Chad and Vicky to keep their mouths shut about the whole situation but, as you noticed, Vicky is not good at that. However, I'll keep a close eye on the situation and make sure you're protected."

That wasn't entirely reassuring but there was no point to worrying about it right now. She just hoped Leland hadn't heard Chad's outburst. He would feel even guiltier about involving her than he already did.

At least her faith in her own judgment had been restored. She had known in her gut that Ramón couldn't be an arms dealer. However, her boss was going to be devastated to find out his wife was aiding and abetting one. Not to mention that she was headed for jail.

The EMTs were still working around Leland as she walked up to the chair where he sat. "What's the prognosis?" she asked.

The woman packing instruments back into her bag looked a question at Leland.

"You can tell her," he said, wincing slightly as the other paramedic tied off the gauze wrapped around his arm.

"He got lucky." The EMT zipped the bag and straightened. "The bullet just grazed his arm—barely touched the muscle—so he won't even have a divot after it heals. We cleaned it up and gave him antibiotics, but I don't think infection will be a factor. Jumping in a pool helped clear the wound of any potential debris. He should try to ice it—twenty minutes per hour—for the next few hours and elevate it when possible to reduce swelling. Other than that, it's just going to hurt like a sonofabitch." She raised her eyebrows at Dawn. "We gave him something for that but I can tell he's not the type who will take it."

Dawn grimaced at how right the EMT was but a wave of relief rolled through her. "Thanks for taking care of him."

The medics nodded and picked up their gear before they headed toward the exit.

She sat down beside Leland. "How badly does it hurt?"

"I can barely feel it." The planes of his face softened as he asked, "Did you get an honest answer to your question?"

"Yeah, Ramón wasn't involved. Vicky deliberately made him sick today so he wouldn't catch Chad moving the guns out."

"That's pretty cold but I suppose she was protecting him in her own twisted way," Leland said. "I'm glad for your sake."

He lifted his hand to touch her cheek, his eyes scanning over her face like lasers. Then, with a low groan, he doubled over, his elbows on his knees.

"What is it?!" Dawn scooted off the chair and knelt in front of him so she could see his face. Terror ripped through her when she saw that his skin had gone pale and his eyes were squeezed closed. "Are you feeling light-headed? Are you going to pass out?" He could be going into shock from blood loss. She braced her hands on his shoulders. She didn't want him falling forward onto his head. She looked frantically for the EMTs but they were nowhere in sight.

His eyes opened to meet hers. "I thought you were going to die. When I heard the gunshot and the glass shattered around you . . ." He pulled her in against him using both arms in a grip like a vise. He was shaking. "I thought Chad was going to kill you."

"I think he was shooting at you, not me." Dawn wrapped her arms around Leland's rib cage, his body heat soaking through the clinging cotton of his shirt. He'd put himself between her and Chad's gun every time he had the chance. He'd tried to draw Chad's attention away from her in the pool. Her heart twisted in her chest. "You were doing a damn good job of protecting me."

"It was my fault he pulled that gun. If I hadn't walked into the gym, he would have let you leave without a confrontation. I set him off." She didn't think he could hold her any tighter but he did.

"You don't know that. He was looking for me and he had a gun hidden behind his back. Who can tell what he intended?"

"I should have overruled Tully and his FBI connection. You should never have been here." His shuddering grew stronger.

She wanted to shake him but he was already shivering, and she figured that might hurt his arm anyway. "Stop beating yourself up. I made the choice to come to work because I wanted to help catch the bad guys." Maybe she'd had something to prove to herself too, since she'd let them get away back in college. "You couldn't have stopped me. It was my decision, not yours."

"It was a bad decision." But he sounded less desolate and the trembling eased.

"Hey, they caught Chad and we're both still alive."

"Just barely." He tipped her head up and kissed her as though he was never going to stop.

Chapter 20

Two hours later, Dawn sat on her sofa with her legs across Leland's thighs, her head resting on his uninjured shoulder while his good arm circled her. Leland's damaged arm was propped up on a pillow with a gel ice pack resting on it. The television was on but muted so they could catch any news flashes about the drug and arms busts. Leland had pounded on Tully again to keep their names out of it because he worried about the same thing Chad had mentioned: retaliation by the cartel. Dawn was pretty sure the DEA and FBI would be quick to take all the credit, but Leland was obsessed with her safety.

"Did I tell you how brilliant you were to jump in the pool?" Leland asked, his breath tickling through her hair.

"About five times, but go ahead and tell me again."

He chuckled, the sound vibrating through her. "Even Tully was impressed."

"Yeah, who knew I would ever need that particular piece of information, let alone remember it? And who knew little old Josh was the programmer behind the dark web node?" Vicky had given up Josh in about thirty seconds when the FBI questioned her. "No wonder Chad wanted the kid to have a good birthday."

"If his claim that he had no idea what he was programming it for is true, would you mind if I hired him? He's got real potential."

"Go right ahead. You can be a good influence on him."

Leland's phone rang. "It's Tully," he said, swiping it onto speaker. "Hey, Gibson, Dawn's listening too."

"I've got some good news." Tully sounded exhausted and elated at the same time. "Chad has cut a deal to give up all his arms-dealing contacts in return for going into witness protection. Turns out the ATF and a couple of other agencies are very interested in where he got his military-grade weapons. So he will disappear as though he never existed, taking your names with him to the grave."

"What about Vicky?" Dawn asked. "She's the crazy one."

"She'll likely go to jail as an accessory," Tully said, "which means she needs to keep her mouth shut to survive. As wacko as she is, she's figured that much out. With a few hints from her interrogators to scare her even more."

Dawn thought of Vicky's hard-nosed approach to the gym's finances and decided that Tully could be right about her boss's wife. Vicky was all about self-preservation.

"Truth is that the cartel is in major disarray," Tully continued. "The DEA grabbed virtually all the top lieutenants when they scooped up Griselda Rodriguez. The rest of the scumbags will be scrambling to fill the power vacuum. They won't have time to go looking for revenge."

"Until the power vacuum gets filled," Leland said, his arm tightening around Dawn.

"Hey, give me some credit. I kept Dawn's name out of every piece of paperwork anyone filed, so she's invisible. You've been turned into 'an anonymous source.' If your name is anywhere in the records, it's buried under so many layers of confidentiality that even you wouldn't be able to unearth it with all your hacking skills, partner."

"I can unearth anything," Leland said, "but in this case I will happily leave it buried. I owe you for today. Thank you."

"For what? I just did cleanup."

"You're kidding, right? If you hadn't ridden to the rescue, all Chad had to do was wait for us to come up for breath one more time." Leland's arm tightened around Dawn.

"Well, I did find your glasses for you," Tully said, brushing off Leland's gratitude. "I'll accept your thanks for that."

Leland called him an asshole in a tone of deep affection and disconnected before dropping his phone onto the coffee table.

"Natalie always said Vicky was smarter than I gave her credit for. I'm glad her brain finally got control of her mouth." Her last worry laid to rest, Dawn yawned and nuzzled into Leland's chest. "I feel too tired to move but too hyped-up to sleep."

"I have an idea." Leland skimmed his hand up to cup her breast, his thumb grazing her nipple through the fabric of her nice, dry, pink T-shirt.

She grabbed his wrist and moved his hand back down to its original position, even as a delicious sizzle streaked through her insides. "You're hurt."

"A mere flesh wound. The rest of me is in fine working order."

She could feel his cock stirring to life under her thigh and smiled. "Oh, no, I'm not going to be responsible for making your gunshot wound bleed again. Besides, that's just the effect of all the adrenaline in your system. You don't actually want me."

"The hell with the adrenaline!" Leland seemed to explode into motion, throwing off the ice pack and elbowing away the supporting pillow. He used his good arm to lever her fully onto his lap before he wrapped both arms around her. "You could have died today."

"You could have too. You're the one who kept acting like a human shield." She kissed his cheek. "And I love you for it." She tried not to jar his arm with her movement.

He went still. "Did you just say you love me?"

Shit! She *had* said that. "It's a figure of speech. It means extreme gratitude." But when she glanced up to see if her explanation had defused whatever discomfort he was feeling, she forgot to breathe. His face was lit with an emotion that looked like happiness. "Are you glad that I said 'I love you for it'?" she asked.

His expression turned serious. "When you're getting shot at, your brain focuses on the most important facts. What I focused on was how empty my life would be if I lost you." He ghosted a hand over her hair. "Maybe it's too soon to say this, but I know from my mother's death that tomorrow could be too late."

Her heart seemed to stop beating as his gaze skimmed over her face before he continued. "I want to see you every day and sleep beside you every night. I want to make love to you in every room in your apartment and my penthouse and anywhere else we feel like it."

Dawn started to say she was good with that program, but he laid a finger across her lips. "I want to go back to Carmella's and eat a whole dinner there with you. I want to take you to my favorite restaurant in Paris. I want to learn what movies and books you like, what TV shows you hate, what you like to cook. I want to wake you up in the middle of the night when I miss my mother. I want to comfort you when you feel a panic attack rising. I sure as hell want to make sure you never get shot at again." He bent down to kiss her slow and deep.

Her heart began to dance, skipping around in a fluttery, exuberant rhythm as his lips moved over hers. He lifted his head, locking his gaze with hers before he said, "I want to love you, Dawn."

"I want you to love me." She summoned up all her courage to say, "Because I love you." It was hard to form those words because she'd been hiding them from herself, so she tried again. "I love you. A lot."

He gave a short, triumphant laugh. "I wasn't sure. You don't give much away. But I hoped, especially after you told me about what happened to you. I thought that meant something."

She combed her fingers through his soft hair. "It meant so much. I told you the ugly truth about me and you didn't run away."

"There is nothing ugly about you," he said, feathering his fingertips over her face so that tendrils of delight rippled over her skin. "Something ugly *happened* to you. It's a very important distinction."

"You're helping me to understand that."

"Even more important is that you turned the ugliness into good. You taught other women how to defend themselves so they could avoid the horror you lived through. You saved Alice's life. Hell, you saved *our* lives."

"*We* saved our lives. It was mutual." She pulled his head back down to kiss him. She couldn't get over the wonder of being loved by this brilliant man who believed she was just as brilliant as he was, in her own way. And now even she was beginning to believe it.

When they finally came up for air, Leland stroked his hand down her back to squeeze her butt. "You can't tell a man you love him and then refuse to make love with him."

"But your arm!"

"Exactly! Shouldn't getting shot while saving your life earn me some significant gratitude?" He raised his eyebrows while giving her a hot smile.

"Okay, but if you bleed to death, don't blame me." She ran her palms down his chest to untie the cord of his sweatpants.

He slipped his hands up under her shirt. "At least I'll die a happy man."

Epilogue

Six months later

"Hard forward!" their guide, Boof, shouted. "Dig in! This one's gnarly!"

Leland wedged his feet more firmly under the raft's side and shoved his paddle deep into the madly frothing water before hauling it back. The bow of the craft rose up as it hit the standing wave and then plunged down the other side like a roller coaster.

"Wahoo!" Tully yelled as frigid water crashed over them. The other side of the raft rode up over a rock so that Derek was tilted upward and nearly toppled down on top of Leland, but then the boat righted itself and settled into surfing the cascading waves.

"Back right!" Boof yelled.

Leland back paddled with all his strength to keep the boat going straight as they headed for a drop. When they hit the lip, they seemed to hang in the air before the raft smashed down into the crazed waves tossing foam at the foot of the falls.

Somehow they got through without flipping or without anyone going overboard.

"Take a break and give me a high paddle," Boof said. "You just made it through Knock Your Socks Off rapids and over Ballistic Falls."

Leland laughed at the dramatic names and raised his paddle to tap it against those of his fellow rafters.

"That was a hell of a ride." Derek's voice held the same exhilaration sparking through Leland.

"We can do it again," Boof offered. "There's a takeout not far from here and we could portage back up."

Tully surprised Leland by saying, "Nope, let's keep going."

"What's with that, Gibson?" Leland asked. "You're usually all about the thrill ride."

"I'm gettin' hungry," Tully said from the bow. "Time to get to camp and have me some venison."

"Okay, guys, this is a calm stretch. I'll steer, you rest," Boof said.

Leland pulled his feet out from under the raft edges and shifted to sit on the inflated thwart that crossed the rubber craft, his paddle resting across his knees. He scanned the riverbanks, admiring the wild forest rising from their rocky soil. He blinked in the slanting late afternoon light that glinted off the water carrying them swiftly toward their camp. His gaze pulled in to rest on the men with him, their scruffy but so-familiar faces framed by helmets and reflecting the same sense of peace and wonder he felt. "I never thought I'd say this, but I'm almost sorry it's our last day on the river." Except that Dawn's absence was a continual ache in his chest.

"Ha!" Tully said. "Told you so!"

Derek laughed. "Yeah, there's nothing like being dumped in freezing-cold water, bashed into a couple of boulders, dragged back into the boat headfirst, and getting abused for falling out in the first place."

"An experience we all shared—even Boof," Leland pointed out, although Derek was the one sporting a black eye to prove it. Leland hoped like hell it would fade before the wedding or Alice would be very unhappy with them.

"Hey, I did it on purpose," Boof protested. "Solidarity, man."

"Think of the positives. No need to shave for four days," Tully said.

"No client meetings and no neckties," Derek said.

"You get to piss in the woods," Boof contributed.

Leland chuckled before he said soberly, "No getting shot at by arms dealers"—he glanced over at Derek—"or crazed computer criminals."

"Yeah, there's that," Derek agreed. "And you know a drug cartel won't come after you here."

Tully looked over his shoulder. "Hey, I made sure to keep Leland and Dawn out of the official reports. You've got to trust me on that."

"I trust Chad and Vicky's sense of self-preservation even more," Leland said. In fact, he trusted Tully, especially as time had passed and no attempts at retaliation had been made.

Movement caught his eye and he glanced up. "Look! Another bald eagle!" He gestured to the huge bird that had just launched itself from a treetop. They'd seen several already but the fierce hook of its beak and the slow power of its wings still made them all watch in awed admiration.

"That never gets old," Tully murmured, his head tracking the eagle as it winged its way across the river.

"I'm going to say this now in case I get bashed in the head by another rock before we reach camp." Derek knocked his fist against his helmet. "Thank you for this time. For this experience. For being the two best friends and partners a man could ask for." He shook his head. "I don't know how I got so lucky."

"Group hug!" Boof yelled.

"I think that might capsize the raft," Leland said.

Tully, however, swung his legs around and enveloped Derek in a bear hug that rocked the boat. "Remember, we've always got your back."

Leland waited until Tully had settled back into the bow before he eased over to wrap an arm around Derek's shoulders for a man hug that kept the raft level. "I understand now about Alice. How you feel. I know you'll be happy so I don't have to wish you that. Instead I'll wish you good health and a long life to enjoy it."

Derek gave him a return squeeze. "Dawn's an amazing woman. I wish you the same."

Leland sat back. "I haven't asked her yet but I'm going to soon. I need to find the right time."

"Fair's fair," Derek said with a grin. "If you want me to wear a wig to help with your proposal, I will."

"Okay, slackers," Boof interrupted. "Time to put your backs into it. This next rapids are Class V plus. You're gonna get rocked."

An hour later, they drifted down the last stretch of calm water before reaching camp. Tully had involuntarily gone swimming in the last set of rapids and they'd barely escaped flipping the raft, so the run had ended well. Boof congratulated them on being true river men.

When the raft came around a bend, Leland spotted a rocky beach with tents set up on it and four people milling around the orange glow of a fire. His stomach rumbled at the prospect of the venison Tully had mentioned. He would appreciate some dry clothes as well.

When they drew closer, he bent forward to squint at one of the people unfolding a camp table. Joy exploded through his body.

"Good God almighty, that's Dawn!" he blurted out, his heart doing a backflip.

"And Alice!" Derek said, his face lit with an almost equal joy.

Tully turned around and smirked at them. "You're welcome."

Just like that the low-level whine of absence Leland had been feeling through the whole trip went silent and he knew. No more waiting. *This* was the right time.

"Put your backs into it, boys," he commanded, digging his paddle into the water. "I need to kiss someone."

⸺

Dawn snuggled in against Leland as they sat in front of the snapping campfire that Tully had built just for them in front of their tent. "I still can't believe that Tully flew Alice and me out here to meet you guys."

She was so grateful, because Leland's absence had been a hole in her gut, always there, always throbbing like a wound.

She felt Leland brush a kiss on the top of her head. "Did you enjoy the helicopter ride?"

"Oh my God, yes! Skimming right over the treetops was a rush and a half." She'd never ridden in a chopper before, so when they'd told her it was the only way to get to this remote site, she'd been a little nervous at first. Especially when she had seen how small the aircraft was.

"I want to bring you back here to go rafting," Leland said. "I can see you in the bow of the boat, looking like a warrior queen as you challenge the rapids."

Dawn smiled and patted the hard wall of his chest. "You think I'm way tougher than I really am. But I'd like to try it since you guys had such a great time."

"Yeah, it was terrific except for one thing. You weren't with me."

Happiness surged through Dawn as she looked up into Leland's face. The reflected flames seemed to dance in his blue eyes. She reached up to run her fingertip over his eyebrow. "I've missed touching you."

He twitched the brow she'd just traced with an expression of dismay. "You missed touching my *eyebrows*? I was hoping for something a little more, er, significant than that."

"For that we have to go in the tent. And I'm so ready."

Leland folded his long legs in and stood, taking her hand to bring her up with him. She started toward the tent that was set away from the main campsite, thanks to Tully's insistence that they needed privacy. But Leland pulled her to a halt.

"We need to talk about something," he said.

She looked up at him. The fire painted the elegant planes of his face in warm gold and dark shadow, both of them moving with its flicker. The light ran along strands of his hair as well, picking up gleams of blond amid the brown. "What is it?" she asked, searching his expression for a clue.

He took both her hands in his. She braced herself for some unhappy news because he looked so solemn.

"Remember when I told you all the things I wanted to do with you? Paris, Carmella's?" He smiled. "And now I've added white-water rafting."

"You've added a lot of things and we've done most of them," she said.

"There's something really big that I want to add." His grip around her hands tightened and he sank down onto one knee. He brought first one of her hands and then the other to touch his lips, watching her the whole time as he made tingles waltz over her skin and butterfly wings brush against her heart.

"Darlin', I want to grow old with you." His voice held a rasp of deep emotion. "Will you do me the honor of marrying me?"

She couldn't stop staring down at his face because it was so filled with love and tenderness and caring. "Yes! Of course I'll marry you."

"Your hands are shaking," he said, looking down.

"Because I'm so happy. It's zinging around inside me." She turned her hands to grab his, trying to pull him up. "Kiss me so you can feel what I'm feeling." Because it was too hard to find the words to tell him.

"Wait! I want to show you something first." He bewildered her by reaching into his pocket to pull out his cell phone. She watched in bafflement as he swiped a few times before turning it toward her. "Imagine me putting this on your finger right now."

She peered at the screen. The photo showed a ring—a large, deep-green, square emerald rimmed with diamonds was set in a wide gold band—nestled in a black velvet box. She touched the screen with one fingertip. "It's absolutely gorgeous but—" Why did he have a picture of a ring on his phone?

"I bought it for you three months ago." He kissed her finger just where the ring would go, making her skin shimmer with the feel of his warm lips.

"Three months?! What were you waiting for?" But more joy washed through her because he'd wanted to marry her for that long. And he'd chosen such a glorious ring for her.

"I was waiting for the perfect moment. The one so memorable you couldn't say no." He stood up and pulled her into his arms, his tall body a solid, comforting mass. "But being apart from you for this trip showed me that waiting was stupid. *Now* is the right moment."

He tilted her chin up with his fingertip. "I love you so much that I know why you were shaking. It's hard to have that much emotion bottled up inside you."

She curled her hand around the back of his neck and tugged his head down, needing to feel those warm, firm lips against hers. "Kiss me and we can share the emotion between the two of us."

"I have a better idea." He bent and scooped her legs off the ground, the flame in his eyes sending tendrils of electric desire curling through her as he carried her to the tent. "This way you can touch more than just my eyebrow."

Acknowledgments

The year I wrote this book was a busy one: I renovated and moved into a new house, and my son got married two thousand miles away from home. Both were happy occasions but demanding of time and mental bandwidth. So I am particularly grateful to all the people who let me lean on them in order to bring this story to you, my readers. I've been in this business long enough to know how very lucky I am to have such an amazing support network. I sprinkle fistfuls of sparkling appreciation over:

Maria Gomez, my fabulous acquiring editor, who inspires me to challenge myself to reach higher with every book. She also motivates me to improve my wardrobe because she always looks so gorgeous.

Jane Dystel and Miriam Goderich, my incredible agents, who never cease to amaze me with their fierce dedication to making my career soar. I'm not sure what good deed I did in a past life to deserve having them in my corner.

The entire brilliant Montlake team, who takes my pile of pages, turns it into a beautiful, finished book, announces its existence to the whole world in creative ways, and holds my hand in the nicest manner through the whole process. They are all rock stars.

Andrea Hurst, my fantastic developmental editor, who evaluates my work with such intelligence, sensitivity, and finely honed critical instincts. Her judgment is unerring; her understanding vast; her professionalism admirable. Not to mention that working with her is pure pleasure.

Scott Calamar and Claire Caterer, my meticulous, sharp-eyed copy-editor and proofreader, who are my strongly woven safety net. They carefully comb through my story to catch all my "egregious errors" and all my tiny mistakes, so that my wonderful readers don't get irritated by typos, time-line discontinuities, grammatical awkwardness, or the fact that the color palette of every character's wardrobe in the entire book was blue and gray.

Eileen Carey, my amazing cover artist, who somehow peers into my writer's brain and conjures up my vision for my book, only much, much hotter and more exciting. She is truly a wizard of imagination and creativity.

Miriam Allenson, Lisa Verge Higgins, and Jennifer Wilck, my beloved critique group, who are there for me in every way all the time. They listen to my whining and wailing with patience and sympathy. Yet they still tell me what needs fixing in the work. I couldn't ask for more magnificent friends and fellow writers.

Sally MacKenzie, my ever-faithful RWA conference buddy, who cheered me on through the final frantic days and hours and minutes of finishing this book when the deadline was coming at me like a speeding freight train. She is both motivator and comforter.

Kristen Richardson and all the warm, supportive folks at Jazzercise Verona, who keep this sedentary writer's body moving and grooving to the music. They get me out of my head and make me so much stronger and more energetic.

Patti Anderson, to whom I dedicated this book, because she was my personal trainer for many years (until she moved to the wilds of Minnesota). She went above and beyond taking care of my body by sharing her hard-earned wisdom about life at times when I desperately needed a lifeline. I will be forever grateful to her for that. (Note:

anything I got wrong about personal training in this book is entirely my fault, not Patti's.)

Rebecca and Loukas, my mind-bogglingly remarkable children, whom I love with all my heart and soul and always will, no matter what. Every day they make me proud of the breathtaking human beings they have become.

My marvelous readers, who keep me going—and even ship me chocolate!—at times when I need encouragement. I know that when I send my imaginary friends out into the world, you will welcome and embrace them with warmth and enthusiasm. Thank you for being there for me!

About the Author

Photo © 2015 Lisa Kollberg

Nancy Herkness is the award-winning author of the Second Glances, Wager of Hearts, and Whisper Horse series, published by Montlake, as well as several other contemporary romance novels. She is a two-time nominee for the Romance Writers of America's RITA Award, and has received many other honors for her work, including the Book Buyers Best Top Pick, the Bookseller's Best award, and the National Excellence in Romance Fiction award.

Nancy graduated from Princeton University, where she majored in English. In addition to her academic work in literature, she was accepted into Princeton's creative writing program, and her senior thesis was a volume of original poetry.

After graduating, Nancy had a varied career that included retail management and buying, COBOL programming, computer systems sales and marketing, and a brief stint as a receptionist at a dental office. Once her children were in school full-time, she sat down and wrote *A Bridge to Love*, her first romance novel to be published.

A native of West Virginia, Nancy now lives in suburban New Jersey.

For more information about Nancy and her books, visit www.NancyHerkness.com. You can also find her on Facebook and Pinterest.